THE DC JOB.

A CASE LEE NOVEL

Book 8

By Vince Milam

WANT TO RECEIVE MY NEWSLETTER WITH NEWS ABOUT UPCOMING RELEASES? Simply click below:
https://vincemilam.com

Other Case Lee adventures (click **Vince Milam's Amazon Author Page**)
The Suriname Job: A Case Lee Novel Book 1
The New Guinea Job: A Case Lee Novel Book 2
The Caribbean Job: A Case Lee Novel Book 3
The Amazon Job: A Case Lee Novel Book 4
The Hawaii Job: A Case Lee Novel Book 5
The Orcas Island Job: A Case Lee Novel Book 6
The Nevada Job: A Case Lee Novel Book 7

Acknowledgments:

Editor—David Antrobus at BeWriteThere - bewritethere.com
Cover Design by Rick Holland at Vision Press – *myvisionpress.com*.

As always, Vicki for her love and patience. And Mimi, Linda, and Bob for their unceasing support and encouragement. Special thanks to Stephen and ML for their gracious hospitality.

Chapter 1

It started with a plea for help. It ended with ugliness and deliverance and relief.

Soft sand muffled my strides under a full moon's light. A camel rested sphinxlike with legs folded under and observed my passing. It tossed a low, throaty grumble in my direction and resumed chewing its cud as the tiny bells adorning its halter tinkled. I paused and checked my back trail. Two men followed: dark objects, distant but closing. There were no other movements, no other sounds in Wadi Musa. The Valley of Moses. The two men's identity—unknown. But smart money would bet they were hitters, killers. If taking me out was their intent, smart money would also bet against that happening.

People had lied to me from the get-go about this job. Lies of omission, lies regarding context. The job itself, cut-and-dried. A diplomat's teenage daughter had gone missing. Find her. Fair enough and a possible can-do, but a keen interest from both the CIA and the US State Department regarding my actions painted a much larger picture. A picture hidden in the shadows, dark and unknown.

So I'd moved forward with a plan, sidestepping the clandestine and diplomatic world as much as possible and focused on finding the kid. All the rest was clutter, white noise. Albeit white noise that could prevent Case Lee Inc.'s lone employee from remaining vertical and healthy.

The two trailing killers were mission related, but at the periphery, and it pissed me off. They weren't kidnappers and were likely unaware of the reason for my Petra trip. They'd been instructed to whack me. Period. I'd taken a late-night walk to stretch my legs and ponder the day's events. The two approaching figures nixed any contemplative time. No long guns, no rifles, were evident as they split up, circling, still distant. But each man's right hand showed signs of gripping a pistol, which tossed these asshats into the confirmed hitter bucket. My .38 revolver, procured from a fixer in Madaba, remained in the waistband of my jeans. Other than several other camels and a half-dozen hobbled donkeys, all to tote tourists, there were no other observers. At my back, Petra's long, winding entrance, terminating at the ancient ruins.

I'd accepted the job for multiple reasons—the rescue aspect, its focused aim, and the country of Jordan as a starting point. A solid, clean, safe place I'd visited several times before. Jordanians were good folks, the food was great, and I'd chalked up quality time while sitting in hookah bars with a cold beer, chatting with the locals in my rough conversational Arabic. All good. But my Arabic language deficiencies hadn't helped the day's events when I focused on the teenage girl's disappearance.

At the moment, I focused on the two hitters. I wasn't sanguine about killers approaching me, but the worry meter remained a long way from pegged-out. These cats were too far for a pistol shot in my direction, but their intent was blatant as hell, and at this point devoid of downside. So I pulled the revolver, held it high in the moonlight, and waggled it as an auctioneer displaying an item. Welcome to the downside, gents.

Both men paused, assessed, and continued on toward a beat-up ex-Delta operator who'd punched enough hitters' tickets to last a lifetime. I sighed, lowered my arm, and considered options. Haul ass for one. Make a mad dash back for the small collection of hotels and shops that serviced the Petra tourist trade. An option—real enough, but dismissed. They'd still come after me, so if these clowns wanted a fight, fine. I turned and headed for an option the two hitters wouldn't like. Not one little bit.

I'd had a semifrustrating day. The fifteen teenagers and two State Department employees had stayed at the same hotel I occupied. Fourteen teenagers returned to DC. Planned as a school trip—a private school in DC filled with diplomats' kids—the State Department took part through funding the lion's share of the expenses. They also provided the chaperones. The hotel manager had confirmed the timelines and logistics but offered zero other input about the missing girl. Not unexpected, but he occupied a spot on my interview punch list.

The group's guide had been another story. He'd waffled too much for my comfort, appearing to dodge any culpability. Something didn't smell right. I'd found him hanging out under a tent awning with the other guides. They cloistered themselves near the camels and cart donkeys, sipping coffee and smoking. Once he'd self-identified as the guide for the teenage group, we sidled away from the other guides and had a chat.

"Do you remember the missing girl?" I asked in English. "Is there anything you can tell me about her?"

"I guide many groups. I cannot be expected to remember every person."

"I understand," I said, and switched to Arabic. "There is no doubt this entire experience has been very difficult for you."

"Everyone wishes to know what cannot be known! The police interviewed me three times. Three times! My honor was questioned. Is this not enough insult? Are you here to add to my worries?"

"I am certain you are an honorable man. The girl's father hired me. Imagine his concern, his torment."

He paused and lit a smoke.

"Such a thing would be most terrible. But I can add nothing that would help you."

"Would you describe your path? Your guided trip with this particular group?"

"I will tell you again. One group is much like the next. Europeans, Americans, Canadians. Many groups. Young people, old people. Groups of families."

"I understand. Where might you take a group of young people such as the one I seek? Surely they will walk farther than old people?"

He shrugged, disinterested. Weird. The Jordanians were proud people, and this guy was an official Petra guide, licensed. I would have expected elaboration about his coveted job, details and insights justifying his official status. I switched back to English.

"Pretend I'm a tourist. Your client. And pretend I wished to see all of Petra's wonders. Where would you take me?"

He pointed a desultory hand toward al-Siq, or the Siq, Petra's main entrance, and shrugged again. I pulled a tourist map of the ancient city and spread it before him.

"Okay. I exit the Siq at the Treasury. Then where?"

"The theater. The royal tombs. The Temple of Dushares."

"What about the Byzantine church?"

"Perhaps. I guide many groups. Every day I guide groups."

I refolded the map and switched back to Arabic.

"When was the girl discovered missing?"

"I cannot say when."

"Where was the girl discovered missing?"

"When we exited al-Siq. Near where we now stand."

Someone was lying. The State Department escort had told me in DC that they'd discovered her disappearance when they returned to the Treasury, before they reentered the Siq.

"And then what?"

"We searched for her. Of course."

Of course. But she was long gone by then. It was a several-hour trek along Petra's tourist trail, from its entrance and back again, checking out the sites over a couple mile distance. Sufficient opportunity for kidnapping the diplomat's daughter, but opportunity limited to specific areas, sites. Otherwise, there were too many witnesses. Whether she remained alive now—unknown. What wasn't unknown—this guy, this guide, was hiding something. Whether direct knowledge or acting upon look-the-other-way instructions, I'd never know. Frustrated, I thanked the guide and headed into one of the world's seven wonders.

An Arab tribe called the Nabateans settled Petra around 200 BC near trade routes. It's estimated twenty thousand inhabitants once occupied the area, with most major structures carved from mountain faces, deep into the rock. In the Byzantine era, a few Christian churches were built, but the city continued its decline until abandoned and forgotten for millennia, tucked away and hidden within the desert mountains. It remained unknown to the Western world until archeologists reintroduced it in the early nineteenth century. I'd visited once, years earlier, when Delta held a training exercise for the Jordanians. A very cool place, and the backdrop for several movies, including an Indiana Jones flick.

The site's entrance was about as dramatic as it gets. The Siq—a smooth-walled crack in the mountain and Petra's main access. Far from a straight-line pathway, the ten-to-thirty-foot-wide Siq weaves constantly, its smooth rock walls soaring four to six hundred feet above you, adding a powerful dramatic effect as you approach the site. At the end of the mile-long hemmed-in path, the Siq empties into a plaza, facing the massive facade of the Treasury carved from a sandstone rock face. Jaw-dropping stuff.

Tourists were few as I made my way along the path, intent on speaking with Bedouin shopkeepers within the site. Although I'd been there before, Petra didn't fail to impress. Once through the Siq, ruins of ancient buildings lie scattered across the several-mile area, although the eye-catchers are the structures hacked from rock faces. Lofty ornate entrance columns, obelisks, and artwork cut and carved from a jagged vertical mountain. Huge smooth-walled sandstone interiors display brown, red, gray, and white swirls. But I wasn't there as a tourist. My entire focus—find the starting point for the young girl's kidnapping. And find the SOBs involved.

Chapter 2

The Jordanian government managed the Petra tourist trade, and they struck a deal with a local Bedouin tribe to operate the rest and concession areas. Under fabric awnings spread across the site you could purchase trinkets and souvenirs, or sit a spell and have a bottled water, soda, or Arabian tea and coffee while an ancient culture surrounded you. I started with the concession area nearest the Siq.

I'd learned through the years that the Bedouin across Arabia maintain certain characteristics. A nomadic people, they will park it when an opportunity such as Petra presents itself. They are both hospitable and aloof, the cultural barriers deep and wide. And they are observant. Man, are they observant. Silent, expressionless faces as dark eyes watched and captured details. Details, intel stored as jewels, shared most often among family and tribal members only. I sought subtleties rather than grand revelations, and I feared my Arabic language skills fell short of glomming onto hidden meanings within a highly nuanced language. But you roll with the cards you're dealt, and I ordered a coffee, sat on a large cushion, and engaged the Bedouin proprietor in small talk. As a westerner who spoke rudimentary Arabic—a rarity—Bedouin doors would crack open, revealing nothing or everything. I prayed my language skill set could capture the latter if it presented.

"Is business good?" I asked as he prepared coffee.

"It has been adequate. It should remain so today, inshallah."

Inshallah. The Arabic version of a southerner in the US stating, "Lord willing." Similar expressions were sprinkled throughout conversations both in Arabia and the US South. Go figure.

7

The proprietor, wearing a draped red-and-white kaffiyeh head cover, removed a small brass coffeepot with wooden handle from a tiny bed of coals and poured thick, sugary coffee into a tiny cup.

"Shukran," I said, thanking him. "Will you join me? I will, of course, pay for your cup as well."

The Bedouin lifted his chin as affirmation, poured his own cup, and groaned as he sat, lighting a smoke.

"It would dishonor me not telling you the reason for this visit," I said, sipping coffee.

The Bedouin acknowledged my alleged candor with a dignified nod. Alleged because, well, he'd judge my truth. As for the judge's ruling, I'd never know. Bedouins were a tough nut to crack.

"The father of the European girl who disappeared at Petra several days ago has hired me. One can only imagine his pain."

"It would be a terrible burden."

He nodded as he stared across the open area, then sipped coffee and took a drag of his cig.

"Is it possible you might offer a personal observation about the event?"

I may or may not have offered a decent translation of "observation," but it was sufficient for his understanding.

"Many Europeans pass this way. It is for this reason I sell coffee and valued artifacts."

"The coffee is excellent, and I am certain your artifacts are priceless. But I, like you, must attend to responsibilities. My responsibility is removing the father's pain as much as possible."

"Of course."

He settled back against another large cushion and watched a few tourists wander past.

"It is said they did not discover her disappearance until after they exited the Siq," I said.

"So it is said. It is not for me to judge, but do you not find it peculiar they would not collect the young people before they exited through the Siq?"

Bingo. Peculiar indeed. This guy confirmed the group had failed to count heads prior to departing Petra and heading into the Siq and back to the hotel. The State Department escorts in DC had stated twice that they'd begun their search here in the plaza, near the Treasury. Waiting until they exited the Siq on their return trip ensured another thirty or forty-five minutes passed before they organized a search. Critical minutes if a kidnapping had taken place. Man, something was bad wrong with this picture. Why would the DC escorts lie about the search's starting point? It made no sense. A butt-covering exercise, stating they'd immediately jumped on it? Maybe. But I doubted it. Something else was in play.

Two hours later I'd hit four more concession areas, traveling a couple miles deep into Petra's ruins, with no luck. I stood at the ancient ad Deir spiritual center, a mile uphill and above the collection of ruins within Petra's flat section. It was the tourist area's farthest reach, with the average visitor not opting for the hot-sun climb.

Someone had whisked her away, made her invisible, setting off my BS meter. Could she have left the group early, made her way through the Siq and back to the hotel where kidnappers waited? Sure. A slim possibility, but one I didn't buy. A back door existed here, an alternative to the Siq. I pulled the map and compared it to the sight below. Not on the map, but visible, was a trail behind the Byzantine church ruins. It followed the bone-dry desert valley north. I pulled my satellite phone and in short order got a Google Earth image of the area. A mile farther, the trail turned into a two-track road.

Another two miles led to the much smaller and less visited site with more Nabatean ruins. And a Bedouin camp. Hello, back door.

The afternoon heat baked as I hustled north, working a trail. Neither a warm trail nor one filled with promise, but it was something. And something beat the hell out of what I'd discovered so far. Heat waves shimmered, my footfalls near silent in the sand. Dry, clean desert air crusted my nostrils, the water bottle I toted drained. I skipped the small collection of ruins and wandered into the Bedouin village, seeking the ubiquitous collection of old men gathered in the shade, drinking tea or coffee. They weren't hard to find.

A tall, crumbled ruin wall supported one end of a large cotton shade awning and backdropped seven weathered faces. Two secured poles propped up the awning's other end. The shaded area held thick seating cushions scattered about, and a young man was pulling dual duty as he made tea and coffee and filled and lit tall brass hookahs when requested. I smiled, spread "masaa' al-khayer" or "good afternoon" all around, and plopped down on a cushion. Polite smiles and sage expressions returned from wrinkled leathery faces, cheek whiskers gray, eyes runny. I asked the young man for bottled water and hot tea. When in Rome, baby.

We exchanged several pleasantries as a blow-dryer-hot breeze ruffled the shade cloth. I downed the water, accepted the tea, and began the verbal dance, stating the reason for my appearance. They met my declaration with slight nods and draws on hookah mouthpieces and silence. Apple-flavored tobacco smoke wafted among us between scorching breezes. The young man behind me prepared more tea. Blocked by cultural nuance, I changed tack, dropped the circular waltz, and assumed they knew something about the girl's kidnapping.

"You are honorable men. My heart tells me you would have nothing to do with such a terrible act."

Wizened faces nodded agreement.

"But what type of man would do such a thing?"

"'Ajnabi,'" one replied. An outsider. Or foreigner. The man who spoke resumed puffing his hookah's mouthpiece as the others again nodded affirmation.

There it was. As close to confirmation as I'd get. The teenage girl had passed this way, her kidnappers observed. A sense of relief washed over me. I hadn't progressed down the kidnap trail, but it was damn sure a trail. The hunt was on, the scent vague. Vague, but there. It was enough to lift me from my worthless status.

"She is but a young woman. It could not have taken many men to do this thing."

A silent pause. One old man slurped tea and said, "No more than three."

A three-man operation. It confirmed the "they" I'd received from my fixer in Madaba. Kidnap the diplomat's daughter, whisk her out Petra's back door, and then what? These men couldn't answer that. But more details, more intel, could lie buried among them. If I could pry it out.

"These three outsiders must have been Europeans. She is a European girl."

"La." No.

I acted surprised, shocked, and shook my head.

"I cannot believe a Jordanian would do such a thing. My heart tells me it cannot be."

"Foreigners," another man repeated, scratching mere outsiders, Jordanians, off the list.

Okay. Not Jordanians. I considered the Israelis. Mossad. They would speak fluent Arabic and were Jordan's neighbor. But these old men and their

11

fellow Bedouins here would have a keen ear and spot Israeli-accented Arabic. And would have said as much, the neighboring Jews not high on their popularity list. No, Arabs had taken the kid. Their accents identified them as foreigners, non-Jordanians. Okay. But I needed more.

"Alssariq," I said. Thieves.

I frowned, assured, and exhibited disgust.

"La." No, again.

"Tajir," the oldest among them said. The others murmured agreement, sipped, smoked, and—consensus achieved—settled back as the veil descended and further discussion on the subject ended.

Tajir. Merchants, shopkeepers, traders. Oh man, try as I might, I couldn't pry further clarity from them to overcome my poor Arabic. And I did try, to no avail. They'd shut the door. I thanked them and assured them I would find the teenager. They returned "Inshallah" several times. God willing. I'd take it, needing all the help I could get.

Confirmation someone had kidnapped her, check. A lead who did it. Check, again. With a huge asterisk. There were over twenty Arabic-speaking countries across the Middle East and North Africa. A three-thousand-mile swath of turf, which made for a gossamer-thin lead.

It was sunset when I returned to the hotel, and a shower, meal, and two Grey Goose vodkas prompted the late evening walk. A walk filled with contemplation of my next steps. I'd head for DC and confront the father, for sure. If he wanted to see his daughter again, I'd make it clear he'd best come clean. Far too much swirled around this gig for a plain vanilla kidnapping. I'd ask the Clubhouse for help. Jules's network might pick up a tingle, a vibration, about the girl's whereabouts now that I had something she could work with. I might even hit up the CIA. They were interested in my activities on this job, so I could call in a little quid pro quo. Because at the moment, I clutched at straws.

The two nighttime hitters continued their slow approach, cautious, likely wondering why I stood still like a moron. So I kicked off activities, turned, and strode fifty paces toward the Siq's entrance. I stopped, checked their positions—each still seventy paces away—and cast an unseen smile in their direction. C'mon in, boys. It's about a mile long, and not a lot of moonlight poured down into that high-walled, meandering, narrow crack. C'mon in. And meet Case Lee.

Chapter 3

The contract offer came in late at night while anchored in a slough off Muddy Bay, an hour north of Charleston, South Carolina. A four-day trip's final night. CC, my mentally challenged younger sister, slept belowdecks with her dog, Tinker Juarez. It was late summer, the night breeze off the Atlantic now cool, stars flung by the bushelful overhead. I worked on my second Grey Goose, ensconced on the throne—an old duct-tape-repaired recliner situated on the *Ace of Spades*'s foredeck. The *Ace* was home. A well-used diesel-driven wooden cruiser, rough around the edges, in need of a severe scraping and new paint job, and filled to the brim with character. The *Ace* and I lived among the sloughs, side rivers, and small towns of the Intracoastal Waterway. The Ditch. It stretched from Virginia to Florida and provided a watery street address.

Satellite-enabled laptop open, I read the offer from my usual client, Global Resolutions. An uber-discreet Swiss company, they presented me with regular contracts. Lucrative contracts, with the lion's share of the money going to Mom and CC. The offers tossed my way seldom ID'd Global Resolution's client, the paying party. This one was different.

Investigate the disappearance of a teenage girl in Petra, Jordan. Respond within twenty-four hours. If accepted, details to follow.

It sounded like a solid gig, an opportunity to find a lost kid. My girlfriend, Jess, was off on her own contract investigation, so it was a good time to put the work boots back on. With little deliberation, I accepted. My right index finger, as always, suspended over the keyboard's Enter button—a personal commitment microceremony that sounded the starter gun for the next adventure. Sending the encrypted acceptance email often tossed me into life's spin cycle. Eyes wide open, I punched Enter.

The immediate response surprised me, a rare sense of urgency. Global Resolutions sent me a name, home address, and cell number. So much for not knowing the paying party.

Jakub Kaminski, political affairs diplomat at the Polish embassy in DC. His daughter, Krystyna, had gone missing. Hmm. I'd expected an industrialist or old money or tech exec as the client. Not a diplomat, or anyone associated with the diplomatic corps.

Poland's government would be all over it. So would the US State Department. Those folks protected their own and, with a missing child among their diplomatic tribe, would have moved heaven and earth to find her. An internet search revealed little. A few tiny news blurbs, read by few, forgotten by all. Oh, well. I'd visit Kaminski and head out to find his daughter. A solid gig with feel-good elements. I could get CC and Tinker home with Mom and catch a flight from Charleston around noon, so I shot Kaminski a text asking for a meeting at his house the next afternoon. I also requested he use his pull and get a sit-down with any players in DC who'd been with the kid or group of kids in Jordan.

I had wheelhouse coffee underway at dawn; the morning held a fine day's promise. Tinker padded up the belowdecks steps, performed a wheelhouse fly-by, exchanged tail wags for behind-the-ear scratches, then up and over the side, hitting dry ground to do his business. With Tinker back on board, I fired the old diesel, pulled anchor, and slipped away. While CC slept, I shot an encrypted message to the Clubhouse.

Missing daughter. Jakub Kaminski. Meeting tomorrow a.m.?

Her reply—succinct and typical—arrived within minutes. Jules wasn't big on electronic communications.

0900

Two hours later, we approached Charleston Bay. CC and I stood together in the wheelhouse, eating breakfast. Crackers, mayo, pickles, canned tuna. Not my cup of tea, but CC loved it and had relished a sly victory knowing Mom wouldn't have allowed it to start the day. It didn't hurt that older brother would do pretty much anything she wanted. She'd hold a cracker with fingertips, carefully smear mayo, fork some tuna on top, and with great care top it with a small, circular dill slice. Then down the hatch. Tinker remained on duty, rotating between prow lookout and wheelhouse begging, moving with commitment between each station. The wind, light, gave the *Ace* a slight roll among the small waves.

"A good trip," she said, tuna cracker assembly in progress.

"It was, my love."

"No! It was a great trip! Tinker Juarez says so too."

"A great trip. Every trip with you and Tinker is a great trip."

"Tinker Juarez."

"Right. Tinker Juarez."

"Sometimes I miss Mom. Not all the time."

"And she misses you, CC. But she knows we make trips." I handed her another cracker. Tinker focused laser-like on our movements. "I just wish I could remember what kind of trips we make."

"Great trips!" she said, laughing and leaning into me.

She inhaled her last cracker and continued lolling against me, turning so her back pressed against my side. A fine morning, perfect. Her hair smelled like grilled steaks—expected, as she'd hung alongside me at the foredeck grill the night before. Not a hair scent Chanel would push, but maybe they should. I liked it. My blood brothers would approve, except for Bo. He was particular about his toiletries.

"Do you think we will see dolphins?" she asked.

"Maybe. They are always moving."

"Like you."

That one stung. Lately, CC had begun questioning my mobile lifestyle.

"If I didn't move around with the *Ace*, we couldn't take these just okay trips."

"These great trips," she said, giggling and rolling her head back to smile at me. A pelican flock cruised past low, their wing movements languid. "I like it when we see big birds. And ducks. And the little dancers."

The little dancers—small shorebirds near our anchor spots. Little feather-ball bodies perched above long stilt legs, who would run to and fro along a mud bank as we eased toward an overnight layover. CC said they were dancing, and some were better than others, but they were all good, and they were dancing for *us*. The love at such moments was so strong my chest ached.

I took a noonish private charter for DC, rucksack packed, .40 Glock loaded. The twin-prop plane's drone made napping easy, and the long Uber ride reinforced DC's beauty. A look and feel due in part, I supposed, to the height restriction on buildings. It fostered a distinct neighborhood feel within different areas. Very cool.

What wasn't so cool—the city's god-awful functional mess. Departments eyeballing other departments with suspicion, envy, distrust. Bureaucrats jockeying for position within the power hierarchy. Rumors, backstabbing, gossip, lies—a freakin' mess any way you looked at it. Large corporations exhibited the same behaviors—as did, perhaps, all large collections of us human critters—but DC swept the dysfunctional awards each year. And for this job, I would rub elbows with that mess.

The diplomatic world, in my experience, remained a relatively benign player. Sure, they were up to their eyeballs with self-importance and the day's realpolitik, but they left me alone. I made a point of returning the favor. But there was a twist. The State Department and its diplomatic corps had an uneasy alliance with the CIA. The Company. I'd seen it innumerable times. Company spooks embedded inside overseas embassies and consulates. My gut said sharp elbows were always in play, and odds of information-sharing a crapshoot. In DC, home to both State and the Company and where the separation was more pronounced, the long knives would become unsheathed. At least overseas, working out of the same embassies and consulates, they might share after-work beers. That wouldn't happen in DC. Unless the Company worked a State asset, squeezing intel from some hapless State employee. An event that never flowed the other direction.

Jakub Kaminski, political affairs diplomat for Poland, lived in the Kalorama neighborhood. Two dozen blocks north of the White House, the area housed most embassies and diplomatic residences. With cocktail and dinner soirées every night of the week, the diplomat class could attend and mingle after a short walk from their homes. You had to be a special breed of cat to enjoy that lifestyle. I wouldn't last a week. Kaminski's place was a three-story brownstone nestled among block after block of similar homes. In his fifties, fit, with close-cropped gray hair and light-blue eyes, he met me at the front door.

"You are Mr. Lee?"

"I am."

"May I see your identification?"

A little strange, but I didn't know the diplomatic tribe's ways. I pulled my passport, he perused it, and I was invited in. A large sitting room held his wife, Anna, and a large silver tray with a silver urn and fine-china coffee cups. I shook Anna's hand and accepted a cup. The areas around her eyes were dark, the eyes lost, hopeless. I couldn't imagine the pain of losing a child, and my heart went out to her and her husband. A dark pall filled the large room, generated through human misery. Its effect on me was immediate—light the fuse, go find the daughter, and make someone pay. The payment part wasn't in the contract, but I'd toss it in as lagniappe. No problem.

"Let me gather some basic information," I said after we'd all sat. "Then we'll see where it goes from there."

"Time, Mr. Lee," Jakub said. "Time. Too many days have passed with nothing to show for it. Action is what we must have. Action."

"Yessir. I understand. And you'll get action. But let's eliminate the obvious. Is it possible your daughter ran away?"

"Absurd," he said. "Completely absurd."

"Your State Department has asked the same question several times," Anna said. "I do not understand why they keep asking this thing. My husband is correct. It is not possible."

Her accent, more pronounced than her husband's, would have been charming under different circumstances.

"So she wasn't the type to head out on her own?"

"Not at all," Jakub said. "Krystyna is a fourteen-year-old girl, yes, but quite mature for her age. You would say levelheaded. She would not run away and do this to her parents."

"Yes. Levelheaded," Anna said. "And do not enquire about a boyfriend as your State Department did. Such a thing is ridiculous."

I bought it. A young teenager in a foreign land, running away as a lark or grand adventure. In London or Paris or Rome, sure, perhaps. But not Jordan's Wadi Musa, Petra's location. I couldn't see it.

Jakub and Anna described the trip her daughter had taken. A school venture, one week long, with two State Department escorts.

"Have you talked with her friends? Interviewed everyone who was on the trip with her?"

"Yes," Anna said. "Everyone she was close with at school and each of the young people she traveled with."

"Nothing came of it?" I asked. "No red flags, no matter how small?"

"None."

"Krystyna is your only child?"

"Correct."

I enquired about grandparents, aunts, and uncles. Family ties that the kid could have contacted. Jakub and Anna had covered those bases.

"Has there been any contact from the kidnappers? A ransom note?"

"None whatsoever," Jakub replied.

"May I see Krystyna's room?" I asked.

Jakub led me upstairs. A young teenager's room greeted me, albeit a young teenager's room tidied up. A couple of wall posters—a Polish rock band and Poland's national women's soccer team—along with a few stuffed animals and books and small, ornate treasure-trove boxes. There was a photo of Krystyna with her soccer teammates, a local team.

"Is she a big soccer player?"

I kept things in the present tense. No point talking about the kid as if she wasn't around anymore.

"Very much so," Anna said, who'd followed upstairs. "And she is quite good. The team captain."

"May I have a couple photos of her?" I asked. "One full-body and one from the shoulders up."

Anna went off to pluck two representative photos while Jakub and I remained in his daughter's room. A small desk clock ticked, and I could hear a passing vehicle on the street below.

"I'll give it my best shot, Mr. Kaminski. That's all I can offer."

"That is all I can ask, Mr. Lee. You come highly recommended. And you come as our last and best chance at finding our daughter."

"There will be a few costly expenses. Private jet charters, things like that."

"Cost is not a concern. My government is funding your efforts. You will leave for Jordan tonight?"

"I have an early morning meeting tomorrow. I will depart after that."

"Is such a meeting necessary? Time is of the essence, Mr. Lee."

"I'm afraid it is necessary. My assets are not government sanctioned. There are assets and resources that nest in my, well, different world."

He got it and nodded as reply, along with the slightest of smiles. Jakub Kaminski had had enough of government-sanctioned resources. He and I walked through the search efforts performed to date, and I prodded and peppered him with questions. Not a lot there. She was gone. But a tingle, an uneasy sense, came with his answers. My gut said he hid something. And my gut was seldom wrong.

I shouldered my rucksack inside the front door, having confirmed Jakub had set up a meeting with the school trip's State Department escorts and a meeting in Amman, Jordan, with the US Diplomatic Security Services, the DSS. The Kaminskis stood side by side.

"Is there anything, anything at all, either of you can tell me that would help? I've got a thin trail to work with, and the more intelligence I have, the better."

"Nothing more," Jakub said. "But I must ask. When you find her, and I understand there is no guarantee." He paused and took his wife's hand. "When you find her, and she is being held by one or many men, who will help you with her escape? I ask this because Poland has excellent special military resources in this regard."

"I appreciate the offer. If it comes to that, I'll let you know. Otherwise, I'll handle it."

"Are you sure, Mr. Lee?"

"I'm sure. It falls into my area of expertise."

I shook hands with Jakub. Anna delivered a brief hug, a kiss on the cheek, and a whispered, "Godspeed."

My Uber ride waited outside. It was a while before my end-of-day meeting with the State Department, so I headed for my central hotel, head filled with the pain those two folks carried and acknowledgment that the clock ticked, and each passing day lessened the odds of finding the kid. And a heart filled with the pain and horror the kid, Krystyna, lived through now, at this moment. If she lived.

As I walked, I neglected the appropriate focus on my back trail. This was DC. A place where you'd best watch your back.

Chapter 4

I dropped my rucksack at the hotel and grabbed a burger before the State Department visit. While munching fries, I called my girlfriend, Jess. Jessica Rossi, a legitimate private investigator. Unlike me, as per our former Delta team lead and current resident of Fishtail, Montana, Marcus Johnson. He proposed I name my one-man organization Shitstorm Guaranteed Inc. Funny guy.

"Hey," I said. "How's Tallahassee?"

Jess lived in Charlotte, North Carolina, and had accepted a contract from a Florida attorney who handled a billion-dollar estate. The siblings had gone to war with each other—cheating spouses, stolen funds, attempted murder. The fun never stops.

"It's cooling off in this part of Florida. Which is a big deal when stuck in a car without the engine running while watching any of a dozen family members do something stupid." She chuckled. "That came across jaded. Let's just say my blouse doesn't sweat-stick to the car seat at the moment. How's that?"

"It's the little things that count. How's Scrabble coming along?"

Jess played competitive Scrabble on her iPad while she pulled surveillance duty.

"It's all good except for the weenies that are getting their butts kicked and decide to quit. Where are you, and what are you doing?"

"DC. I've accepted a contract to find a disappeared girl. A fourteen-year-old Polish diplomat's daughter. She went missing in Jordan."

"Have you been there before?"

"Yep. Nice place, good folks, no worries."

I kept all danger flags from our conversations. It was, maybe, the only major bone of contention between us during our monthslong relationship. Jess worried about me. I got it. So gallivanting into harm's way stayed under wraps as best as I could manage it. But Jess had a talent for digging.

"Your voice says there are worries. This job doesn't involve structuring a peace settlement while you dodge bullets in that part of the world, does it?"

"If you heard worry, it's because the trail is thin and I have no clue if she's dead or alive. I just left her parents. If I track down a body, this job's final act is informing her parents. In person. I can't imagine what that would be like for them. Mercy."

Her voice lowered and became empathetic.

"It's horrible. For them and for the messenger. I speak from experience."

Jess had been a detective in the Charlotte PD.

"What was she doing over there?" she asked.

"A school excursion. A private school here in DC."

"What's the consensus on who might have done it?"

Jess marched through the five *W*'s, gathering intel. As a former detective, it came naturally for her.

"No one, me included, has a clue."

"That's not a good start. When was this disappearance?"

"Four days ago."

"The clock's ticking, bub."

"Yeah, no kidding."

"So you're headed for Jordan tonight?"

"Tomorrow. I'll check in with the State Department chaperones late today and visit a prime asset tomorrow morning."

"The enigmatic Jules of the Clubhouse?"

"One and the same."

"When do I get to meet her?"

"Not a good idea."

It wasn't. Jules represented a world loaded to the fill line with spooks, hitters, and miscreants of all stripes. Dangerous folks, and I wouldn't risk Jess brushing against that world, my world.

"A man of mystery. Fine. Then I won't share the salacious details I'm uncovering as we speak. Details on full display through a wide crack in the curtains at a cheap motel, delivered to my wide eyes with fine German binoculars. Good grief, these two must have been former gymnasts."

"Don't get any ideas."

"Too late. So why was this teenager disappeared? Or does that fall into the same bucket as who might have done it?"

"It does. Again, no clue."

Jess sighed.

"Ransom note?" she asked.

"Nope."

"I feel for you, Case. A lot of signals point toward a dead end. Don't get too bummed about it if you come up empty."

"The look in the parent's eyes tells me I won't accept that option."

"And good for you and your tenacity. But it's also a Mr. Lee attribute that, I would add, pulls you into dark places. I don't want you going there."

"I'll do what I told the father. Give it my best shot."

"Just keep those shots figurative. Please."

We chatted on about more personal items. Where our next rendezvous might be, DC sites, Tallahassee food specialties. Good stuff, life-binding, and we ended the call on a solid note. Time for the State Department, US diplomacy's heart and soul, in the close-by Foggy Bottom neighborhood.

The Harry S. Truman Building. Eight stories high, not counting the basement and subbasement, and a million-and-a-half square feet, clad in a limestone exterior. Eight thousand people worked there, forty-four elevators humming all day. There were two among those eight thousand I was interested in. The school trip chaperones.

The Glock, holstered at my side and hidden with a sports coat, was problematic once I'd spotted the metal detectors set up for interior access. I told the receptionist in the vast lobby about my meeting and suggested a lobby sit-down would be more than adequate. He made a call, confirmed the appointment, and said they'd be down soon. Bullet dodged.

Jill Evans, midforties, styled hair, Brooks Brothers business suit, tall and thin. No smile and a perfunctory handshake. She pointed toward a table and chair across the large room. In short order Peter Winston joined us, again midforties, and again a Brooks Brothers suit. And styled hair. One of those just-ran-a-brush-through-it looks that cost a full Benjamin, not a strand out of place. The same height as Evans, with a marshmallow build. He, too, lacked any sign of bonhomie.

"We agreed to meet with you as a favor for Jakub Kaminski. You are a private investigator, correct?"

"I am. And thanks for meeting with me."

"We could not find any background on you, Mr. Lee," said Winston. "That is most unusual."

Well, sashay over to Langley and chat with the Company, scooter. They have lots of background on me.

"Yeah, well, I keep a low profile."

"It would seem your enquiries should be directed toward DSS."

The US Diplomatic Security Service. DSS. Three hundred offices around the world, protecting our diplomatic corps. More than once I'd considered the relationship between DSS and the CIA, both ensconced within US embassies. High odds they didn't play well together.

"I intend on having a chat with the DSS chief in Amman. But right now I'm trying to get a feel for on-the-ground details."

"The DSS has all that information," Evans said, her chin lowered, eyeballing me as a pinned insect under glass.

"I'm sure they do. But it doesn't sound like they've gotten much traction, does it?"

Two silent, officious stares returned.

"Okay," I said, plowing ahead. "Do you two chaperone many of these school excursions?"

"We guide these types of trips. Not as chaperones, but as goodwill ambassadors," Winston said.

"And yes, we make several such trips a year," Evans added. "It is important that young people see the world as it is rather than rely on the garbage they might read or view on the web."

Winston pursed his lips and nodded concurrence.

Yeah, whatever, folks. Now help me find the kid.

"I understand it was a five-day trip, and Petra was the last day before everyone headed back for Amman and the flight home."

"Correct."

No doubt Evans's one-word answer would constitute this meeting's theme.

"Did Krystyna have any special friends with her on the trip? A close buddy or several friends she hung out with?"

"No," Evans said.

That smelled of BS. Teenage kids collected in cliques.

"How was the trip up to that point? Up until you traveled to Petra?"

"Good."

"And when did you and Mr. Winston discover Krystyna was missing?"

Winston spoke up.

"When we gathered at what is known as the Treasury. Before we entered the long walk through the mountain and back to the hotel. We immediately initiated a search protocol, of course."

"And no one saw anything? The Jordanian guide? The vendors inside Petra?"

"If you are insinuating, Mr. Lee, that we were in any way remiss in our efforts, you would be sadly mistaken," Evans said. "There is the strong possibility Krystyna does not wish to be found. She simply ran off. Teenagers the world over do such things."

Uh-huh. In the middle of a vast desert in a country where you didn't speak the language in a culture for which you had no natural affinity. Right.

"Let's pretend she didn't run off. Let's pretend someone captured or kidnapped her. Who would want to do such a thing?"

"I cannot imagine," Evans said. Winston nodded in agreement.

"What was the Jordanian response?"

"Admirable," Evans said.

"What does admirable look like?"

"I understand they expended a great deal of time and effort on the situation," Winston said.

I didn't doubt it. This was a major black eye for Jordan's burgeoning tourist trade, although the press coverage had been minimal. I poked and prodded for another ten minutes, getting nowhere.

"Okay, then," I said. "I'd appreciate it if you would confirm my meeting with the DSS guy in Amman, Nick Halpern. Jakub Kaminski said he's done so, but a little push from you folks would help."

Neither answered. Alrighty, then. Love, hugs, and kisses all around. As for Halpern, I didn't expect a lot more than what I'd just experienced. All signs indicated I was on my own.

Chapter 5

Back at the hotel, I checked messages and rechecked news about Krystyna. Slim pickings on the news front. Oh well, kids go missing all the time, and Krystyna, although a diplomat's daughter, fell into the large global bucket of missing teenagers. I opted for a long walk—clear the head and stretch the legs. I headed for the National Mall area and the Jefferson Memorial. A four-mile round trip as dusk approached, with marvelous monuments well worth a meander past. Rush hour traffic had passed as government employees headed home. What was left of the tourist crowd, already reduced with school in session, thinned even more as nighttime descended.

The Vietnam Veterans Memorial appeared as a rift in the earth, with sixty thousand names inscribed on the black granite walls. I stopped and ran my fingers across a few names, an act that never failed to bring connectivity and sadness and appreciation. The Lincoln Memorial, always worth a visit, stood near empty. The words inscribed on the limestone walls were anything but. The Washington Monument, the world's tallest obelisk, stood bright and illuminated, dominating the view. The Korean War Veterans Memorial made me pause, as usual. At night, the ghostlike oversized figures stabbed with poignancy.

Two other ghostly figures, live ones, tailed me. I'd picked them up while leaving the Lincoln Memorial. This was DC, so the menu of folks who might tail me contained multiple columns and plenty of options. I'd waded in spookville's waters often and had enemies, semibenign players, and no friends among the espionage tribes. More than a few spooks had tried to kill me. They no longer walked among us.

High odds these cats related to my visit with Kaminski and had picked up the trail as I left his home. I'd let my defenses down, ignored my radar, and now we headed for the Potomac River at night. Great. Just freakin' great.

I'd dropped down along the foot-and-bike trail near Ohio Drive, thirty feet from the river. A misty rain began falling, there was minimal road traffic, and one jogger headed toward me from the opposite direction. Dim street lamps at lengthy intervals cast circles of light. The men trailing me could have been follow-that-guy players, keeping tabs. Or hitters. Hard to say at the moment, but best to force the issue rather than the cat-and-mouse routine.

I stopped at the center point between two street lamps and faced the river. If this vignette turned ugly, I wanted maximum darkness. The last thing I needed were witnesses to any violence. I turned my head left and smiled and nodded and waved a friendly hand at the jogger as she went past. She did a quick hand-raise as a response. I followed her progress to the right, toward the two men. Their silhouettes, thirty feet away, were 1950s central casting. Both men were large and blocky, with large, blocky suits. One had stopped and adopted my position, facing the river. He wore a fedora. The other, with close-cropped hair, continued toward me as the jogger weaved past them. There were no exchanged pleasantries between the men and the jogger. My right hand rested on the holstered Glock. Two vehicles passed in opposite directions at my back and lights blinked across the Potomac. Otherwise, the night stood still.

I positioned at the walkway's edge and gave the approaching man plenty of passing space. Both his hands were closed, no weapon evident. My adrenaline meter redlined. I had no plans on pulling the Glock, an overreaction to an undetermined threat. That would change in a heartbeat if this cat's hand filled with a pistol. If he wanted a physical tango, I'd accommodate that as well.

He shot a brusque nod toward me when a few steps away and began to pass by. Events exploded as he struck. Abreast, his left hand thrust out and grabbed my coat's lapel. A preliminary move, seen often enough—anchor the victim while the right hand came to bear. Wasn't happening. Rather than pull away, I lunged into him. Caught his right wrist with my left hand and slammed my forehead into his nose. Cartilage crunched as he grunted with pain. The headbutt should have staggered him. It didn't, but it loosened his grip on my jacket. I kept a death grip on his wrist and swung over his lapel arm with a right cross. A solid shot against his jaw. I've leveled more than a few large men with that punch. It hardly fazed this guy. Blood gushed from his broken nose, and footfalls sounded as his partner dashed our way. A split-second glance at my opponent's right hand showed a small metallic object, not a knife. I shot a rapid glance toward his approaching partner. The minimal light highlighted glinting steel in one hand. A blade. Enough of this crap.

Within a half-second, I filled my hand with the Glock and pumped two rounds into my grappling opponent's chest. The pistol's sharp blasts boomed across the area and carried over the Potomac. A vehicle's bump and rattle sounded as it jumped the curb behind me. Then another vehicle. Cops—but no flashing lights, no sirens. I kept a grip on my opponent's wrist as he fell and swung the pistol right amid the expected "Drop it!" cries from the cops. The fedora-wearing thug slammed the brakes, slid against the wet pavement, and stopped five paces away. His knife clattered on the walkway as he thrust his hand into his suit jacket where a shoulder holster could hold bullet-laden steel. I didn't wait for verification. A single trigger pull, another cacophonous blast, and a .40 caliber hollow point drilled into fedora-guy's forehead. I anticipated screams and gunshots from the cops. Shots aimed at me.

I snapped my head toward the rear and captured two large black SUVs stopped on the grass with doors and back hatches flung open as dark-suited men spilled out. What the hell?

"Stow the weapon, Lee!"

I didn't. This was too crazy, too bizarre.

"Stow the damn weapon, asshole!"

Two dark-suited men snatched up fedora-man and tossed him into an SUV's rear area. They then hustled toward me and repeated the operation with the man I'd shot in the chest. Another man wore a small headlamp and collected fallen weapons and spent brass. Another used a fire-extinguisher-looking canister and sprayed the walkway with what smelled like bleach. They worked around me as if I wasn't there and moved fast, efficient. A lone bicyclist headed in our direction stopped, assessed, and turned around. See no evil. Within sixty seconds they'd stowed the expired hitters, doors shut. The SUV with the bodies took off. The remaining vehicle, one rear door still open, waited. An operator stood behind the SUV's hood, voice lowered.

"Get in, Lee. The director wants to see you. But put the weapon away first."

Mind reeling, I stood stock-still after lowering my hand, pistol still gripped. A vehicle passed, its tires rolling over wet pavement. It slowed, rubbernecked, and rolled on. Sirens sounded in the distance. These were Company operators, and I wouldn't park my butt in one of their vehicles without an excellent reason. The man who'd addressed me pulled his phone, punched a single command, spoke softly for ten seconds, and hung up. On cue, my phone vibrated. I pulled it and checked the source. Marilyn Townsend. The CIA's director of clandestine operations.

"Director?"

"Enter the vehicle, Mr. Lee. Time is short."

Too weird, too planned, too strange, and I couldn't wrap my head around it.

"What?"

"Get in the vehicle. You are exposed to a great deal of unpleasantness from local law enforcement. Climb in, Mr. Lee."

I did. And holstered the Glock. The SUV jumped the curb and we took off. The guy riding shotgun passed me several pretreated wipes.

"Blood," he said. "Your face and neck."

No doubt. Two up-close-and-personal pistol shots would have thrown blood splatter my way. I cleaned up with caution, aware the disinfectant wipes could also contain some weird drug that would knock me out. I salved my concern knowing the director was expecting me in a conscious state. Maybe. You just never freakin' knew.

We crossed the Potomac and followed the river north, toward Langley, and exited at Rosslyn, weaving down side streets. We parked in front of a small pub and behind another large black SUV. She would hold court inside, tucked into a corner.

Marilyn Townsend, the world's most powerful spy. We went way back. During Delta days, as a Company field agent, she'd worked with our small team around the world. Together, we'd taken out bad guys. We'd respected her abilities and attitude and mission focus. When our team retired and moved on, she'd worked her way up Company ranks. Her identity as the current Director of Clandestine Operations was a well-kept secret, known to but a handful. It was better that way. Let CIA political appointees and professional bureaucrats deal with Congress and the president. Townsend remained deep in the shadows and performed the heavy lifting.

Years passed after she and I separated. I took on shadow gigs after a bounty hunter murdered my wife, Rae. And began bumping into Company assets, which included the occasional sit-down with Townsend. Several times over the years, the Company, under Townsend's direction, had played me like a Stradivarius. I'd assumed after our last encounter—when she'd hired me for a domestic job on Orcas Island—that we'd never see each other again. I had mightily pissed her off during that one. Ours was a yin-yang relationship with mutual respect, a dollop of trust, and a jaundiced eye cast in both directions.

A half-dozen black-suited security personnel stood as I entered and approached the pub's farthest corner. The barkeep asked what I'd have as I passed. I informed him a double Grey Goose on the rocks would do. The black-suited seas parted without comment—unusual and disconcerting—and I spotted Townsend at a small table, nursing a glass of wine. She smiled at me. Which added to the weirdness. I'd never use the term "friendly" with her descriptive.

"Director. You're looking well," I said, sitting.

"And you as well, Mr. Lee." During our Delta exploits, it was "Marilyn," and "Case." Days long, long past. "Thank you for joining me."

The barkeep, johnny-on-the-spot, arrived with my drink. Unbeknownst to him, six fingers pressed against the triggers of automatic submachine guns as he approached our table, deposited my drink, and left.

"I would like to offer you help on your current endeavors, Mr. Lee. Company assistance."

She smiled again. Oh, man. Through the looking glass, baby. Through the freakin' looking glass.

Chapter 6

"You look well, Mr. Lee. How have you been?"

"Let's see. I just whacked two guys before they did it to me. Then the clean-up squad arrived and removed all traces of those edge-of-your-seat activities. And now I'm sitting here with no clue what the hell is going on. So, all in all, I'm doing pretty doggone peachy."

She tossed a tight-lipped smile my way and sipped wine. I downed a healthy slug of vodka.

"Are you hungry?" she asked. "I well imagine this establishment could provide a nibble or three."

Forearms on the table, I leaned forward.

"What are you doing, Marilyn? Besides weirding me out?"

The bell over the pub's door rang, and another Company spook entered. He waded through the security detail and whispered into Townsend's ear. She nodded, he left. A half-dozen other patrons sat in the joint—all were either oblivious to the black-suited security detail packed in a corner, or patrons whose interest in cloak-and-dagger doings near CIA headquarters had long ago waned.

"If a recent unpleasant event had happened, and it didn't, those would have been SIA assets."

The Bulgarian State Intelligence Agency. Great. The Bulgarian secret police occupied an ugly corner in the espionage and covert action space. They'd attempted to assassinate Pope John Paul II and often acted as Russia's hit squad. And now I sat on the SIA's shitlist. Lists under constant expansion. It included Russia, China, Iran, Chechnya, Sudan, and, on occasion, the good ol' USA as represented by the woman sitting across from me. Just freakin' great.

"What did that one guy have in his hand?" I asked.

"A poison injection device. You were to be killed," Townsend said.

"The other cat wielded a bladed steel injection device. And reached for his pistol."

"Let's not rehash events that didn't occur. Are you sure you aren't hungry?"

"I'll have a plate of truth, a side order of motivations, and a tall glass of relevant players."

As expected, she sidestepped my request and plowed a Company furrow—her standard operating procedure. I'd have entered a state of personal shock and awe if she'd come clean.

"You met with the Polish diplomat. A Mr. Jakub Kaminski."

"I did."

"You have taken a contract to find his daughter."

"I have."

"Would you have any preliminary thoughts on her disappearance?"

"Yeah. I don't have a clue if she's dead or alive. If dead, there's a lot of desert in Jordan for burying a body. And if alive, this is a strange way for a kidnapping to play out. Kaminski hasn't heard a word from any kidnappers about ransom."

"Ah."

She sipped wine as her three-dimensional chess pieces shifted about. I'd take a stab at gathering intel, with low odds anything fruitful would come of it. Townsend didn't view quid pro quo as a legitimate device, although she'd delivered once or twice when it furthered her efforts.

"What do the Bulgarians have to do with all this?" I asked.

"Perhaps nothing."

"Bullshit."

She chuckled. Calling BS on the world's most powerful spy wasn't an activity taken lightly, but she and I had shared knife-edge exploits the world over during Delta days. We'd lived in tents and hovels and eaten MREs together, mission-focused, with no backup other than our wits and trigger fingers. A gritty and dangerous existence, and the years hadn't faded our connection. Not that we were bosom buddies, then or now. But still.

"Allow me to broad-brush a larger picture," she said. "One that might provide you context."

"Okay."

"We are interested in the diplomatic swirl around this girl's disappearance. Our brethren in the diplomatic ranks can be less than candid about their inner workings."

The royal *we*. Townsend was interested, which covered all the bases for the CIA.

"Turf battles?"

"In part. And perhaps in part because of their own initiatives."

"Initiatives you aren't privy to?"

"The intelligence flow adopts many shades of both truth and obfuscation."

"There's an answer I should stick on the fridge."

"Your sarcasm aside, it is an accurate statement."

I downed the vodka and raised the glass toward the barkeep across the room. He glanced up and nodded back. You've gotta love the language of a good bar. Short, sweet, to the point. And very unlike the conversation I held with Townsend.

"Could we get back to the Bulgarians? Did the Russians send them after me?"

"Unknown. It would appear the two Bulgarian assets we have in custody remain uncommunicative. A common condition with your encounters."

"Can the critiques, Marilyn. Over the last several years the Company has used me as their chew toy. Your chew toy. New Guinea, the Caribbean, Sudan, Orcas Island. So stow the demeaning 'tude unless you and I relish spending the next hour comparing notes on who did what to who."

A fifteen-second unblinking eye-lock ensued, broken when the barkeep arrived with my fresh drink. Townsend asked him if fresh coffee was available.

"We have an espresso machine. I can thin it out and make you a cup."

"An espresso sounds good. One sugar. And a cognac."

"Would you like the snifter heated?"

"I would."

He waded back through the black-suited sea. Trigger fingers relaxed.

"A fresh start, then, Mr. Lee," she said and sat back, fingertips against the tabletop.

"We can give it a try, Director."

"I would offer assistance with your quest."

"What does that look like? And I'm guessing it's pointless to ask why."

"*Why* is far outside the scope of your endeavors. That said, I would appreciate brief communiqués during your efforts as you look under rocks and, I would suppose, dig in the sand. As for assistance, feel free to communicate with me, day or night. I can bring substantial forces to bear. I do not say that lightly, Mr. Lee."

I'd asked her for help in the past. Requests turned down as she drew no perceived benefit from aiding me. Whatever the benefit this time, her offer had potent possibilities. The Company operated globally, big time. By law they were forbidden from operating on US turf, but two large black SUVs on body disposal duty a short while ago shot that stricture all to hell.

"Who's your head knocker in Amman?" I asked. "I'll be there day after tomorrow."

"How was your meeting with State? A Ms. Jill Evans and a Mr. Peter Winston, I believe."

Marilyn Townsend's all-seeing eye. A tiresome display waved about too often. I remained silent, weighed options, and settled on feeding her, with the hope that the Company help might include bailing me out from a tight spot if needed. Hope springs eternal, although experience pointed toward a pipe dream rather than anything substantial. But you never knew.

"Both Evans and Winston were defensive. Guarded. And they didn't appear too broken up over the girl's disappearance."

"Ah."

Her coffee and cognac arrived. She stirred the former with a tiny spoon and inhaled the latter's aroma before taking a sip.

"I'll meet with their DSS guy in Amman. I'm not holding high expectations, but you never know."

"Mr. Nick Halpern," she said. She reached into her suit pocket and extracted a small business card. "I would appreciate it if you also met with my operations officer after you meet with Mr. Halpern."

She slid the card across the table. The otherwise blank card displayed a phone number and the name Jonas Bancroft. It was clear the Diplomatic Security Service and the CIA weren't playing well together on the Krystyna Kaminski case. Not my problem, and they could have at it with their behind-the-curtain global pissing match. My job—find out what happened to Krystyna and, if possible, bring her home. If the Company could help me do that, fine. If feeding Townsend intel fostered their assistance, fine. If the DSS and Company issues stepped out from behind the curtain and affected my efforts, not so fine.

"I'll meet Bancroft after Halpern," I said. "Now, the water remains muddy on your side of the table. On my side, it is crystal clear. Find the girl. Whatever else is going on is gorilla dust, and I don't want any part of it."

"Nor do I wish you to be a part of it."

"Good. I appreciate the offer of help. I may take you up on it. I'll feed you pertinent intel as it crops up. Does that cover the mutual back-scratching?"

"It does." She sipped cognac as her demeanor mellowed. "You and I do not require adversarial exchanges each time we meet. Our mutual paths stretch too far back."

"Yeah. I know. And I'm not happy when we butt heads. But you've gotta admit your outfit has gnawed and shaken me like a rag doll on more than one occasion."

"A matter of perspective, and a complicated one at that."

"Roger on the complicated."

I downed my second drink. Yeah, we had a complex relationship. I respected Marilyn and back in the day edged toward liking her. But today was a different world. She was the world's top spy. I was a beat-up ex-Delta contractor. She lived and thrived in a world where nuance, misdirection, lies, and leverage reigned. Spookville. I tried, not always with success, living a simple life. Good and bad, right and wrong. Live and let live as long as you don't hurt anyone. Mess with my family, friends, or me, and I'd bring the hammer down. Simple stuff. The vast chasm between Marilyn's world and mine contained a few shaky footbridges, worn and tenuous. Bridges built on mutual respect and acknowledgment of each other's skill sets, I supposed.

And built on our history together, a binding glue with a strong dash of nostalgia.

We sat in comfortable silence for another few minutes as she finished her espresso and cognac. When she retrieved her cane and tapped it twice against the hardwood floor—signaling her protection team who stood en masse—we shot each other an old-days smile.

"Call or text me, Mr. Lee. You, among few others in the world, have my number. Our devices are both encrypted, so do not hesitate."

"Roger on that, Director. Will do. Both with intel, if relevant, and a request for help, if needed."

"Allow me to discern relevancy. Now, watch your back. You occupy an unpopular position within your current contract."

Yeah, no kidding. Townsend and her squad left the bar. I didn't, and sucked ice cubes while paying the tab. My phone pinged with a text message. The Clubhouse in Chesapeake, Virginia. Jules was the grittier version of Townsend. A self-described simple broker of information, she was anything but. A working man's conduit into shadowland. She serviced a varied clientele, including the Company. She'd saved my bacon frequently, and we shared mutual fondness. Sorta. Jules was a strange duck in anyone's book, and Clubhouse interactions often teetered on the bizarre. Came with the territory. Her text message, disconcerting in the extreme, stipulated a venue change for tomorrow morning's meeting. An unwelcome first, which added to this contract's weirdness.

Tomorrow a.m. location. Ask for Antoinette.

It included a Chesapeake address, not distant from the Clubhouse location—a Filipino-run dry cleaner in a shady part of town. I checked the address and street view on Google. A tiny diner, run-down and tucked between a small-appliance repair shop and a boarded-up secondhand clothing store. The Antoinette bit was Jules being, well, Jules.

Weird layered on strange, spiced with peril. An issue had occurred inside the Clubhouse today. One resolved with Jules's usual method—her double-barreled shotgun, which always rested on her desktop and pointed toward any and all visitors. She had put it to use. Good or bad use depended upon, as Townsend stated, perspective.

The Filipinos below her operated the dry cleaner rent-free. In return, they guarded the rickety stairs leading up to the Clubhouse door and performed clean-up duties when required. I'd checked the steel-walled Clubhouse for telltale signs of lead shotgun pellets splatting steel and discovered more than a few. Once the offending party met his or her maker, the downstairs staff would climb the stairs with rags, bleach, and a body bag. They'd tote away the unfortunate soul who'd crossed Jules to a tight Filipino community on Chesapeake's edge where a certain individual raised pigs. Large, hungry pigs, who'd eat anything, including bones and teeth. Adios, unfortunate soul. Dollars to doughnuts the next day's venue change reflected ongoing clean-up efforts.

One helluva start for this job. Jakub and Anna Kaminski were hiding something. Well, Jakub was. Anna, not so much. Strange reactions from State, as both Jill Evans and Peter Winston pulled a tight-lips routine layered with suspicion and ill will toward me, the guy contracted to find the girl they'd had a hand in losing. Then two hitters whacked, two more notches on the figurative pistol grip. An act taken neither lightly nor one filled with remorse. Them or me, a simple choice. A quick Company clean-up sweep and the offer of assistance from Townsend. And now, a Clubhouse issue resolved with a twelve-gauge problem-solver. Oh, man. As they say in New Orleans, "Laissez les bon temps rouler." Let the good times roll, baby.

Chapter 7

Early a.m. on board a long-range Gulfstream headed for Chesapeake. A charter—pricey as hell, but the clock ticked. The Polish government were footing the bill, with the possibility other governments chipped in. High odds the Bulgarians weren't a contributor. The Gulfstream was a hot model, capable of ten-plus hours of high-speed flight without refueling. It would take me nonstop to Amman, Jordan, after the meeting with Jules.

The Chesapeake diner's peeled-paint door opened onto a small room with three patrons having breakfast. One old man, head in hands, stared at his coffee. A middle-aged couple, dressed with hard times, glanced my way and continued their low conversation. Their faces attempted upbeat expressions as they talked with each other, but they couldn't hide the underlying lines of despair. To their credit, the stiff-upper-lip act showed they hadn't given up. Yet. It touched me, seeing folks down on their luck like that.

It was a Vietnamese-run establishment. The matriarch eyeballed me and offered a table with a tight smile.

"I'm here to see Antoinette."

Her hand shifted from an offer into a palm-down finger-beckoning gesture. I followed her through the swinging kitchen door, past a man and a woman working a griddle and fryer, and out the back door. A tiny concrete pad, surrounded with a high wooden fence, held a table with two chairs. And Jules. The matriarch closed the door behind me.

Jules and I both grinned. At her left hand, a fresh steaming cup of tea, the tea bag string evident. Her right hand hid inside a long leather case, halfway unzipped, which lay across the table, pointed at me. A sure as the sun rises in the east, she fingered the trigger of her shotgun. As per Clubhouse protocol, I emptied my pockets and displayed a roll of Benjamins.

47

Information cost. A slow pirouette followed, with an important announcement.

"You'll notice the Glock in my waistband, Jules."

"I shall make an exception this time, dear boy. Sit."

Clubhouse rules prohibited entrance with a phone or weapon. Cash only, plus intel handwritten on index cards. Nothing else. Except licorice, a Jules addiction, which I hadn't brought. As I sat, she slid her hand from the long leather case, plucked the tea bag from the mug, allowed it two swings as a pendulum, and tossed it over the fence at her back. She kept her one eye focused on me during the process and smiled. Blowing away some guy may have lifted her spirits. She showcased a strange rounded brown-leather cap, no brim—another first. Her DIY haircut stuck out from underneath it, and she wore a new eyepatch, reddish-brown. Color coordination with the cap, I supposed. She carried a peculiar countenance on her best days, and now resembled a bygone-era shaman. Had to be the cap.

"I take it, Antoinette, you don't favor bleach's aroma," I said.

"It is true, the Clubhouse lacks large-scale ventilation. By tomorrow, I shall be ensconced back into my regular place of business. Be most assured. As for the nom de plume, why not? Allow me a bit of frivolity."

The Clubhouse's steel walls didn't allow for any windows. And prevented buckshot from exiting.

"Who was it?" I asked, not expecting an answer. I was wrong.

"A member of your opposition."

"Not sure what that means, Jules."

"Which is, once again, one among many reasons you so delight this wretched creature. May I offer you a cup of tea? The kitchen staff appears capable of boiling water."

She chuckled, snatched a quarter-smoked cigar from the table's edge, and fished in her work shirt pocket for a kitchen match. Struck on the tabletop near her abacus—she'd brought the Clubhouse accounting system with her—cigar smoke billowed, and the Clubhouse was open for business.

"That whole opposition thing is kinda important, Jules. Two men tried to kill me yesterday in DC. And you received an unwanted visitor."

"And your attackers' status?"

"They've joined the ranks of the dearly departed."

"One would hope none of our national monuments were affected. You didn't employ explosives, did you, dear?" she asked with a grin.

"Funny."

"Tell me all about your yesterday. Leave nothing out."

I did. The entire kit and caboodle. Relaying intel about Townsend wasn't a big deal—the CIA was a solid Clubhouse client. Because Jules knew things. Boy howdy, did she know things. Government clandestine services relied on electronics, computer science, and a standard human asset network. Not Jules. She eschewed electronics, not trusting them. What she did have was a non-garden-variety foreign network of spies, thieves, fixers, hustlers, hitters, and general miscreants. Plus corrupt or talkative politicians and officials spread across the globe. And the politicians and officials' handlers. Jules knew things.

"Day one on your new contract," she said, her eye locked birdlike on me.

"Day one."

"One can only speculate on the wonders today might hold."

"It holds a long, boring flight. I'm outta here, headed for Jordan after our meeting. A ten-hour flight, landing in Amman at three a.m. their time. There's not much room for wonderment."

"He said, filled with jaunty confidence. I do so love your bright perspective. Are you sure you won't have tea?"

"No, thanks. Now, about the opposition. What can you give me?"

Always a good question. Jules doled out expensive intel with precise measurement.

"Your Bulgarian descriptive was most helpful. My sinister visitor yesterday evening proved Albanian. It would appear we reside within an eastern European motif. For the moment."

"My accepting the contract affected you." No kidding. A hitter showed at the Clubhouse. The connection bothered me. A lot. "I'm so, so sorry. This has never happened before."

"Fear not, dear. It is appropriate for the Clubhouse to stake a fresh flag occasionally. A large flag, snapping in the breeze, that reiterates Clubhouse rules."

"I feel terrible about it."

"Do bear in mind I had accepted his meeting. The pretense appeared valid. A new client on the horizon. Think no more on it, Case Lee. Let us discuss the landscape as it relates to the poor girl. With your experience, how would you assess her current condition?"

"I don't feel good about it, at all. Days have passed and no ransom contact with Kaminski. She didn't plan a walkabout. It wouldn't fit the profile I got from her parents and the intel in her room. The one thing that gives me hope is the entire event was too well coordinated for a simple abduction. Had to be. You know the Jordanians scoured their country, plus the efforts from DSS and others."

"I concur. You may wish to question DSS's tenacity, however."

"Yeah, I got that vibe at State. But their DSS guy in Amman must have put in the effort."

"You ignore, again, the one big thing, dear boy."

Nothing was ever as it seemed. The one big thing. Simple words, complex as hell on the ground.

"Maybe. The deal is, I'm avoiding all that stuff as much as possible. I'm focused on the girl. Find her, or what became of her."

"Stuff?"

The Clubhouse's world—stuff, things, actions, rumors, and mindsets that occupied dark corners and dangerous recesses. I hadn't said it as a pejorative.

"You know I don't mean it like that. It's just that I can't have shadow movements distracting me and still maintain a decent shot at finding her."

"Hmm." She sipped tea.

"Let's get back to the eastern European theme. Those places have a track record as Russia's hired muscle. Not that the Russians don't have plenty of muscle themselves. I speak from experience."

I'd tangled with them from New Guinea to Nevada. A tough bunch.

"There may well be a connection," she said. Her cigar had gone out, and she fished for another kitchen match in her shirt pocket. "How might such activity connect with the diplomatic world? And more importantly, how does it connect with the poor child? I'm afraid you must wade through more *stuff* to find answers."

She fired a found match. Cigar smoke wafted about our small area. She had a solid point. My contract triggered outside events. Deadly events, both on DC's streets and inside a small room above a Filipino dry cleaner in Chesapeake. Jules was right. I'd deal with bad guys three-sixty-degrees moving forward. Damn, Sam.

"I need a fixer in Amman."

"No, you do not. Multiple sets of eyes will await your arrival."

"I can't go into this naked."

Naked—without weaponry. In particular, weaponry that went bang.

"I am afraid au naturel is mandatory. They will seek excuses for hindering you, so leave your firearm with me for safekeeping. As consolation," she said, hand in a front pants' pocket, "there is a gentleman in Madaba who will equip you once you have run the gauntlet in Amman."

She chuckled and slid an index card across the table. It had a name and number. I memorized it. No physical artifacts left the Clubhouse, even under outdoors-behind-the-kitchen conditions.

"Madaba is twenty miles outside Amman."

"Indeed it is."

Man, I hated that. I'd land, get a few hours' sleep, meet with the DSS and Company operators, then drive to Madaba. Naked. I stretched my neck and plowed ahead.

"What's the deal with the Company? She wants me to gather intel on State. That's pretty doggone weird."

"Is it? Two large organisms, both with the motivations of any organized hive. Stay safe, grow, thrive, claim new territory."

"You suggest State is crafting something that gives them more power. Perhaps at the Company's expense."

"I do not suggest any such thing, Poirot. I am suggesting she wants you to find out."

Marilyn Townsend. She. Neither Jules nor I used her name when we conversed—a private protocol. We sat silent while she puffed. Fresh patrons must have entered the diner as kitchen activity sounds increased through the closed door.

"Why did you take this contract?" Jules asked.

"Seemed like a cut-and-dried gig."

"Shall I repeat the question?"

"Okay. A cut-and-dried gig sprinkled with do-good."

"I would suggest doing good constitutes the prime ingredient. Which is, again, why you delight me so. I have no other clients with similar motivations. A breath of fresh air, dear boy. Now," she said, lifting the abacus's edge from the tabletop, "if you would be so kind as to provide the names of the DSS individual and Company officer in Amman, we shall consider the Madaba contact details an even trade."

Fair enough and done. I placed the Glock alongside her sheathed shotgun.

"I'll return for it," I said, standing. "Wish me luck."

"Communicate as the need arises. And it will. You enter the eye of a storm, Case Lee. Godspeed."

Chapter 8

The Amman flight, customs, and immigration were uneventful, and I checked into an excellent hotel. I'd grabbed some shut-eye on the flight, and the hotel bed afforded another three hours. Good to go. The Amman Diplomatic Security Service guy, Nick Halpern, met me over breakfast. At least my breakfast—he didn't stay long. A perfunctory handshake, a nod when the waiter asked if he'd like coffee, and a dive into the heart of things.

"You are here to find Krystyna Kaminski."

A statement, not a question.

"That's the plan. What can you tell me about the Jordanian efforts?"

"They have been quite thorough. The young woman decided to run away, and in case you didn't know, there is not a great deal anyone can do about that."

"I don't think she ran away."

"You would be wrong."

"I could be. Let's pretend I'm not. What has DSS done about finding her?"

"We have poured a great number of resources and valued time into the effort. Now, I have a concern."

"Okay."

"I am concerned your efforts, whatever they might be, will upset our host country. Our relationship with Jordan is excellent, and avoiding conflict is a major priority."

"I don't seek conflict, Halpern. I am seeking intel and would appreciate anything you could deliver me."

He sipped coffee and stared over my head. This guy was an asshat. And defensive. A defensive asshat, useless with respect to my mission. He deigned to resume looking at me.

"You are on a fool's errand, Lee. The young woman is gone. Young people disappear by the thousands all over the world, every day. Whatever you plan on doing here, make it quick and quiet. Travel to Petra, leave, and collect your payment. You gave it the old college try."

Breakfast was excellent, and I took my time enjoying it, staring at Halpern as I chewed. He turned in his chair, legs crossed, stared across the room, and sipped coffee. Asshat. I finished the meal, wiped my mouth, sat back, and sipped coffee.

"Does the embassy keep any spare explosives around, Halpern?"

His head snapped my way, eyebrows furrowed, mouth open.

"What?"

"Nothing. Just a thought. You know, my greatest challenge so far is getting past the grief and consternation shown by you and your fellow State employees in DC, Evans and Winston. Krystyna Kaminski's disappearance has clearly torn you people up. If you could work through the vale of tears and tell me what you've done in Jordan to find her, I'd appreciate it. Because from where I'm sitting, it looks like State, and you in particular, haven't done jack shit."

He stood, tossed his napkin on the table with a huff, and turned.

"One last thing, Halpern." He halted his turn, now sideways toward me. "I'm aware pissants like you enjoy messing with people as personal retribution. Passport issues, no-fly lists—the usual crap. So before we depart company, know this." I lowered my voice as we locked eyes. "I can get anywhere in the world. No problem. And if I get wind you flipped any State

Department switches, I'll pay you a home visit here in Amman. At night. Sabe?"

With eyes as big as saucers, face bright red, he completed his turn and stomped away. I never have dessert with breakfast, but that tasted sweet. At least for a while, until my anger dissipated and blood pressure lowered. Way to go, Lee. Once again, making friends and influencing people. Smart. Real smart. On the flip side, it was often best to draw a few lines in the sand. It kept things simple. I liked simple.

Bobbing in the DSS guy's departure wake was reinforcement that lies had paved my path. Kaminski, Evans and Winston in DC, Halpern just now, and likely Marilyn Townsend. The Polish diplomat and Townsend lied through omission. Kaminski knew more. A bunch more. Townsend less so, but she understood framework, and I didn't. The State people just flat-out lied.

The waiter cleared dishes and poured me more coffee. His smile and demeanor reminded me why I enjoyed the country of Jordan and, in particular, Amman. A clean, organized city filled with good, pleasant folks. I pulled my phone, the Company's head spook in Jordan on the call list. Wasted effort as he appeared, as if on cue, alongside my table.

"Jonas Bancroft," he said, extending his hand. "May I sit down?"

I stood, we shook, and I pointed toward the empty chair.

"Are you guys taking a number out in the lobby?"

He chuckled and stated, "Yes, please," to the waiter, in Arabic, when offered coffee.

"I observed your exchange with State. You must realize he has now scratched you off his Christmas card list."

"Another cross to bear."

"Shall we compare notes, Case? May I call you Case?"

This cat was good. Bonding and rapport straight out of the chute. Well-trained spooks were an interesting lot. Bancroft had received word to cooperate with me from on high. He wouldn't know Marilyn Townsend—he wouldn't even know her name—but someone way, way up his food chain told him to meet with me and cooperate. Which put Bancroft, for the moment and subject to change, on the plus side of the ledger. Written in pencil.

"Case works."

"And call me Jonas. Great. What can I help you with?"

"What's with all the weirdness wrapped around a missing teenager?"

"Just that. Weirdness. Halpern received marching orders and has played his cards close to his chest."

"Well, I've talked with the escorts, Jill Evans and Peter Winston, and now Halpern. I'd say the first nine items on a ten-item marching order is a simple 'keep your mouths shut.'"

"Hence the weirdness. Look, Case, I work with State every day. We share offices. I have friends who work that side, and they're good people. Don't paint everyone with a Nick Halpern paintbrush."

I didn't. I'd run into plenty of State employees over the years, and most were fine, others just okay. And I was aware the Company and State shared offices—the Amman US embassy was an enormous structure, surrounded with vast grounds, and contained within a massive wall. I could well imagine it was a tight-knit US community. Which translated into this current State ops, whatever it was, being even more tight-knit and secretive.

"I've got no animus toward State," I said. "But whatever game they're playing, they're serious. Dead serious."

That was a sufficient descriptive for Bancroft's understanding that killing was on the menu. I wouldn't get into the DC event or let slip intel about

Bulgarians—he worked under a need-to-know basis from both the Company and Case Lee Inc.—but my statement would come across loud and clear.

"Any thoughts on what's driving this?" he asked.

"That was my question for you."

We both sipped coffees.

"What if I baseline the two organizations?" I asked.

I would swim in the shark-filled spookville pool with this guy for a quick sprint, well aware I sucked at it. Best bet—leverage Jules's words as a launching point.

"I don't follow," he said, smiling, pleasant as could be.

"You're both large and living organizations. With deep concerns over your operating environments and the ability to grow, expand, gain power. Right?"

"We provide accurate, comprehensive, and timely foreign intelligence related to national security."

"Yeah, it's a great official tag line, and kudos to the Company copywriters. But is there an operational turf battle between you two I don't know about?"

"It's a big embassy, Case. Within an enormous US government. There will always be a lot of sharp elbows."

A perfect spook answer, not telling me jack.

"Then let's talk State."

"The Department of State leads America's foreign policy through diplomacy, advocacy, and assistance by advancing the interests of the American people, their safety and economic prosperity." We exchanged unblinking stares for a few seconds until he added, "Alright, I'll admit they've got better copywriters than we do."

We both chuckled and smiled. He'd opened the kimono a sliver and exposed Jonas Bancroft, human being. Maybe. That was the thing with clandestine players. You just never knew, and if you had a lick of sense, you'd never trust them.

"What's State got cooking right now?" I asked. "Any new initiatives that would relate to a lost teenage girl?"

"None that I've heard of. That's an honest answer. Here's another honest answer—they are a lot more political than we are. I mean, they deal with the political class. We do as well, but not as a full-time member. State does as a card-carrying member. We may need to explore that angle."

"Nope. Exploration is off the table. I'm finding out what happened with a Polish diplomat's daughter. Period. What have you got as it pertains to State that helps me?"

"I'm afraid you won't like the answer."

"You're right. So why are you and I meeting? I've got places to go and people to see."

"I'm here for support. Those are my marching orders, and I intend to carry them out. Would you like an asset or two to travel with you?"

Amman CIA officers. They'd offer less than this guy, and I didn't relish spook car mates for my Petra trip. And they sure didn't need to discover the Clubhouse fixer in Madaba. Jules would find out and have my butt.

"I appreciate the offer, but no. I'm fine."

"I'm glad we met," he said, standing. "You have my number. Call me twenty-four-seven. I'm a handy guy to know in this part of the world."

"Thanks. I'm sure you are."

We shook hands and he eased away, lifting a chin and smiling at hotel staff during departure. He'd left behind a big red button. Push it, slap a hand on it, when needed. Help would be on the way. I gave it a fifty-fifty shot.

Alright. A rucksack and bottled water waited upstairs, a decent SUV rental sat out front. Off to find the kid.

THE DC JOB

Chapter 9

The Madaba drive had me glued to the side- and rearview mirrors, checking for tails. I'd crawled under the SUV before departing and disabled the rental car company GPS, knowing full well my new CIA friend could have planted another one I wouldn't find. Electronic tracking aside, my primary concern was the on-the-ground dangers. I couldn't pick up any tails, but the relief factor never kicked in. They could still lurk, hidden and coordinated, so relaxation—particularly without a weapon—wasn't on the menu.

My fixer had instructed me to hang out at the Greek Orthodox Church of St. George, a tourist spot. The church housed a remarkable mosaic map showing the known Byzantine world from the fourth or fifth century and drew a consistent stream of visitors. While waiting, I overheard a half-dozen languages.

Madaba was famous for both stunning mosaics and proximity to Mount Nebo, a holy site for Jews, Christians, and Muslims alike. The place where God showed Moses the Promised Land. The land of milk and honey. I'd visited Mount Nebo years earlier during a break in our training exercises with the Jordanians. I'd been lucky with weather that day—clear, cloudless, calm—and viewed the Dead Sea, Jericho, and far in the distance, Jerusalem. It drove home how people's historical context varied around this good earth. I marked US history from 1776. Here, events three thousand years ago were woven into the warp and woof of everyday life. It was a vastly different worldview, with ancient ties, and I reveled in it.

One of my tasks during those days was accompanying a Jordanian government archeologist as he inspected our proposed training sites. He was a fine older gentleman, and on our first trip I followed him like a doofus, checking out the operational terrain. He'd stop occasionally, bend down and pluck an item from the ground, inspect it, and toss it over his shoulder. The third time he did this, I hung close and retrieved his discarded item. It was a pottery shard, several inches across, with remnants of a simple design.

"Having us trample through here isn't a concern?" I'd asked him, displaying the shard.

"Byzantine," he'd said. "Not so old."

As I waited at the Madaba church and reminisced and keyed on individuals around the area, an older gentleman with gray hair and a brisk stride passed and, without pausing, said, "Follow me. At a distance."

I did and kept a thirty-pace separation. We wove through narrow streets, past local souks selling produce and sundries, losing him here and there as he, no doubt, checked my back trail. At a tiny coffee- and teahouse, he darted inside. I followed.

A half-dozen tables with rickety chairs, a young man, and a small goat occupied the interior. We sat and ordered tea. I couldn't take my eyes off the floor's barely discernible mosaic patchwork, interspersed between ancient bare cement and covered with dirt and dust. My fixer, Yosef Ali, noticed my preoccupation and asked the young man for a quick cleanup. He complied and shooed the goat outside, dumped a bucket of water on the floor, and wiped with a dirty mop. Intricate designs with animals and events appeared with shades of cream, blue, red, and black—all created from thousands of fingernail-sized tiles. I thanked both Yosef and the young man. I couldn't help myself. How often would I sip tea on two-thousand-year-old mosaic flooring?

"I have what you requested," Yosef said as he lit a smoke. We spoke Arabic.

"Excellent. Where are they?"

"Perhaps you meant it."

"It?"

"Yes. I have it here."

"It?"

"A pistol. As you requested."

"I requested a selection so I could choose."

He wagged a forefinger at me.

"La, la, la." No, no, no. "Such a thing is quite impossible here in Jordan."

"Do you have any rifles?"

"Such a thing is quite impossible."

I'd procured tools from a variety of fixers around the world, and their abilities ranged from A, on the full-service side of things, to Z, token assistance. This cat nestled somewhere near X. And I gave him that leeway because he could at least offer a weapon. The young man arrived with both the tea and a burlap bag-wrapped item, which he set on the table. He then went and stood at the door, again shooing away the goat, which had wandered back in. I unwrapped burlap as Yosef sipped tea.

A well-used but serviceable .38 Smith & Wesson revolver, along with twelve loose cartridges. I inspected the weapon, dry-fired it, and loaded it with half the cartridges. The other six slid into my jeans pocket. Beggars, choosers, baby.

"How much?" I asked.

"Five thousand US."

He received my finger wag.

"La, la, la, la."

"It is an exceptional weapon," he said. "Used for many decades in Jordan."

"It is an old revolver. I expected a modern semiautomatic pistol. And rifle."

"Such things are quite impossible."

"I do not even know if this old pistol will shoot."

"Why would it not shoot?" He lowered his voice as the young man at the door glanced back over his shoulder. "Of course it will shoot. It is a pistol. You pull the trigger and it shoots. The modern pistols do not have this weapon's reliability. It is a fine, fine weapon."

He had a point about reliability, given this environment's fine sand and grit. But five large was too much. He knew it, I knew it, and we both knew the haggling process was a way of life here.

"Perhaps it is better if I travel without a weapon."

I sighed and stared at the mosaics.

"Perhaps this is true," he said, "if it is not an issue for you to sit near death each moment."

We both sipped tea, and he smoked as the bell ending round one sounded. I tired of this each and every freakin' time in the Middle East. Transactions were a zero-sum game. A winner and a loser. It wore me down. Which was the whole damn point.

"I also enquired about information regarding the diplomat's daughter in Petra," I said, kicking off round two.

"This is so."

"Do you have such information?"

"Of course."

Translation—maybe, sorta, rumor has it.

"If I value this information, I could, perhaps, pay one thousand US for the weapon."

Another litany of back-and-forth ensued with feigned hurt and astonishment, and we settled on three grand plus whatever intel he possessed. I had to scoot on down the road.

"What can you tell me about the girl?"

"What do you seek?"

"Is she alive?"

"She remained alive as they captured her."

The underground rumor mill had ground out two baselines—she was captured and lived through the experience, and more than one person whisked her away. Nothing to hang your hat on, but a small ray of hope. And hope was all I had working.

"Who are they?"

"Who can say?"

"But more than one person."

"So it is said."

We could circle that maypole for hours, so I changed direction.

"Would they have taken her to Amman?"

"No," he said, shaking his head. "Such a thing would be foolish."

"Where, then?"

"Who can say?"

Israel's border lay less than twenty miles west. I couldn't see it, but stranger things had happened. But the Bulgarian and Albanian connections didn't point in that direction. Eighty miles to Saudi. A possibility. The same distance to Egypt, another possibility. And there was the port of Aqaba and the Red Sea. Possibilities aplenty, and each one complete speculation. This was one guy, albeit a fixer who kept his ear to the ground, who had tossed whispers and rumors on the table. Better than nothing, but not by much.

I thanked Yosef, unrolled Benjamins, untucked my shirt and covered the pistol now slid into my waistband, and hustled to the parked SUV. Three hours south stood Petra, where answers might nest. The pistol's cool steel against my side comforted, my radar remained tuned up, and I headed out. Twenty miles later, I pulled off the highway and into a deserted desert wadi, or valley, for a weapon check. I looked for Bedouins and found myself on ancient historical turf without a soul in sight. The .38 fired on the first trigger pull, hitting the aimed-at rock high and to the right. With three more shots I gained confidence it would hit where I aimed. I took two shots with my left hand because, well, you never knew. I reloaded my last six cartridges and scooted onto the highway, good to go.

Given my DC experience, hitters in Petra remained a distinct possibility. Now armed, I could handle that. What I had a poorer grip on was what was really going on. No identifiable bad guys motivated to kidnap the diplomat's daughter. The Bulgarians, and Jules's Albanian, were proxies. Whoever pulled their strings were part of a larger picture that included State and the Company. I forced a mental push and kept the larger picture as background noise. I wanted the bastards who'd taken the kid. On-the-ground enemies. The bigger stuff, the amorphous grand plans of others, would remain outside my scope. Or so I thought.

Chapter 10

I picked up my pace toward the Siq's entrance. The two killers followed suit. I shoved aside thoughts of the afternoon's meeting with the old Bedouins under the large shade awning and their take on the kidnappers—merchants, shopkeepers, traders. More pressing matters dominated the moment, with personal survival topping the list.

 Twenty paces from the mountain's entrance, I dashed. They wouldn't. I'd entered a killing lair—dark, tight quarters as vertical mountain walls extended several hundred feet upward, hemming me, and them, in. No, they'd hit the entrance and pause. Ahead lay a thousand yards of sand-floored narrow darkness that turned, shifted, waited. Yeah, they'd pause and speak in hushed tones and then move forward with an attack plan, their movement as snakes on a winding hunt.

I marked five hundred yards with a boots-on-sand count and slowed. Time to find an ambush spot, a place where I could bushwhack the SOBs. Or at least the tail end guy. A close-quarters firefight wouldn't happen as they held superior weaponry, and the noise would echo out both ends of the Siq. Bedouins would rouse from their sleep within Petra. That didn't bother me as they'd remain silent—far too clannish to report anything to the national police—and retrieve old, rusted, hidden weapons just in case things spilled out in their direction. Multiple pistol shots would also wash out the Siq's opposite end toward the nearby cluster of tourist hotels and administrative buildings. And national cops. Couldn't, wouldn't happen.

As it was, two weapon blasts were iffy. I'd haul it and exit the Siq, grab my rucksack in the hotel room, toss everything in the SUV, mount up, and roll. There was only one legitimate direction, which would lead to its own set of problems. Man, these two clowns had screwed things up.

While smooth, the rock walls weren't uniform. Undulations, bulges, and tiny outcrops lined both sides. Moonlight splashed the wall's upper reaches as a rare shaft of light highlighted the sand trail. I scanned and collected options at a slow pace for a hundred yards until the perfect spot appeared. Ahead, moonlight. Where I stood, black darkness. On my left, a large boulder forced the trail tight against the opposite wall. And twelve feet up on the right, a small, smooth ridge. A shelf.

People place deer-hunting blinds high in the air because their prey don't look up. These killers would follow suit and focus on each small pathway section before a gentle or sharp curve hid the next stretch. Radars on high, they'd move from turn to turn with one leading, the other holding back. It's what pros would do. High odds these were pros. Pro or not, seeking their quarry overhead wouldn't happen.

I first searched behind the trail-intruding boulder and sought another weapon. I used my boot toe and kicked hard-packed sand between the boulder and the wall. An abrupt toe-stop offered promise. Like a dog digging between its back legs, I uncovered several rocks. The first, too small. The second was almost too large, but would do. Five pounds, larger than my hand, and with a jagged edge. Back at the trail's other side, I tried scaling the wall and failed, boots slipping on the smooth surface. I tucked my shirt in and dropped the rock inside, cool against my skin, freeing my other hand. Slow, steady finger- and footholds brought me to the ledge. I stood and surveyed the hunting grounds while plastered deep into the dark. I retrieved the rock, pulled the pistol, and waited.

It took them thirty cautious minutes as the sheer mountain walls cooled and emitted an eerie stone-on-stone low growl at random intervals. The lead killer's near-silent footfalls were discernible several paces away as he paused before the path's turn and my elevated location. Unable to view him, I had no doubt he performed a wary peek into my stretch of pathway. I'd gambled his partner would hang back and perform the same tactic as he watched the lead hitter peek and move forward at the path's next turn, well past me. If I was wrong, Plan B entailed rapid gunshots from above. Higher risk, and noisier, but doable. These were two dead men walking, sent to kill me, and this fandango's outcome was carved in stone. No hesitation, no remorse. I threw the kill switch—hidden and tucked away and dusted off too damn often, but still sure and swift. Adrenaline meter pegged, all senses maxed out, an executioner wrapped with a deadly calm.

There he was, his head six feet under my perch, pressed close against the wall as the path dictated. A jet-black silhouette against light sand footing, his right pistol-laden hand led the way. He hesitated, halted, and twisted his head sideways. His animalistic sixth sense had kicked in and hinted at my presence. A frozen vignette with life-ending action a hair's breadth away. It lasted fifteen seconds. Then he moved on, focused on his certainty that I was ahead, and overrode his danger-looms instinctive alarm bells. He moved quicker toward the next turn, thirty paces ahead. When he entered a moonlit section, his footfalls were replaced by those of the trailing killer who edged around the pathway corner below me, stopped, and watched the lead man negotiate the turn ahead. I couldn't see him below yet, as it required another step or two before he'd appear under my feet.

I remained frozen, eyes shifting between the lead cat's progress and the blackness below. The mountain sounded a spooky grumble of cooling rock, and the lead hitter hesitated at the sound as he peeked and assessed the pathway's next stretch. Then he made the turn and disappeared from sight, cueing his partner. The trailing hitter moved with more assuredness—his partner having cleared the way—and passed below me, his pace smooth and calculated.

I didn't leap. The accompaniment of boot-on-rock sounds held too high a risk. I made no foot movement at all. A simple forward free fall, silent, rock arm raised, absolute focus on my enemy's skull. The stone's edge drove home with vicious power. I released the weapon as it struck and tucked and rolled upright while shifting the pistol into my right hand. No need. He was dead before he hit sand. An almost noiseless kill, it signaled a role reversal. The hunted now became the hunter.

I reached the next pathway corner with long, fast strides. A quick look-around highlighted the lead hitter moving with care twelve paces ahead. I'd cut the distance, ensure a closer shot. I made the turn and trod with careful steps, approaching his back. He either heard my footfalls or his instinct spoke, and he turned his head to check his back trail. Perhaps he figured his partner approached. I'd never know.

I took one last step, sighted, and put a bullet in his head. The weapon's blast deafened within the enclosed space as the sound echoed, reverberated, long past the trigger pull. Not good. I dashed forward and checked the dead man's jacket for ID and pulled a passport. I jogged toward the other killer and performed the same, producing a penlight and recognizing the Cyrillic writing on both passports. Russians. Oh man.

Immediate plans flashed neon-bright—haul ass. I did, running toward the Siq's entrance, sprinting around turns and dashing down straight sections until I was spit out among the resting camels and donkeys and otherwise quiet tourist assembly area. The pistol blast must have sounded this far, carried through the stone mountain crack, but at the moment no people wandered about, curious. It might not have lasted, so I made quick strides for the hotel, pausing to spit on my hands and rub my face, lifting my shirt's tail as a hand towel. Blood from the rock's crushing blow would have splattered evidence on me. How much, unknown, but passage through the hotel's lobby created enough concern that, as I approached the building, I stripped off my shirt and reversed it.

In my room's mirror, it proved a solid choice. The blood on my face had smeared with the spittle, sufficient that I appeared as a sunburned tourist. My shirt, khaki, was another story with dark blood spots aplenty. A quick wash-up, rucksack packed, and I headed back through the lobby, tossing a smile at the two desk clerks. Another nutty tourist doing something weird.

Behind the wheel, I opened my satellite phone's GPS. Egypt was out. Too many variables. Saudi—no way, Jose. Which left Israel. Their clandestine organization, Mossad, unbeknownst to me at that time, had contracted my services for a recent gig. I was a known entity. Security in Israel was tight as a drum, no avoiding checkpoints, and Mossad would want a brief chat, a serious chat, about why I'd appeared in their country. So be it. Six-plus hours to safety—a five-hour Tel Aviv drive where I'd arrange a charter jet and haul it out of this part of the world, with Mossad's interrogation an additional hour.

In my wake, two dead Russian hitters. It's dangerous leaping to conclusions, but their arrival wasn't much of a leap. Their initial efforts with proxies, Bulgarians, had failed. So they'd taken matters into their own hands. They'd pull out all the stops next time. Part of my mission moving forward— ensure there was no next time. I gave those odds fifty-fifty.

There was a little-used desert road that would take me the twenty miles to Israel's border. No traffic, a clean escape. And a bellyful of frustration. I'd confirmed three men kidnapped the diplomat's daughter and likely whisked her out of Jordan. Why? And to where? No freakin' clue. But answers, partial answers and fresh trails, would come from Jakub Kaminski. He'd held back. If he wanted a prayer in hell of finding his daughter, he would come clean. I'd make that clear. So a return to DC, back to a lair filled with spooks, diplomats, and politicians. This time, I'd walk in with eyes wide open. The one big thing, Jules's admonition, was writ large into this gig. In their world, nothing was ever as it seemed.

Chapter 11

I drove without headlights, the moon providing sufficient illumination. Around a curve in the road, lit up like a desert beacon, stood the border crossing. I'd considered a cross-country track that would have avoided both the Jordanian and Israeli authorities until situated inside Israel, but land mines eliminated that option. Sprinkled across border areas throughout the Middle East, the explosive devices lay buried, thick as sand fleas. Some were antipersonnel, others antitank. All would ruin your day.

Sighting the Jordan-Israel crossing prompted a pull-over and prep. Between the Jordanians, who might search my vehicle, and the Israelis who most definitely would, it was weaponless travel time again. I'd have to risk the five-hour Tel Aviv drive. I strode a few paces into the desert and tossed the pistol's bullets. My boot heel excavated a decent-sized hole, I dropped in the pistol and two Russian passports, and ancient sands covered hot evidence. I considered keeping the passports as currency at the spookville poker table but nixed the idea—such an act put me in their world. No, thanks.

Headlights back on, I approached the Jordanians. Two border guards stood duty, and they gave my passport a perfunctory stamp and sent me through. Word hadn't reached them about the dead men at Petra. Once authorities discovered expired bodies, border crossings would be a different ball game. But for now, clear sailing.

The Israelis were anything but perfunctory, as expected. Past travels there had braced me for the inevitable. Two of the four border guards led me inside a small, well-lit building, along with my rucksack. The other two guards performed a fine-tooth-comb act on my vehicle. Inside, one guard emptied my rucksack while the other asked questions. Lots of questions. Then he made a phone call.

When he'd completed the call, which altered his attitude not one whit, he explained I could travel to Tel Aviv under the condition I remained on the major roads and stopped only for gas, food, and rest.

"Can do easy," I said, smiling. He didn't return the casual sentiment.

A few miles along, I pulled over and arranged logistics. There was an available charter jet at eight a.m. that would get me to Athens. A few hours layover and a second, long-range jet would take me to DC. Good enough. It allowed time for a short catnap and the inevitable interrogation at Ben Gurion Airport's private charter terminal. Mossad, having instructed the border guard, would insist on a chitchat.

Miles of nighttime desert, occasional small-town lights in the distance, and a sense I'd hit a dead end. Krystyna Kaminski had disappeared. What little intel I'd captured provided no path forward. The lack of a ransom demand removed classic kidnapping from the table. And abduction left the door wide open for a litany of probabilities, beginning with Krystyna's murder. Some would construe the other possibilities as just as bad.

I drove along, empty and despondent, with two more dead men in my wake. And for what? Had I gained anything from it, other than two additional souls notched in Case Lee's personal dossier? Nope. Did it aid my efforts to find Krystyna? Nope, again. Their deaths tossed a pinch of emphasis on gathering insight into whatever moronic grand scheme those on high had concocted. I'd get it from Krystyna's father, maybe, and leverage it for gritty intel on her abduction. The rest, the grand scheme—nothing but muted attic thumping among spooks, diplomats, and politicians.

The private air terminal at Ben Gurion Airport was a 24-7 operation, so I found a comfortable lounge chair and grabbed some shut-eye. Several hours later, a few strange foot taps against my boot jerked me awake. A man and a woman, both midforties, stood together and waited until I sat up. The Mossad welcome wagon had arrived.

"Case Lee," said the woman. "It's a pleasure meeting you. I am Aubrey. My partner is Joe."

"I'm glad you two went with classic Hebrew names. Were Buffy and Renaldo already taken?"

Aubrey smiled. Joe didn't.

"Do you mind if we pull up chairs?" Joe asked.

"And if I did?"

"We would still pull up chairs," Aubrey said, displaying a pleasant expression.

"Then have at it. I need coffee."

The private terminal lounge had, as almost all did, a single-serve coffee maker. I chose the dosage closest to rocket fuel, carried a steaming mug, and plopped back down facing two of Mossad's finest.

"You are looking for Krystyna Kaminski," Aubrey said. "Tell us how well you are doing at your job."

"Not well at all."

I'd feed them intel on what I'd learned. Arabic-speaking abductors. That would keep the Bulgarians and Russians out of the conversation but would give them a crumb or two for their current efforts. And just maybe, they'd let me catch my plane.

"Sorry to hear that," she said.

I sipped coffee and waited. They'd ask the questions. I'd play spook dodgeball.

"You and Mossad have an interesting history," Joe said. "I believe we all worked together rather well in the past."

"Yeah, about that. I was pretty doggone explicit with your asset in Bolivia about not hiring me again."

"So we understand," Aubrey said. "And yet, it was a fruitful relationship."

Fruitful for them and nothing new there. The Company, MI6, Mossad, and who-knows-else had either leveraged me or played me like a freakin' drum over the years. Take your pick.

"Speaking of the past," Joe said, dropping the pleasant demeanor. "What happened with Uri Hirsch?"

"Last I saw him was in Brazil. Rio de Janeiro."

A lie. The last time I saw Hirsch, a Mossad agent, was in the US. Stretched out with a rifle bullet in his head.

"He has disappeared."

"Hirsch ran with a rough crowd."

"As did you. And yet, here you are. Fine and healthy."

I kept my yap shut. My blood brother—Marcus Johnson, former Delta team lead, now a rare black rancher in Montana's big empty—had delivered Hirsch's bullet. I'd come close to liking Hirsch, but he'd pulled a pistol on me and made demands that weren't going to happen. When Marcus strode up after his shot, I'd asked him if he had any idea who he'd killed.

"Yes. A man aiming a weapon at you in a hot fire zone."

End of story and classic Marcus. As for bullets, I'd take one for him anytime, anywhere, and further discussions with Mossad on Hirsch's disappearance wouldn't happen. A short conversational pause ensued as we sipped coffee. The private terminal came alive as pilots and crew flowed through.

"There were two Russians in Petra yesterday," Aubrey said, one hand holding the mug's handle, the other underneath. She'd maintained her pleasant bearing and now displayed Mossad's all-seeing eye. Not a surprise—they blanketed the Middle East. "Were there any issues with them?"

I feigned no knowledge of the Russians with pursed lips and a shoulder shrug.

"No issues with any Russians."

In an hour or two they'd get wind of my lie once Jordanian authorities found the bodies. And I would be cruising at thirty-five thousand feet.

"No issues. This is good," she said. "And very unlike the recent situation in DC when, in fact, there *were* issues. Two of them, both resolved with well-timed assistance."

"Do you people all hang out with each other and draw straws? Who's next in line to keep tabs on harmless ol' Case Lee?"

"You people?" she asked.

"Spooks."

"Ah."

I rose and retrieved another cup of java after asking Aubrey if she'd like another. She declined. Joe could get his own coffee.

"It would appear your Jordan trip was a waste of time," Joe said when I returned.

A solid conversational tack, delivered to prompt a denial and, hence, intel. Fine by me. It was throw-them-a-bone time and get on a plane.

"Krystyna Kaminski was abducted at Petra and taken away."

"You would know this how?" Joe asked.

"Bedouins. The abductors spoke Arabic."

The two Mossad agents shot each other a quick glance.

"Why would they kidnap this girl?"

"There's been no ransom note. They captured her. I don't know why. I don't know where they took her. And I don't know if she's dead or alive. Does Mossad have any insight?"

There—two bones for them to gnaw on. Arabic-speaking abductors and no ransom demands. I wasn't expecting *my* question answered. They shot each other another quick glance, this time with a tight nod from Aubrey to Joe. A nod that might signal time to cement our mutual comrades-in-arms relationship. Or time to spit on their hands, hoist the black flag, and begin slitting throats.

"We would like to help you, Case," Aubrey the good cop said, setting her mug on the small table between us and leaning over her knees.

"Okay."

"Most people think a nation, be it Israel or the US or France, speaks with one voice. In many ways, that is true. But there are layers."

"Here we go."

She sat back up and laughed.

"You could do better hiding your lack of interest in such topics. I would hate having you in a class on geopolitics."

"I'm a simple guy."

"Then I will pretend you are a simple man. You have heard the expression the right hand does not always know what the left hand is doing?"

"Yep."

"Krystyna Kaminski's disappearance obviously involves diplomats, and by extension, politicians."

"Okay."

"The signs are clear. How much help was your Mr. Nick Halpern in Amman?"

"Do you people ever give it a rest?"

"No. We cannot afford to do so. Your Mr. Halpern is hiding something, this much is clear. The diplomatic corps does not act without permission. Permission from elected and appointed officials. No?"

"I suppose."

"Krystyna Kaminski is a small piece of the puzzle. A tiny piece. But her disappearance offers an entry point for answers. You, Case, are the perfect person for making such an entry."

"What I'm hearing is Mossad wants intel on the bigger picture. You and the CIA both."

"There are also others who wish understanding. Other friends."

I retrieved my mug, took a sip, and eyeballed Joe. He remained silent, without expression. Aubrey had shifted into ABC mode. Always be closing. My plane had landed, taxied, and sat refueling outside the large terminal window.

"So here's the deal," I said after draining my mug. "I don't care about any of that stuff. That's a fact. My job is to find the girl, an effort not looking too bright right now. But let me level-set this entire situation."

"Please do."

"The most powerful clandestine outfit in the world plus the clandestine outfit some consider the world's best are both thrashing around, seeking intel on some concocted high-level bullshit plan. Neither you people nor the Company have the secret handshake for conspiracy-of-the-month tree house access, and that bothers you both. A lot."

Aubrey and Joe remained silent.

"Have you considered talking with Kaminski? He might provide insight. I hope he does, because then I drop off the high-interest page for you people."

"We have talked with Jakub Kaminski," Aubrey said, leaving it at that.

Clearly it wasn't fruitful. The Company would have gone through the same exercise. I might have better luck if I could convince Kaminski yours truly remained his last and best shot at recovering his daughter. Although, at the moment, I was unconvinced my efforts would succeed.

"Right. Back to level-setting. You spooks, all of you, view me as a tool. A lowlife contractor. One side wants to work me. I get that. The other side sees me as an easy target with no repercussions. I get that, too. Both sides want to either discover the big secret or prevent its discovery." I leaned forward and locked eyes with Joe first, then Aubrey. "Neither side gives a damn about the girl. She's another tool. Not to me. And that's the great schism. Let's not pretend otherwise."

I leaned back in my padded chair. Silence reigned for fifteen seconds until Joe spoke.

"What would you suggest, Lee?"

You gotta hand it to Mossad. Unlike the Company, they would get down to brass tacks in a heartbeat.

"The Middle East is your backyard. Unleash your bloodhounds with the intel I've provided. Find a trail. Feed me. I'll take it from there."

"You have not delivered us much," Joe said. "Several Arab men, no ransom."

"It's all I've got."

"And?" Aubrey asked. "Mossad's benefit?"

"If I stumble across the magic decoder ring and capture legit intel on the big secret, I'll feed it to you."

With pursed lips, she mulled it over for a few seconds.

"This is an acceptable proposal," Aubrey said, confirmed with a tight nod toward Joe. "If we find information about your missing girl, I will be in contact. You have my word."

I halfway believed her. She pulled a blank business card from her purse and handed it over. It displayed a handwritten phone number.

"I'll return the favor. Let me write my number down for you," I said and unzipped a side rucksack pocket where I'd stashed a pen or two.

"No need," she said. "We have it. I would add something else. I care about the girl."

A private terminal employee strode over and let me know the small jet was ready for boarding. I stood, shook hands with code-names Aubrey and Joe, and headed across the tarmac. I wasn't a happy camper.

For an idiot who claims to avoid clandestine muck and mire, you're now ass-deep in it, Lee.

Chapter 12

I texted Jules in Athens during a couple-hour layover and asked if she'd courier my Glock, disguised as a box of documents, and have it delivered at my DC hotel. She'd do it with no follow-up needed. Jules would read the tea leaves and feed her network hints that the lost Polish diplomat's daughter search had gone sideways. From hotel check-in forward, I'd have 24-7 protection. This gig had slipped into the acute danger bucket, beginning with the Bulgarians and reinforced with the Petra Russians. Anyone who messed with me once I'd made the DC hotel would deal with my .40 caliber friends. How long that situation lasted depended upon Jakub Kaminski, recipient of my second text message. I asked for a six o'clock meeting at the hotel bar. He responded in the affirmative.

Make-or-break time. I had no desire to pull the plug on this effort; Krystyna's disappearance had ceased being a job once the old Bedouins confirmed her abduction, tipping me into the borderline obsessive pool. But I required some meat, inside background details. I'd walk away if Jakub Kaminski couldn't or wouldn't deliver the goods. No other option, and I hated the thought.

An uneventful flight, DC traffic out the wazoo, and check-in at the hotel in Georgetown. The desk clerk handed me a courier-delivered package. I smiled and waved off the bellhop, toting my own rucksack. It wasn't a typical luggage piece for the upscale hotel. A quick shower and shave, with the now locked-and-loaded Glock near the bathroom sink and within instant reach. An old habit.

I grabbed a small corner table at the rooftop bar, the DC heat long past and autumn around the corner. Already crowded, the bar filled with hotel guests who leveraged their connections with the DC crowd, plus resident politicians, bureaucrats, and lobbyists. The usual cast of characters. I eyeballed the crowd and sought spooks. DC spooks upped their game and blended in, big time. Picking out one or two or half-a-dozen was well nigh impossible. A couple in their thirties laughed and chatted over thirty-dollar glasses of wine—possible card-carrying members of the Company, SVR, MI6, Mossad, DGSE, or a dozen other spookville tribes. And there I parked it like Custer, although I had enough sense to understand I was surrounded.

I ordered a Grey Goose on the rocks. Twenty bucks, which would have bought four or five exact same drinks at innumerable small-town bars along the Ditch. I waited for Kaminski, scoped the crowd, and overheard self-important conversational snippets. It didn't bother me—I had long ago accepted DC's ethos and acknowledged it was the nature of the beast whose belly I now occupied. They were by and large good folks, but their environment buttressed a sense of significance.

I couldn't hold back a wry smile, knowing the single mom in Knoxville who plucked up a Costco rib eye, checked the price, and settled for the cube steak, would have a far different opinion about this crowd's self-importance. Same with the guy in Wichita Falls who, instead of a fishing trip with his kid on a Saturday, planned to crawl under his pickup and bust knuckles while changing out a rebuilt starter. And that mom and that dad wouldn't hesitate telling this crowd how the cow ate the cabbage. Which, I supposed, drove my smile.

Jakub Kaminski arrived, scanned the rooftop, and found me. We shook hands and sat. His drink matched mine, substituting Wyborowa vodka for Grey Goose.

"Please tell me you have information," he said, pleasantries shoved aside.

"Several Arabic-speaking men took Krystyna at Petra."

"So she is alive!"

"I don't know that."

It was painful interacting with this man's anguish. The lines on his face, the circles under his eyes, the desperation in his voice. I could not imagine the pain, having experienced nothing similar.

"Where was she taken?"

"I don't know that either. And I don't know who or why, but I believe you do, Jakub. If you don't come clean with me, I'm through. There's no more I can do."

A hard truth within a brutal situation. But truth made up the lone hole card on the table, and Jakub Kaminski held it.

"Is there anyone else you could enlist for help?"

"Yeah. If I knew more about what's going on. I have solid intel they abducted Krystyna. Have you received communications from kidnappers since I last saw you?"

He shook his head and stared at his drink.

"Which puts us back to square one." I held back on the hitters, both here and in Petra, but tossed a tickler on the table. "What do Russia and the former Eastern Bloc countries have to do with this?"

His head snapped up, a nerve hit. He shot furtive glances across the chattering crowd, which, with his arrival, was now guaranteed to include clandestine players.

"I'm your best bet at finding Krystyna," I said, taking a sip. "And your best bet *will* walk out of here in sixty seconds."

The last thing I wanted was a personal Jakub Kaminski pile-on, but the clock ticked, and each lost moment lowered the teenager's odds. As he stared at the drink again, his back stiffened, his posture became upright, the fear and agony in his eyes tempered with fire. He returned a tight nod. At last, he became what I expected. A fighter.

The Poles are hard biscuits. Have been for centuries. In the late seventeenth century, the Polish king led the largest cavalry charge in history against the Ottoman Empire at Vienna and crushed them. Nazi Germany ran over them at the onset of World War II as the Poles lacked modern equipment. But they saddled up anyway and charged German tanks on horseback. A fair number of Polish fighters survived the invasion and escaped to Britain, contributing to Allied efforts. They joined the British and piloted aircraft during the Battle of Britain, and fought in North Africa, Italy, and Normandy. My Delta team trained with their elite soldiers. Hard biscuits.

"Opekuny," he said, voice flat and hard. "A Russian word. It means guardians."

I nodded back and waited. The rooftop chatter continued, now blocked through intense concentration.

"First, you must understand this," he continued. "If word of this is made public, Krystyna and Anna are dead."

"And you. I get it."

"I do not matter. They would kill Krystyna, if she is still alive. They would also kill Anna. This is a hard fact, not speculation. Do you understand?"

"Understood."

He gave a last look around the rooftop bar, and we locked eyes.

"The Guardians comprise a collection of nations in a top-secret endeavor. They wish to coordinate and control the information available to their populations."

"You mean the internet?"

"Please keep your voice down."

We both shoved our drinks closer and leaned across the table, heads twenty inches apart. For any spooks watching, skullduggery was at play. Too bad.

"Tell me about the Guardians," I said.

"A secret coalition among national leaders and diplomats."

"And their spy organizations," I said.

There were too many floating pieces that required nailing down. Keep it simple.

"Yes, correct. Although there are nuances."

"Let's talk nuances later. What countries?"

"Russia, Poland, Romania, Serbia, Bulgaria, Albania."

"Okay. Six countries. Got it. What are they doing?"

"Again, coordinate and control the information available to their people on the World Wide Web."

"The internet."

"Correct. I will emphasize Poland is no longer involved."

Brass tacks appeared.

"So they took Krystyna as a warning to keep your mouth shut."

He glanced around the room again, face hard, his gaze flintlike. We locked eyes again.

"Yes."

"Why did your country back out?"

"Poland lived under the Soviet boot for forty-five years. Freedom is precious to us. This includes freedom of information. For this reason, we left the Guardians early in the process."

"Okay. Now, just so I'm clear, this secret organization includes all facets of government. Politicians, diplomats, spy organizations. Right?"

"Correct."

"And Krystyna is the red flag for anyone else thinking about leaving the organization, or telling the world about it."

"I believe that is also correct." He downed his vodka, leaving a few ice cubes. "I have been a foolish man, believing your efforts would succeed without revealing the truth. My sincere apologies."

"Let's save all that for later. Why are other nations outside this now maybe-not-so-secret organization interested? Because they are."

"Yes, this is true. Now I must explain nuances."

"Will it help to find your daughter?"

"Perhaps. First, very little in political or diplomatic circles remains a secret. This is not a bad thing, as it often brings greater understanding."

"Jakub, you're headed into the weeds. Let's stick with the real and now."

"Yes, of course."

The server approached, and we ordered two more drinks. Continued rooftop conversations surrounded us under the now nighttime sky. Servers carried appetizer orders past as the crowd's alcohol consumption prompted appetites. Quick glances confirmed the expected—drizzle food. Minimal sustenance, the plate decorated with assorted sauces and colors drizzled from plastic bottles.

"Diplomats from several Western nations approached me, yours included, about the Guardians. I explained Poland had withdrawn, but confirmed the organization's goals, which they had discovered through diplomatic circles. These Western nations' political and diplomatic layers viewed the Guardians' efforts as having potential benefit. They considered it as a grand experiment, one which, if the results were positive, could fit the West."

Alarming, but so far above my pay grade I blocked most of it out. Most, but not all. The SOBs, the masters of the universe, screwing with the free flow of information.

"I've learned the West's clandestine organizations weren't invited into the fold," I said. "They want to know what is going on."

"I understand this as well. I have no great insight into why they remain uninformed. Kept out of the loop, as you might say."

An explanation would have added some clarity to muddy waters. Were the clandestine services simply pissed they weren't invited to play? Did they have other plans, perhaps parallel efforts? I sat back and sighed through pursed lips as our drinks arrived. I'd learned nothing that offered a lead, a trail. They'd captured Krystyna as a potent signal for other Guardian members to keep their mouths shut. Her disposition remained a mystery. I remained stuck, axle-deep, and saw only one option. Light the fuse and pick up a piece or three after the explosion.

"Alright, Jakub. We're still faced with dead ends. So let's blow it up."

No wide-eyed questioning look, no wrinkled brow showing concern.

"If I am required to put a gun to a man's head, any man, I will do this." He paused, expressionless, eyes unblinking. "I want my daughter back. The rest of the world can go to hell. Yet this conspiracy must remain out of the public eye. It is a death warrant for my family."

"Roger that, and leave the firearms to me. I want you to pull the conspiracy trigger with the CIA and Mossad. You've gotta know those folks here in DC."

"I do, yes. But I do not understand. Why not have Poland's secret service contact them?"

I wanted Jakub delivering the intel. It added legitimacy. More legitimacy than Poland's secret service or I brought to the table. He represented the diplomatic layer, which is what the Company and Mossad wanted. These were treacherous waters, piranha-infested waters. I saw no other options.

"I want you to make the contacts. You bring more righteousness to the situation. We have to stir things up, Jakub. But to protect your family, you must tell both the CIA and Mossad about your fear if the Guardians' efforts become public. They both must keep the conspiracy among the clandestine and diplomatic corps. No public disclosures. And no politicians. Politicians think a kept secret is telling fewer than fifty people. Do you understand?"

"I will do this first thing in the morning. You should know your name may come up."

"That's fine."

It was. Word would filter up to Townsend. I'd receive a little gold star, which, along with three bucks, would get me an overpriced cup of DC coffee.

"And I will request added protection for my wife, Anna, from both my country and your CIA. I believe things will move very fast once I make these contacts."

"Yeah, maybe. But let me emphasize a couple of points, spoken from hard-earned experience. Once we do this, your daughter becomes a pawn for a much larger audience. A global game piece. Filter everything you hear from now on with that certainty. What I'm hoping for is fallout. Intel we can use to find her."

"A pawn? This is not a game."

"They'd say the same thing. And you'd both be wrong. This type of crap is their reason for existing. They love this stuff. The bustling hallways, top-secret whiteboard sessions, gaming theory played out." I drained my glass. "You'd best understand this, Jakub Kaminski. We, you and I, don't play that game. Our job—find your daughter. Everything and everyone else can kiss our asses. Are we clear on that?"

He smiled, a first since I'd met him.

"We are very clear on that. You may assume I have taken the same position."

"Good. Contact me with anything you hear or see. Feed me. Understood?"

"Understood. I cannot thank you enough, Mr. Lee. For the first time since Krystyna disappeared, I have hope. It is not much, but far better than hopeless agony."

"Keep an ear to the ground, Jakub. Every bit of intel helps. Now, do you have protection for your way home?"

"Yes. There are two well-trained countrymen who now sip tea and watch us. And you? What about your protection?"

"I carry mine with me."

Chapter 13

I ordered coffee and a brandy and contemplated actions and fallout from kicking the hornet's nest. *Something* would happen, but I had no clue in what form or function. Whatever happened, there was no assurance, none, that it would assist with Krystyna's location. Helluva plan, Lee. Rock freakin' solid.

A sounding board and professional insight topped my priority list. I dealt with the latter first and sent an encrypted Clubhouse message requesting a midmorning meeting. Her reply, succinct as always, made me wonder for the umpteenth time if she ever stopped working.

1000

Done and done, and on to the sounding board. Marcus Johnson, ranching near Fishtail, Montana. As solid as they came, and a person who excelled at planning and execution. He answered after two rings.

"When do you plan to grace me with your sorry butt?"

It neared fly-fishing and bird-hunting season in Big Sky Country. I was overdue for a visit.

"What happened to 'Be still, my heart. It's the wondrous Case Lee'?"

"Hold on."

I could hear, in sequence, the phone laid down, bourbon glugged into a glass, a light groan as he settled into his recliner, and one then two clomps as western boots hit hardwood. His Zippo's clack announced a lit cigar. He came back on the line.

"There. When Jake hears those boots drop, he hits the couch, the day over."

Jake was Marcus's bird dog.

"Did you and Jake have a hard day punching doggies?"

"No one says that, you moron. Try it in Fishtail's bar, and check out the crowd's reaction."

"Has there ever been a crowd in that place?"

"When there's a band. Then we might get twenty folks. We'd get larger crowds if word got out the wondrous Case Lee's arrival was imminent, but I keep that under wraps. What's going on?"

I delivered a high-level overview.

"Alright. As I understand it, you're swinging a sword at entities so far above your head you'll need a fire-truck ladder."

"Fair enough. But I've run out of options."

"Try focusing exclusively on the kid."

"I'm with you, but it's a challenge when bad guys keep trying to whack me."

"You want any cheese with that whine?"

"There you go again, showing your soft side."

"Those hitters are part and parcel of the find-the-kid focus. Can you capture one instead of delivering a headshot?"

"The Company swept away the first two. They didn't inform me about anything but their nationality."

"Big surprise, there. And the two in Petra?"

"I took out one with a World War II .38 Special. It proved an inopportune time for exchanging personal details."

"And the other?"

"Used a rock."

"Subtle. Alright, then accept you've got a target on your back."

"I do. It's the whole moving-forward thing that has me stymied, Obi-Wan."

"You've kicked off a deep-shadow shitstorm. Crumbs will fall off the table over that."

"Maybe. I'll get some insight tomorrow about those crumbs."

"The Chesapeake witch?"

Marcus held no truck with Jules, a clandestine anomaly and an enigma. Either of those put her on his suspect list. As a combo package, he viewed her with both distrust and distaste.

"I've got to get you two together for a date."

"I'd rather lick a rodeo parking lot clean. Let's get back to the kid."

We did. His focus on why the whereabouts of Krystyna was still such a mystery held water.

"If they killed her, why wouldn't they drive that stake into the parents' hearts?" he asked. "If they kidnapped her, where's the ransom demands? So you might consider her limbo status as a form of torture. That'd be a hard swallow for parents, not knowing."

"Man, I know it. And if those crumbs I might access don't bear fruit, my fear is that it's over."

"Son, it's not over until *you* say it's over. We both know that."

It helped. A confidence builder, and it buttressed my commitment. Marcus was an excellent leader, acknowledged and appreciated.

"You're right. It's not over. Something might appear over the next twenty-four hours with the spooks kicked into high gear."

"Just one last thing, Case. If or when you pick up a trail, move fast. Time isn't on your side. Execute with terminal efficiency. And always remember: if you need help here in the States, call me. Twenty-four-seven. I'll be there."

We signed off. I felt better, less lost. Marcus had a way with such things. And I would ask for help if needed. A cool head in tight situations. I paid the tab and took the staircase, headed downstairs for my room. I heard no door clangs above or below me in the stairwell, a sign I was alone, although I made the trip with the Glock pulled. I arranged an a.m. flight for Chesapeake's regional airport. The desire for a brisk walk came strong but wouldn't happen. Not now, not in DC. So I paced, stretched, performed calisthenics, and fretted. Then I called Jess.

"Sorry about the late hour," I said. "How's Tallahassee?"

"Are you back from Jordan?"

"Yep. Quick trip."

"And?"

"And I found out three men took the diplomat's daughter. Bad guys who spoke Arabic. Which leaves one massive swath of turf as possibilities."

"How'd you come by that information?"

"Bedouins."

"Well, aren't you Mr. Lawrence of Arabia? You think she's alive, then?"

"No way of knowing, although my gut says yes."

"Listen to your gut, bub. And next steps?"

I hated dancing around gritty details with Jess. I felt bad doing it, and she sniffed out the dance steps in a heartbeat. It was an issue, and one we hadn't found a balance for. I could reveal everything, but often these jobs held revelations that endangered those in the know. I wouldn't place her in that position.

"I'll go see the Clubhouse tomorrow for insights while I'm waiting for fallout from an action I've taken."

"You mean you stuck a pole in a snake pit and stirred."

"Something like that. Tell me about your gig."

"We'll circle back for a little snake pit exploration, but I don't want you to hurt yourself squirming. Guess what I had for breakfast?"

"Tell me."

"Red velvet pancakes."

"Oh, man."

"Yesterday I had a special hot dog for supper."

"How special?"

"A bacon dog topped with homemade mac and cheese and crushed Ritz crackers."

"Double oh, man."

"Yes, indeedy. There's a gym with a climbing wall near the hotel, and I've made good use of it. I sweat and strain and work off that fine, fine lowbrow food."

"I should get down there some time."

"Let's do it in the fall or spring. The gardens here are stunning. As for the job, it's one horror show after the next."

"It's why you get the big bucks."

"Let's see. There's a cokehead son banging his brother's wife while one daughter, who loves knitting, has tried to hire a hitman and take out several siblings she doesn't like. She *does* like the cokehead, so there's that. Speaking of snake pits, tell me about your leads."

"I don't have any."

There it was, my private stone-cold reality. No point waffling on the subject and no point obfuscating the current status with smokescreens about possibilities. I had jack, nada, and any forward movement was dependent upon shaking the spookville tree. Jess's voice lowered into a more empathetic tone, appreciated on my end.

"You're stuck, and it happens to the best of us. Would you mind if I toss out some thoughts?"

"Go for it, madame. I could use the help."

"I'd add the possibility—and that's all it is, a possibility—your on-the-ground focus has overlooked other trails. This isn't a fault, my Georgia hottie, but it reflects your background. It works for you. It fits your style. But you may consider a sniff or two down alternative trails."

"Okay. You've got a point. But I don't know where else to put my nose to the ground."

I didn't. While I wasn't a complete idiot and acknowledged other directions, other perspectives, there weren't any on this job's horizon. At least not any I could point a finger toward.

"There are always the friends, family, and associates trail. Those personal linkages often hold opportunity."

I explained Jakub and Anna Kaminski had scoured that potential trail. And I may have used a brusque tone doing so. It wasn't directed at Jess, but rather at my own limits and failures.

"Don't get prickly, bub," Jess said. "I'm trying to help."

"I know. Sorry. The frustration factor is cranked pretty high at the moment."

"What about the old tried-and-true money trail?"

"All these players are associated with governments. They're already on the payroll."

I didn't add, "Including the hitters sent after me." I wasn't positive about that, but high odds they weren't hired guns.

"What about the bad guys who took her? The ones you said spoke Arabic?"

Jess had a point. A great point. The government players, in particular the Russians, may well have contracted the abduction to private players. Kept their hands clean. For them to whack an ex-Delta private investigator was plain vanilla stuff, well within their bailiwick and attempted more than once in the past. But fingerprints on a diplomat's daughter's abduction would open an international crisis can of worms. Man, I was an idiot.

"Jess, I wish you were here. I'd grab you and plant a big kiss. You might be onto something."

"Ooh-la-la. Sweep me off my feet, and carry me up the stairs, Rhett."

"I'm not kidding. That's a legit trail. Money exchanged hands. The money trail."

"You'll have to take it from here. My expertise with money trails comprises ferreting out recent high-end purchases as indicators. Things like new cars, boats, houses, and mistresses. I'm not sure what the money trail looks like among you James Bond types."

"I do."

"Do you mind sharing, man of mystery?"

"I know a guy. He lives in a hole."

"Ah. Of course. I'll say this, lover. You aren't boring. There may be challenges in other areas, but boring isn't one of them."

"I'll assume that's a good thing."

"We'll see."

We signed off after I thanked her again. Spirits on the rise, I dialed Israel. While Jakub would meet with Mossad, and open the kimono about the Guardians, he'd deliver his revelation high up the Mossad food chain. Which could translate into time delays before they took action. If they took action. Meanwhile, the clock ticked. I now had a direct line to a field player in Mossad's backyard. Aubrey answered after three rings. It was five in the morning there.

"Sorry about the early hour, Aubrey."

"It is not so early. I am glad you called."

I revealed what I'd learned from Jakub Kaminski. She remained silent while I performed the intel dump, then dove in.

"Have you shared this with anyone else?" she asked.

"The CIA," I lied, protecting Jakub.

It would cease being a lie by morning when Jakub met with the Company. I kept that card facedown because, well, I dealt with shadow players. You just never knew with that crowd. Without a claim others already knew about the Guardians' conspiracy, Mossad might strategize and conclude it best Jakub had an accident in the immediate future, leaving Mossad, and me, as this intel's sole keepers. Weird, cold, but true. You just never freakin' knew.

"I would suppose you had an obligation to do so," she said.

"Yeah. Something like that."

She hesitated, wheels turning.

"You may want to know the two Russians in Petra we had mentioned were found dead."

She stopped there. I remained silent.

"Is this news a surprise for you?" she asked.

"Nope."

No point hiding the fact I'd lied about it when we met in Tel Aviv. Hell, by lying I was speaking spookville's language.

"It may help you to know we identified them as SVR assets. We performed facial recognition on the corpses."

"Okay."

I already sat high on Russia's SVR hit list, so their deaths added little to my overall concern. What little I'd learned when dealing with the SVR in the past pointed toward situational frameworks. They thought in terms of the immediate situation. They'd even lent a hand on an Amazon-based job. On the flip side, Russians had long memories. I wouldn't receive any Christmas cards from them in the immediate or long-term future.

"I must admit you do not sound too concerned," she said, skipping past my Tel Aviv lie and mining for more intel.

"The SVR and I have a long and stormy history."

"Ah. Well, it reinforces your information from Mr. Kaminski. The Guardians—what a silly name. Far too Hollywood, do you not think?"

Bonding and rapport. I had zero inclination to play that game, but she mucked about in the right sandbox, the Middle East, and I could use any help available.

"Yeah, pretty doggone Hollywood. Is there anything you can tell me about the girl? Any signals?"

"I am afraid not, although your information about these Guardians may produce value. I will, of course, share with you anything we find."

A fifty-fifty shot, but better than nothing. One thing for certain, Mossad would act. In what form, unknown. But another fuse lit, and the fallout potential real.

"I'm counting on you folks, Aubrey. Everything I've shared with you only matters to me as it relates to the girl's disappearance. I can't emphasize that enough."

"I understand. And, again, I will share with you anything we might find."

"I'd appreciate it. Let me ask you about the abductors. Do you think they were clandestine players?"

"I would not think so."

"Run-of-the-mill hired thugs?"

"I would think something along those lines, yes."

Alright. Maybe not confirmation, but it reinforced a possible money trail. Excellent stuff. We signed off with more half-assed promises, and I again paced the room. The next day had potential. Potential fallout from spookville. A potential money trail. A visit with Jules and a subsequent visit with someone who could track financial transactions. I was prepped and heeded Marcus's words. Prepare to move with terminal efficiency. Fine. Let's rock and roll.

Chapter 14

Chesapeake's run-down section appeared grittier than usual as hooded expressionless eyes greeted me, as always, inside the dry cleaners. I laid the rucksack, Glock, phone, and wallet on the counter. The rucksack disappeared behind the counter, the rest covered with dirty laundry. No smiles, no nods of recognition. A protective emotional shield, perhaps, for the Filipino family that ran the place—one day, they figured, my carcass might constitute the Clorox-and-cleanup detail.

Through an obscure door and up squeaky stairs. Two knocks, the electronic door lock clacked open, and I entered the Clubhouse. Jules had assumed her usual welcome position—the shouldered double-barreled shotgun pointed at my midsection, supported with elbows on the old wooden desk, her one eye sighted along the two barrels. Her DIY haircut, short and wild and gray, hid the eyepatch's band, now returned to the usual black color. There was no sign of Antoinette the shaman. I performed the standard pirouette with pockets turned out, one hand filled with Benjamins, and felt more than uneasy during the process. Jules's trigger finger had recently greeted an Albanian with a brief squeeze. Or two.

"A sojourner returned from the Levant," she said, pointing the shotgun toward an uncomfortable empty wooden chair. "Tell me about your brief travels, Marco Polo. Leave nothing out."

I did. Jules pushed back from the desk with a foot, the old chair protesting as she leaned, and a kitchen match fired along the chair's arm as she lit a fresh cigar. She never took her eye off me. Once I'd completed my soliloquy, she deigned to speak.

"I cannot help but notice you bear no gifts today."

She referenced her addiction. Licorice. After my descriptive with killers, Bedouins, conspiracies, and lit fuses in the clandestine world, she responded with a typical Clubhouse head feint. Standard operating procedure.

"Sorry. Been busy."

"Yes, you have, dear boy. I must inform you that your current situation appears marvelous, heady, and ensconced in my bailiwick. How uncomfortable for you."

"Yeah, well, I was stuck and had to shake the tree."

"You count on dropped acorns. A deed done and no time for retrospection. An injection of situational chaos, one that fits you."

She smiled and puffed. The old *Casablanca* movie poster still adorned one steel wall, the room's lone decorative item. Her desk held a green-shaded lamp, her abacus, and an embedded Ka-Bar knife used for cigar trimming.

"I'm not big on chaos, Jules. But the clock is ticking, and I've got no trails. Well, I have one. But haven't pursued it yet."

"That being?"

"Follow the money. Like I said, Mossad reinforced a hunch the kid's abduction came through players outside the clandestine world."

"And your plan regarding this scent?"

"Our subterranean mutual friend."

"Excellent. You should know I, too, shall pursue those avenues. A personal effort that acknowledges times have changed. You might note that cryptocurrency has become the coin of the ne'er-do-well realm these days. A transactional system designed for anonymity. One, to my knowledge, never broken into."

"I'd appreciate the help. Between you and Hoolie, something may pop up."

"Perhaps. How is your amour?"

Another classic Clubhouse misdirection. Off-ramps designed to unsettle her client or provide her contemplation time while we talked through more mundane matters.

"She's fine, and on a job in Tallahassee. She's the one who pointed me toward the money trail."

"Ah. Professional expertise. Does she remain happy with your relationship?"

"Jules, I've got a missing kid, government hitters on my butt, a cockamamie global conspiracy, a weird-ass conflict among spooks and diplomats, and one thin lead. Could we, like, focus on that, please? I've gotta get to Topeka and make a drive."

I'd texted Hoolie earlier and asked for a meeting the next morning. He'd texted back an affirmative. The clock ticked as each passing day lowered the Krystyna odds. I wasn't frantic yet, but getting there.

"It would appear you have the situation well in hand," she said, feigning hurt. "I shall snatch my shovel and dig. You should depart and conquer the world."

"I need *your* professional expertise. I'd appreciate it if you, my lifeline, shed some light. I have no freakin' clue about context or backstory or motivations with all this. You do. You always do."

A mea culpa of sorts, and sufficient to mollify her. Her feigned hurt disappeared, and what passed for Jules animation came into play. She adopted a professorial tone.

"As you well know, I focus on human assets. The informational tsunami available on the internet can occasionally be useful, but the real treasure lies with raw human interactions. I state this as acknowledgment my internet breadth of knowledge is lacking."

"Our mole rat friend will handle that," I said, regarding Hoolie.

"Indeed. However, I have read the tea leaves and can provide context. It may help you with your quest for the young lady."

"Read the tea leaves or already received input from your human asset network?"

Jakub had met with the Company and Mossad that morning. It was ten o'clock. Her network may have picked up intel already.

"This would not be your concern, Poirot. You understand the Clubhouse is seldom wrong regarding these matters?"

"I do. And I appreciate it."

She tossed her now-dead cigar into an under-desk trash can, opened a drawer, and retrieved a fresh one.

"Item one. Our acquaintances of a more totalitarian nature have a firm grip on the information their citizenry receives. China, Burma, Iran—the usual cast. The collection you have uncovered, this Guardians cabal, hopes to follow suit, albeit in a manner more coordinated and hidden."

"Okay."

"Your Polish diplomat rebelled. Hence the poor innocent swept away to parts unknown. This cabal wishes their efforts to remain secret and use the young lady as a warning."

She rolled the cigar's sealed tip against the embedded razor-sharp Ka-Bar knife. The cigar tip fell and rolled to a stop near the abacus.

"I shall now foray into perspectives that may disturb you," she continued, chuckling. "Do try and listen. A mild admonishment, dear boy, with the hope it shall prevent you from relating everything to your endeavors."

"Endeavors like finding the girl and staying alive. Important stuff, that."

"This is not about you. It is not about the poor child. It is about human nature and organizational tug and pull."

She headed into esoteric turf, but I didn't mind. I'd glom on to a few revelations and use my boots-on-the-ground perspective. As she knew I would.

"This Guardian group works in concert. Now without Poland, of course. By 'in concert,' I refer to politicians, bureaucrats, diplomats, and secret services pulling as one. Very similar to China and others. This secretive cabal's uniqueness is its transnational aspect, with multiple nations working together."

"Okay. I get that. What about the conflict between the Company and State and how it affects the lost girl? I mean, sure, there are organizational fights. But most of the time the US political class and State and the CIA work together."

She chuckled and fished a kitchen match from her work shirt pocket.

"You are such a delight. With tactical efforts, you remain unsurpassed. Within the higher echelons—strategic, global—you display a remarkable innocence."

"Maybe because so much is BS."

"A crude descriptive," she said. The match fired, and she puffed the cigar. "And one I wouldn't argue against. Yet it represents a major component of the Clubhouse business model. In part, I am but a simple miller who grinds informational grist and feeds those concerned with global matters. I delight in the work."

A rare Clubhouse confession.

"Good for you. Off to work each day with a smile on your face and a song in your heart. Now, about the girl."

"We shall arrive there anon. Western diplomats received wind of the Guardians' endeavors. Unlike clandestine services, diplomats hold casual chats among themselves. Few secrets remain hidden over cocktails."

"Jakub Kaminski mentioned as much."

"An honest declaration from the Polish gentleman. Once Western diplomats received word, they passed information about the cabal to their closest allies—politicians and bureaucrats."

"But not their secret services."

"Correct."

"That doesn't make any sense."

"It makes perfect sense."

I dangled in the wind, and Jules knew it. She puffed on the cigar, amused. I wasn't, but I held my tongue.

"Governing the masses is inestimably easier when information is controlled," she continued. "Our totalitarian acquaintances know this all too well. The dirty little secret is Western political leaders and their diplomatic corps see very little wrong with clamping down informational flow. Publicly, this isn't discussed."

"I'm shocked."

She ignored my snark and continued.

"Western politicians and diplomats will view the Guardians' grand experiment with keen interest. Life would show vast improvement for them if they implemented such a system in the West. Western nations would, I surmise, create their own cabal. Something of a NATO for internal internet control."

She sat back, the chair squeaked, and she blew cigar smoke toward the ceiling. Jules waited for questions from the classroom.

"Stupid question," I said, "but do any of the players give a rat's ass about free speech?"

"The assessment of your question is correct."

Man, I despised this stuff. Most folks wanted to be left alone, with me topping the list, living our lives as we see fit. And something I'd learned through the years, the internet had plenty of back doors and armies of smart, willing people who would use those doors. They'd rally, in a heartbeat, against governments filled with people who sat a long, long way from genius status.

"Okay. I'll keep things simple."

"Best of luck with that, dear."

I ignored the comment and plowed ahead. I'd confirm high-level motivations as they related to actions on the ground. All the rest remained mission white noise.

"Russia and China and others wouldn't want their Western internet traffic access filtered. They inject disinformation here constantly. I get that. They'd like a one-sided deal. Control the input for their countries but still have unfettered internet access to the West. Hence the secrecy with the Guardians' efforts."

"Correct."

Lightbulbs began flicking on in my head. Dim, but growing.

"But here's what I don't get. The Company also lives for that stuff, spreading disinformation around the globe, including within the US. They wouldn't support this whole deal."

"Give the gentleman from Savannah a gold star."

"And, if this idiocy came to pass, it sounds like Western secret services have a much smaller role."

"And there you have it, dear boy. They will fight tooth and nail to prevent such a grand plan from taking effect. Otherwise, they shall be relegated to the digital children's table. They will be forced, once again, to focus on human assets. Which, you will be happy to know, leads us back to your endeavors. Although it must be said, now that the Company, and

Mossad, have both been informed of the conspiracy, you will no longer be the belle of the ball."

"So now they won't lend me a hand finding the girl?"

"I did not say that."

"What are you saying?"

"The poor child remains a tool. As do you. Meanwhile, higher-level actions take place. You stirred things up."

No actionable intel revealed, no new trails, and the frustration factor cranked up.

"Okay. First, to hell with the higher-level actions. I don't care. I've got a plane to catch. Hoolie expects my arrival. Let's cut to the chase, Jules, and forget about my usefulness as a tool. What about Krystyna?"

"She is now useful for *both* sides."

"How does that play out?"

"And here, dear boy, is where the responsibility falls on you. The Clubhouse has provided context. Now my favorite client must discover the details."

A discovery process with, so far, a big fat zero stamped on it.

"I'm not having a lot of luck on the details, although there might be fallout from Jakub Kaminski's morning meetings I could use."

Jules remained silent. It didn't sound like fallout would head my way. No longer high on their popularity list, the Company and Mossad would view me with diminished value, a side activity. I exhaled a heavy sigh. Yeah, the bigger picture now had more clarity and context. It was possible this high-level intel might help, but I couldn't see it. It did little for me and nothing for Krystyna. Oh, man. Time to wrap up this meeting as my gut roiled over ineffective efforts. A bitter pill, and a sliver of personal failure and fear entered my heart. Fear for the effects of my shortcomings on the girl.

"As you said, both sides have now set Krystyna up for leverage. Maybe there's something there I could use. That, and the money trail." I sighed again. "Slim pickings, Jules."

Her entire demeanor changed. Any outward lightheartedness and good humor disappeared.

"Gird your loins, brave Ulysses. I have faith in you. I doubt she is dead. She will reappear, perhaps, within a horrific context."

"Any thoughts on what that might look like?"

She leaned across the desk, one eagle eye drilled into mine.

"Your imagination is as good or better than mine. Just know the Clubhouse does not approve such actions in any way, shape, or form."

I closed my eyes and stretched my neck. A deep inhale and exhale, and back to business. Jules waited until I'd finished, then spoke.

"Do not despair. Have faith in your own inestimable abilities, Case Lee. Know I will do anything within my power to help. Trust me. As always, trust this wretched creature before you. I shall keep my ear to the ground and pursue whispers and rumors." She pointed her cigar at me as added emphasis, her eye on fire. "They have broken the rules and endangered a nonplayer. An innocent, a child. This cannot stand."

She pressed a hidden switch, and the steel door at my back clicked open. Our meeting was over.

"Find her. Find her and those who took her. Deliver a personal statement from us both. Allow no mercy to course through your veins."

Chapter 15

Another charter flight for Topeka, Kansas, and check-in at an upscale and busy downtown hotel. I considered a partway drive and getting a motel room in St. Marys or Junction City. But with a bright neon target affixed to my back, I nixed the idea. A tiny Kansas town offered the opportunity for a professional hitter's long-range sniper rifle. I kept that option off the table.

Thoughts of the kid and the horrors she was living through dominated my perspective. Jules was right. Bring down the hammer. Events now convinced me the two DC State employees, Jill Evans and Peter Winston, were in on the entire deal. So was the State numbnuts in Amman, Nick Halpern. Man, that frosted me. But they sat too low on the conspiratorial totem pole to have any knowledge about Krystyna's whereabouts.

This job's entire context reeked of arrogance, stupidity, and people out of their league. Without breaking a sweat, the cat I would see in the morning would find a way around whatever internet mechanisms they planned to use. There were thousands more like him, spread across the globe.

Marilyn Townsend knew about the Guardians conspiracy by now. Jakub Kaminski had spilled the beans with his CIA contact, and word would have filtered up. Way, way up. My name was in the mix, and Townsend owed me one. That was my perspective. Whether *she* saw it that way was hard to say.

The hotel bar, with my back against a wall, offered the night's entertainment—vodka on the rocks. Helplessness as a prime emotion sucked. All I'd nailed down were Arab abductors. They'd whisked Krystyna away to a godforsaken location. Yeah, I could use my imagination for what lay in store for her, but I didn't dwell on it other than the awareness she lived in abject terror, frightened out of her mind. Those bastards. Every SOB who took part—Russians, Bulgarians, Albanians, State Department personnel, leaders and politicians—deserved more than an ass-whipping. While my blood boiled, I couldn't allow my fervent desire for payback to interfere with the core mission. But all I had was a mole rat meeting lined up about a long-odds money trail scent. The clock ticked while I groped for a lifeline, ineffectual as hell. I called Jess.

"What's up, Red Ryder?" she asked.

Since we'd been dating, I'd helped her transfer to an encrypted cell phone that provided free-flowing conversation.

"Fighting the blues."

"That's not good."

"I'm taking medicine for it."

"Are you still stuck?"

"Sorta. Your tip about a money trail has plopped me in Topeka. I'll get together with a guy tomorrow."

"Ah. The classic Topeka clandestine rendezvous. I should have seen that coming."

"It's not in Topeka. He lives farther west, in an abandoned Atlas missile silo."

"Of course he does. Down here, I'm meeting a wackadoo family member tomorrow at their tennis club. Same same."

I smiled, the first one in too long.

"You run with a better class of people than I do."

"I wouldn't claim that."

"Well, a more stable class of people."

"I wouldn't say that, either. But you've got tenacity on your side, bub. Shake those blues and maintain hope."

"I'm maintaining a potent desire for retribution."

"Here's a thought. Table those feelings and start grinding. Neither of us are Sherlock Holmes, but being a grinder is the next best thing."

She was right. Suck it up, Lee, and plow forward. We chatted about our schedules, potential trips, food, entertainment, and clothes. Well, she talked about clothes. And shoes. Jess's release mechanism was online shopping. "It's either that, or I'll get too far in the bottle," she'd once told me. I got it. We signed off, and I felt marginally better.

I shoved a chair under the room's door handle, locked the bathroom door, and piled all the blankets and pillows into the bathtub. With the Glock within easy reach, I settled into my personal sanctuary, fell asleep, and dreamed about wandering the Siq at night, hearing voices cry for help. They came from every direction, and I scrambled back and forth and upward, seeking without success. My eyes snapped open at two o'clock, and it was a challenge to regain sleep. Helluva way to live.

It was wheat-planting time in Kansas. As I drove west, dust plumes from tractor-pulled planters dotted the horizon. It was a clear day, the weather fine with a hint of morning coolness. I'd disconnected the rental car's GPS the day before and now kept a keen eye on the rearview mirror. No sign of a tail. Such assurances wouldn't help salve Hoolie Newhouse's concerns— a man paranoid to the point of mental instability.

While the guy lived underground in a Cold War remnant, and all the weirdness and freakish mannerisms aside, Hoolie was one of the best. A computer and internet geek extraordinaire. He contracted for multiple clients, an item never discussed. His response to my encrypted text message for a meeting included him stating he'd unlock the door. A farmhouse door. Hoolie had built it years before on top of the command center for an old ICBM Atlas missile silo, dug from the fertile Kansas soil.

117

I rolled over gravel county roads the final five miles. A simple aluminum gate spanned the entrance to Hoolie's fallow sixty-acre plot. No wheat for Hoolie—it would infringe on his personal buffer zone. I left the vehicle, smiled and waved toward the general area ahead, and opened the gate, which allowed the hidden cameras ample opportunity for visitor inspection. His small farmhouse sat at the end of a two-track road.

I parked on a large circular concrete pad, fifty yards from the farmhouse. Below me, underneath the concrete-and-steel cap, an empty missile silo extended one hundred fifty feet straight down. Back in the sixties, at the height of the Cold War saber-rattling, they could launch a massive Atlas rocket carrying a thermonuclear warhead in ten minutes. The US Air Force replaced the fixed-launch missiles as the Soviet Union fell and new technology became available—nuclear submarines, cruise missiles, stealth bombers. The Air Force sold off the abandoned launch sites. Most remained part of the ground-level terrain as farmers plowed around the silo cap and the nearby launch control entrance. Wheat fields were reclaimed, although a few launch sites were purchased by folks like Hoolie.

The clapboard farmhouse was unlocked, as promised. The interior, pristine, although the secondhand furniture—every bit—lacked cushions. You couldn't effectively wipe down cloth cushions with disinfectant. A pantry door off the kitchen opened on a steel-lined shaft, sixty feet down. At the bottom, it widened into the former launch control area. A circular steel stairway led down, wrapped around a central pipe. I'd descended a few steps and began the Clubhouse-like routine.

"Stop there."

I did. Somewhere below, Hoolie aimed an automatic high-powered weapon at me.

"Hoolie. It's me. Case."

"Is anyone with you?"

"Nope."

"Was that a rental car?"

"Yep."

My voice echoed in the steel-cased space.

"Did you disable the GPS on it?"

"I did."

"Is the GPS on your phone disabled?"

"It is."

"Next time, don't wave at the cameras like that. It would alert anyone watching."

"Hoolie, there's not another soul for miles."

"What about satellite surveillance, dude? Are you so sure about *that*?"

"No. No, I'm not. Sorry."

"Turn your phone off."

I did.

"Done, Hoolie."

"Come down."

As I descended, the large space below opened up. Desks, computers, and server stacks appeared as lights blinked and fans hummed. Hoolie lowered his weapon and smiled.

"It's good to see you again, dude."

"You, too. How's life treating you?"

"It's a battle every day. They keep at it, pressing the digital walls inward."

I wouldn't broach the "they" declaration. It would lead down hours-long rabbit holes. But his statement provided a tickler regarding barter between us instead of my usual credit card payment.

"Coffee?" he asked, smiling.

"Sure."

Coffee prep was our version of a Japanese tea ceremony, which included no handshakes, bottled water, and disinfectant. Hoolie was a germophobe, and small hand-sanitizer bottles littered his multiple desktops. He wore jeans and a long-sleeved T-shirt, face and head and eyebrows and heaven-knows-what-else shaved.

"You've got new glasses, bud," I said, also smiling.

On my last visit, white adhesive tape had held together his thick black frames in classic nerd fashion.

"Dude. I had to. My eyes are getting worse."

"A daily vitamin D dose might help," I said, and pointed up the spiral staircase. High odds Hoolie hit sunlight as often as Punxsutawney Phil. I liked the guy and wasn't making a lifestyle jab—but it would do him good to get out more and risk the satellites and drones and whatever government flying dragons were after his white-on-white butt.

"You never can tell," he said. "You never can tell. While the coffee preps, how about trying out my new Walther? It's a .380."

He laid the rifle against a desk and padded across the pristine room to a surgical-clean kitchen area and fired a water-filled kettle.

"No, thanks."

A dim tunnel with an open blast door connected his work area and the missile silo. His shooting range, where he'd stand at the massive empty chute and fire away. You required double ear protection as each shot reverberated and echoed and deafened.

"So what's cooking, dude?"

"Help with a money trail in exchange for a massive conspiracy. An internet-restricting conspiracy.

"Cool! Let's get after it."

We did.

Chapter 16

I started and ended with the core mission, sandwiched around the Guardians conspiracy. To his credit, Hoolie's first question focused on Krystyna.

"Oh, dude. What a mess. Are you sure she's alive? And why do you keep getting into these situations? Aren't there mellow jobs out there? You're always OG to the max, doing your badass thing."

"I'm not sure she's alive. But smarter people than me think so. My gut says so as well."

I refrained from addressing his other questions and had no clue what OG meant. He poured coffee from a French press and slid my mug across a clean, disinfected metal desk. I remained standing. Taking a seat would spread my germs too far afield in Hoolie-world.

"So you think the Russians took her?"

"I think they may have paid someone to take her. But the deal is, Hoolie, it could have been anyone."

"I need a starting point, dude. There are lots of banking transactions, and lots of banks."

"Can you backdoor the banks in Arab countries and Russia?"

Hoolie could hack any system, anywhere.

"That's still too wide a playing field."

"Alright," I sighed. "Look at Russia. And Jordan. Are you sure it's too much to ask checking out all the Arabic-speaking countries?"

"Dude."

"Alright. Focus on Russia and Jordan... and Poland, too."

Poland was a long-odds rabbit hole, but desperate times, desperate measures.

"What are the parameters?"

"Focus on two payments from the same sender to the same entity or person. That underground world operates on a retainer up-front and second payment upon delivery. Delivery of the girl."

"With no other transactions between the sender and receiver over, let's say, the last six months?"

"Yeah. Stick with that."

He squirted sanitizer on his hands, rubbed, sipped coffee, and shook his head.

"It's old school stuff. The world, and your world in particular, has moved to cryptocurrency."

"Bitcoin and such?"

"Yes. And there's no backdooring those transactions."

"Give it your best shot, Hoolie. You're all I've got right now."

He nodded, sipped, and went off on the conspiracy. I didn't mind and didn't attempt to corral him in. His diatribes held potential for a nugget or two I could follow. Desperation, again, reared its ugly head after his statement about cryptocurrency.

"This is nothing new," he said, waving a hand. "The cross-nation coordination is new, for sure, but manipulating the internet goes on every day. Look at China. Or Iran, or any other authoritarian regime. And it's not just them. India shuts the internet down in parts of their country all the time for political unrest, rioting, you name it. By the way, do you have any issue with me spreading the word?"

Hoolie's personal network—like-minded super-geek individuals spread across the globe. They weren't small time, as evidenced by the equipment stacks blinking and chassis fans humming within Hoolie's domain. The cat had a million-dollar setup.

"Give me five more days. Then spill the beans wherever it's appropriate. Except for the general public and the media. Don't do that."

I didn't need Jakub and Anna's blood on my hands. And if I hadn't found her in five days' time, well, she was gone, gone.

"Will do. Oh, I'll spread it among the right technical people. But forget the media, dude. They won't touch this."

"Too conspiratorial?"

"Too many power players. Stepping on the wrong toes. They don't do that anymore. But this is a big, big deal. You know how it works now, right?"

Into the technical abyss, but I was so low, it didn't matter.

"Not really."

"Well, they can shut the entire World Wide Web down through ICANN. That's the Internet Corporation for Assigned Names and Numbers. It has seven members, and if five of them get together in either El Segundo or Culpeper with their private keys, they can shut it down. ICAAN controls DNS Authentication. But they won't go there."

"What's DNS Authentication?"

"Domain Name System."

"So who are these seven people?"

"I can't remember their names, but it's not important. They're from the US, China, Canada, Great Britain, Czech Republic, and even Trinidad and Burkina Faso. But again, these conspiring nations won't go there. They don't need to. Plus, they still want *their* information getting to their people. Dude, I can't believe they'd try something this stupid."

"Why stupid?"

"I'll get to that. What they'll do is go after ISPs and telecom companies. Governments license ISPs—Internet Service Providers. Those companies snap to attention when the licensing body requests they interfere with DNS traffic for specific sites."

"So you can't access certain sites?"

"You've seen the messages," he said, pausing for coffee. "Error messages. This site can't be reached. This site may have moved to a new address."

"Yeah, I've seen those."

"They can also tell the ISPs to throttle back speeds for certain websites. The user sits there and watches the little twirly icon work until it times out. Happens all the time."

"What about the information they allow through? Spooks are masters at nuanced and subliminal messaging."

"AI, dude. Artificial intelligence. With enough computing horsepower and well-tuned AI, they'll pick up and block most of that. We've seen this coming. But having it organized to such an extent, through secret agreements, well, *that* one is out of left field. The stupid buttholes."

"Okay. Why stupid?"

"Because..." he said, shifting toward a desk covered with computer monitors and several keyboards. He viewed a monitor and clacked away for sixty seconds, laser-focused. Standing straight, he continued. "Because there are multiple avenues available, including encryption. Your phone and laptop are encrypted. Drives the overseers nuts."

"What if they block all encrypted communications?"

He shifted back into the kitchen area and poured himself another cup, lifting the French press in my direction as an ask. I shook my head.

"There are ways, dude," he said, a tight grin plastered. "There are ways. But I'm not getting into those with you. Sorry."

I wouldn't have understood anyway, although I took heart from the knowledge that folks like Hoolie wouldn't be denied.

"Anyway, I'll chase money transfers under the parameters we talked about. Your barter proposition stands—no charge for my digging. But don't hold your breath. I'm telling you, cryptocurrency rules, especially in your world. I appreciate the inside scoop on the Guardians and their interested parties in the West. What stupid people. Stupid, stupid people."

I stood stymied, with hopelessness again peeking through the door. Hoolie shifted to another desk covered with monitors and keyboards and went to work. He expected my imminent departure. Up the circular stairs, out the farmhouse, skedaddle on down the road. If Hoolie, and Jules, were right about the underworld using cryptocurrency, me and Krystyna were screwed.

"Who's the world's expert on cryptocurrency?" I asked.

"It's based on blockchain technology," he said without looking up from his computer monitor. "Your question should be who's the world's expert on blockchain technology."

"Okay. Who?"

"Satoshi Nakamoto."

"Where is this person?"

He looked up from his endeavors and pushed his glasses back up his nose.

"No one knows. There's one school of thought it's a collection of people. Blockchain technology was invented about ten years ago, dude. And no one has identified Satoshi Nakamoto. He, she, or them wrote the documentation with British English. So some think a group of Brits invented it. Others see British spelling as a false trail. Whatever, Satoshi Nakamoto disappeared ten years ago after offering the world blockchain technology."

127

He returned to perusing a monitor while his fingers flew over a keyboard.

"What do you think, Hoolie?"

"It doesn't matter what I think."

It did to me. I circled the subject with kid gloves.

"At fifty thousand feet, Hoolie, what is blockchain? Other than it's used with all the cryptocurrencies."

"Blockchain is immutable. Unalterable. A digital record of transactions. Individual records, called blocks, are linked in a single list, called a chain." He continued his work, staring at one of three monitors near his keyboard. "It's decentralized—not stored in one place. That, plus cryptographic algorithms, make it immune from attack. It's impossible to hack. And transactions are untraceable."

I drained my coffee, set the mug on a nearby desk for Hoolie's hygienic ministrations, and considered a hack-proof technology's backdoor. I flung a Hail Mary pass.

"Here's the deal, bud. It matters to me what you think. Between you and me, what does Hoolie Newhouse think about this person or group of people's identities? I understand it's been ten years since anyone heard from Nakamoto. But where do *you* think I could find this person or persons? Between you and me."

He stopped work and swiveled his chair toward me. Pushed his glasses up again and stared for a full ten seconds. I maintained a benign smile.

"There are a few of us who play that game. It's entertainment, dude. Nothing factual."

I nodded and let him speak.

"Do you want a shot in the dark?" he asked.

"I'll take anything I can get."

I meant it.

"Slab City. Look for Red."

"What's a Slab City? Can I use one of your keyboards and look it up?"

His eyes went wide. I'd proposed spreading Case Lee germs on his equipment.

"No, dude. C'mon."

I held up both hands, palms out.

"Sorry. My bad. Is Red a name?"

"Maybe. Or not. No one knows, dude. It's all speculation and rumors. Like I said, a game to pass the time. Give me twenty-four hours on the bank transactions. I'll text you."

"Thanks, Hoolie. Sincerely."

He waved a dismissive hand, back at work, fingers flying. I climbed the circular stairs and left Hoolie-world behind, closing the farmhouse door behind me. In the far flat distance, a dust cloud. Another farmer sowed his wheat fields. My next actions held laughable long odds, but sitting idle, waiting for Hoolie, wasn't an option. I'd head for Slab City. It was that or call it quits if Hoolie came up empty—a better than fair chance according to him. And calling it quits wouldn't happen because a new trail—weak and amorphous and relegated to legend and tribal tales—had appeared.

Chapter 17

I hauled it a mile down the gravel road and pulled over, surrounded with fresh-plowed and planted fields. No barbed wire fences, no structures, no people for miles. Wheat country, prepped to embrace winter's rain and snow and sleet, spring's new growth lifeblood. With satellite-enabled cell phone and laptop, my rented SUV's hood in the middle of nowhere became Case Lee Inc.'s world headquarters.

First, the where and what Slab City research. Twenty minutes later, I had a weak grip on the place. Oh, man. Ninety miles southeast of Palm Springs, California, and near the Salton Sea. Self-proclaimed as "The Last Free Place in America" for some, "The Most Lawless Place in America" for others. Take your pick.

Slab City was a chunk of California desert on an abandoned WWII artillery training range, free from an electrical grid, running water, garbage service, or sewer. And free from laws. Scattered old trailers, collected-scraps structures, you-name-it housing—a haven for squatters, anarchists, eccentrics, drug addicts, outcasts, artists, and folks with "issues."

With several hundred full-time residents who braved the hundred-twenty-degree summers, Slab City swelled to several thousand in the winter as swaths of the northern US became untenable for outdoor living. The timing was right—while people came and went from Slab City year around, the winter influx wouldn't have started, leaving full-time locals. As a find-Krystyna destination, it made little sense. Hell, it made *no* sense. A spot on the map identified by a man who lived underground in an abandoned Kansas missile silo. Pointed out with rumor and speculation among Hoolie's ilk—a skewed and contorted collection of computer geniuses, hackers, and conspiracy mongers. Not a crowd to pin your hopes on. It defined desperate, and I circled the rental vehicle, scooting gravel with boot toes as the Kansas wind blew a low, faint whistle.

Jess was right. Be a grinder, you idiot. This is all you've got to work with. So do the work.

DC, Petra, Topeka. And now Slab City, searching for Satoshi Nakamoto. Or Red. Oh, man. Too weird, too disjointed, but we lived in a weird and disjointed world. The lone shiny glimmer, a pinpoint, was the nature of a place like Slab City. A place where people went who didn't want to be found.

Even so, what a freakin' weak trail. A search for Red with minuscule odds he or she or they existed and then asking him or her or them to break their own unbreakable technology and help a stranger find a teenage girl. Yeah, that oughta work.

I planned next steps with grind-time acceptance. Grab a charter jet, Topeka to Palm Springs. That process would take several hours, if not more. Topeka wasn't charter jet central, and it would require the charter company to send a plane from Kansas City or St. Louis and pick my useless rear end up. The flight itself was three-plus hours. Which translated into overnight in Palm Springs and hit Slab City the next morning. While time passed and wisps of hope faded.

Then there was the on-the-ground aspect, aligning my mental makeup to an investigative wander among hermits, junk artists, drug-addled dwellers, miscreants, and the more-than-a-few-loose-screws crowd. I wasn't a solid fit. But I knew someone who was. Someone who would move among that crowd with aplomb, a smile on his face. Someone who lived along the flight path between Topeka and Palm Springs. Bo Dickerson. Our former Delta team spearhead, a warrior fearless beyond measure, a man who occupied an alternative universe, a cosmic cowboy, an unforgettable character. And my best friend.

Bo lived in Albuquerque, New Mexico, with his FBI girlfriend, JJ. They'd met on the island of St. Thomas, US Virgin Islands, and fallen in love, proving opposites attract. She was a button-down federal agent who'd accepted an Albuquerque transfer, escaping what she considered a Caribbean island's confining spaces. Bo moved with her, and they'd settled into a loving lifestyle. I called Bo.

"My Georgia peach," he said, answering after one ring. "The planetary vibrations have heeded my cry for succor and nourishment."

"What's the matter, Bo?"

"Jezebel has fallen ill."

Bo's prospecting donkey, Jezebel. He'd taken up gold prospecting once he and JJ had settled in, focusing on arid southwest mountains. As the greatest tracker any of us in Delta had encountered, the new career seemed rife with possibilities and a natural transition. At least for Bo. His job on St. Thomas was as a snorkeling guide.

"I'm sorry, bud. What's her status?"

"Tranquil and accepting. The vet, however, isn't sanguine about her situation. We've talked at length."

"What'd the vet say?"

"I meant Jezebel and me."

"Right. Man, I'm sorry. Where'd things go bad?"

"During a profitable egress from the Mogollon Mountains. An unknown arachnid bite, a desert mountain nibble of a mysterious plant—who can say, goober? Who can say?"

"How can I help?"

"Positive and healing thoughts cast into the maelstrom. Where the curative process lays."

"Will do, bud. I'll say a prayer."

"Thank you. Now, tell me of adventures, narrow escapes, and loving touches."

"I need your help."

"Where and when, my brother?"

The standard response among us four blood brothers from our Delta Force team. Bo Dickerson, Marcus Johnson, Catch. Where and when, locked and loaded—no other questions or clarity required. Such friends blessed me beyond measure.

"Today. I can pick you up at the Albuquerque airport and head for Palm Springs. But I don't want you joining me if Jezebel's life hangs in the balance."

"My mental ministrations can be administered from afar, so worry not. What cooks on the California desert?"

"I'm seeking someone in a place called Slab City."

"The name resounds with a forlorn urban motif. We can stay tonight with my uncle. He and I have not eyeballed each other in several years. It would be a good thing."

Bo was an only child, born and raised in Oklahoma. Both his parents had passed, and I was unaware he had any living relatives.

"You sure? I mean, short notice and all that."

"I'll call him."

"What about JJ?"

Thin ice. JJ had crawled my rear more than once about Bo joining me on jobs. She'd laid down the law and demanded I leave him alone if bullets might fly, and explained in no uncertain terms my life would suck if anything happened to Bo. But she and I had a tight, tight bond. We'd been through hell together during a terrorist attack on St. Thomas, and an indelible attachment had formed. Still, she had left *no* ambiguity about Bo's recruitment for my endeavors.

"A visit to a relative and a benign act. One that was kicked off through a request from my tight-as-night bosom buddy. I cannot, and would not, hide that from her. But the familial connectivity may well mitigate her ire."

"I'm not sensing much surety there, bud."

"Surety is a fool's mission. Loose hand on the universal tiller, Magellan, and allow the cosmic winds to blow. JJ will be fine. Jezebel drifts along her own path, be it toward healing or an alternative dimension."

I smiled as another far distant dust cloud kicked up, another farmer working his field out across the flat horizon. Bo Dickerson, me, Slab City. Alright, and my spirits received a marginal lift—because I'd be seeing my best friend again. We signed off, and I chased down an available jet. Sure enough, it required a deadhead flight from St. Louis to Topeka and would arrive midafternoon. While the clock ticked. But there wasn't much I could do about it.

An hour later I sat in the private air terminal lounge, drinking coffee and preparing for the wild goose chase express. Bo texted confirmation his uncle would put us up for the night. I sat like a disgruntled lump and stared out the terminal window, sick and tired of being sick and tired, when Marcus Johnson called.

"I thought I'd check in and see if there were any fresh developments," he said while chewing. "Are you in the States?"

"Kansas."

"You had a powerful hankering for flat?"

"A money trail scent brought me here. What are you munching on?"

135

"A liverwurst and onion sandwich with plenty of mayo. I'm back at the ranch house for lunch."

"I take it you don't have a date tonight."

"I take it you still don't appreciate the finer things in life." He paused and sipped iced tea—his standard midday drink. "So, any progress toward finding the kid? And I don't need to remind you each day's passing puts you farther from your goal."

"The last thing I need is a reminder, bud. And the trail is a far cry from solid. Man, I'd take hard-to-see at this point. But it's all I've got."

"Tell me," he said.

I did. He grunted and groaned a few times as commentary between sandwich bites while I reviewed the situation and my visit with Hoolie. I didn't mention Bo. Now, Marcus and Bo loved each other, albeit with a concerted squint—especially Marcus toward Bo. Within tight spots and fights and full-blown battle, both when we were Delta operators and since, Marcus would select, among all the people on this good earth, Bo Dickerson as his spearhead. The Montana rancher held unadulterated and great respect for the cosmic cowboy's abilities within conflict's realm. Outside that framework, another story. They sat on opposite ends of the worldview spectrum.

"Alright," he said after I'd finished. "While you provided the situational assessment, I perused Slab City on my laptop."

"And?"

"And if your goal was find and explore Wingnut Central, mission damn near accomplished."

With that comment, he'd cracked open the Bo door.

"I've asked Bo to join me. I'll pick him up in Albuquerque if this jet ever shows."

A long exhale on the other end.

"Life is filled with wonders, and here's another one. That's a semisolid plan. Bo's the man for the job, both in terms of situational connectivity and ferreting out the mysterious Red. But your status, to use a technical term, still sucks. That's not much of a money trail."

"No, it's not."

"And something else—your team lacks leavening."

I should have seen it coming. Marcus would insist he join us. He had the time. Ranch activities ground down and entered a low-key phase, a pause before winter when managing cattle marked everyday battles. But I didn't mind at all. It was always great seeing him, and the leavening aspect held water. He'd bring a cool head and decisive attributes to the mission. If you could call it a mission—he and I and Bo knew this was a steep and obscure and borderline futile path.

"What are you suggesting?" I asked, smiling.

"I'm checking flights now."

"No need. I'll send a jet. My client won't bark at the expense. They never do." Marcus hadn't wasted breath on where and when. He would head for California's desert, come hell or high water, and there was no point tossing out protests. "How long before you can hit Billings? And are there any blizzards or fast-moving glaciers to contend with up there right now?"

"Ninety minutes. You should do stand-up. I'll see if I can get you a gig in Fishtail. How are you situated on weaponry?"

"I'm packing the Glock. If you wanted to show up with the inferior H&K, that should cover the bases."

He and I held differing views on semiautomatic pistols, with his preference the excellent German-made Heckler & Koch.

"You're not accounting for the known unknowns. You've got a target on your back, son. There's nothing new there, but let's at least prepare for the unknown odds of tangling with bad guys."

"Do what makes you happy."

"What would make me happy is your career change."

"Don't start."

"I'll wait until Palm Springs and then fire on all cylinders. Meanwhile, I'll cover weaponry requirements."

"I'll text you flight info," I said. "And one other thing, Marcus. I appreciate it. As always. Can't tell you how much I look forward to seeing you again."

"You, too, Case. You, too."

Two phone calls and arrangements were made for a charter flight from Billings. Marcus would land soon after me and Bo. Overnight with Bo's uncle, and off for Slab City while another wall calendar day was X'd through, another exercise in futility chalked up. Somewhere in the world, a fourteen-year-old kid waited. Waited for someone to rescue her. Waited for me. Oh, man.

Chapter 18

Bo and I hung out at the small Palm Springs airport and waited for Marcus's charter. One of the few airports I hadn't hit, it was a gem. Open air except for the immediate boarding area, hot but not scorching, it displayed sun sails stretched overhead, grass patches, lounging benches, a shop and bar or two—it defined doing it right. I always admired the ability of Californians to inject a certain something, a cool factor, into so many Golden State scenarios. Even Bo, who lived life skimming materialist surfaces, was impressed.

"You do travel in style, goober," he said, stretched across a bench, head resting on his rucksack, and lifting a hand toward the overhead sun sails. "First the private charter, and now this."

"Then there's my personal other side of the coin, bud. Gritty locales and long stretches of bad road and prop planes circa the 1950s."

"Spice for life's gumbo. You know, I may traipse over here with JJ once winter hits. I'm capturing an elegant texture vibe. A throwback to the cocktail era."

When Marcus's small jet arrived, he exited with a rucksack and packed duffel bag. An airport employee attempted off-loading the duffel from him, but no dice. The duffel held potent weaponry, and Marcus Johnson wouldn't release his grip on operational toolsets. He wore a straw Stetson with gray hairs peeking out below the brim, western footwear, a western-cut blazer, and a hard glare toward the immediate environment. In his book, he'd entered an operational area.

While Bo and I had hugged and laughed and tossed jibes at each other in Albuquerque, Marcus refrained from such exhibitions. We exchanged solid handshakes and side-pats and sincere smiles.

"I'm liking this travel style," he said as we headed for the rental SUV. "Billings doesn't offer direct flights to, well, much of anywhere."

"Our favorite goober is full of surprises," Bo said, poking me in the ribs. "Including this brief foray into digital intrigue and mystery."

After disabling the rental SUV's GPS, we headed for La Quinta, forty-five minutes southeast, where Richard and Mary Lee Dickerson lived. The sun eased low in the sky, dusk not far away. Five minutes into the trip, Marcus, riding shotgun, lowered his window. His Zippo's clack proclaimed cigar time. Bo, in unison, fished in his rucksack and pulled a small pipe and container of weed, firing a bowl.

"Glad to see you guys still abide by society's rules," I said. "It would please the rental car company."

"You travel with stand-up citizenry," Bo said. "Forthright men, undaunted by societal slings and arrows."

"And armed to the teeth," Marcus added. "After I studied this Slab City place, and with knowledge there's a fair-sized contingent who'd like nothing more than to eliminate one Case Lee, you two will come to thank me."

"I've taken the opportunity for digital perusal as well, fearless leader," Bo said. "A grand adventure awaits as we sleuth among the grand scheme's detritus. A place, perhaps, tinged with resignation and a dollop of despair, but a powerful brother- and sisterhood bond weaves throughout our destination."

"What's woven throughout that place are drug addicts, hobos, and escapees from the law."

"Seekers, master and commander. Artisans with perspectives tilted from the norm. A different world, and one to be relished."

Marcus grunted in response and added, "One to visit and then head for a disinfectant bath."

"Anyone heard from Catch?" I asked, attempting a conversational lane change. "I'm thinking his wedding can't be far off."

Juan Antonio Diego Hernandez, aka Catch, made up the fourth member of our still-living Delta team. He and his fiancée, Willa, were residents of Portland, Oregon. Catch—so-named because his ability to take care of, or catch, unexpected surprises during conflict always impressed. He was a bear of a man, the best shot we'd ever encountered, and another brother, near and dear.

"We chatted a couple weeks ago," Marcus said. "He asked about pickup trucks. He's in the market."

"You would know," I said.

"I would know about working trucks. From his questions, he's headed for what I believe people term 'pimped out.' Not a ranch vehicle."

"The Catchmobile," Bo added. "One of a kind. Like him."

"Amen," Marcus and I said in unison.

The gated La Quinta neighborhood held a golf course, manicured landscape, palm trees, and Spanish-style houses. Richard and ML—Bo had explained Mary Lee went by her initials—met us in their driveway. It was quite the setup. Off-white stucco house and walled yard, red tile roof, and an expansive single-level house. Richard, retired from a California real estate business, was an absolute gentleman. ML, an elegant and good-humored lady, was a committed hostess. She handled three rough men's arrival with absolute grace and assurance. Richard and ML were clearly fond of Bo, with hugs and laughter exchanged. The house interior was airy, the theme white and classic. The overall look would fit a magazine photo shoot, mixing comfort and elegance. Quite the place. ML had supper cooking while Richard insisted he make us cocktails. Together, they pulled off a rarity—making the three of us feel instantly at home.

Drinks in hand, we sat among white wrought-iron and padded patio furniture, as roses and bougainvillea draped the white stucco perimeter wall. Our view—palm trees and clear skies and nearby soaring desert mountains draped in alpenglow.

"Where do you live, Case?" ML asked as we settled in.

"On a boat. I travel the Intracoastal Canal from Virginia to Florida."

"It sounds fascinating. What an interesting lifestyle," she said.

"Well, ma'am, interesting doesn't do it justice," Marcus said.

"Bo tells me you men are engaged in a peculiar quest," Richard said. "It involves Slab City."

I didn't mind discussions about the job with Richard and ML, as long as the grisly and danger-inducing aspects remained absent.

"My client hired me to find a diplomat's captured daughter. Several strange events have pointed to Slab City."

"Rescuing a diplomat's daughter?" ML asked. "That is wonderful. Bo said you were a private investigator. I believe his term was 'firefighter for life's foibles.' I hope I'm remembering this correctly, Bo." She smiled in his direction and sipped her mai tai. He raised his mojito as agreement. "So Case, is this a typical engagement for you?"

"The jobs vary quite a bit. I'm not sure any are what you'd call typical."

"Understatement of the year," Marcus added.

"Would you mind sharing how the road led to Slab City?" Richard asked.

"They abducted her in the country of Jordan. I believe certain players made payments to her captors. Information from an associate suggests someone in Slab City may help."

"What was the motivation behind the young lady's capture?" ML asked.

"It's somewhat convoluted and involves diplomats and other government players from around the world."

No point waltzing spookville into the mix, but Richard sniffed it out.

"It sounds very cloak-and-dagger," he said. "If you don't mind me asking, do you work for the CIA?"

"No."

"But they are his close personal buds," Marcus said. "Except when they're not."

"Our Georgia peach rides tornadoes," Bo said. "It's an admirable profession, although he still fights the universe's tug and pull. He can't help it, being among the straight-and-narrow crowd."

"It sounds exciting," ML said as she rose and padded through the large sliding door. Supper prep sounds soon filtered back through the door. She dismissed offers of help with a polite but firm hand.

"And you, Marcus," Richard said. "I understand you ranch in Montana."

We chatted about ranch life, JJ and Albuquerque, La Quinta's appeal. Supper was excellent, as was the company, and everyone faded off to bed except for me and Bo.

"Great folks," I said. "You're lucky to have them in your life."

"Great folks, stated without reservation. They'd like JJ."

"And vice versa." Coyotes yipped in the distance, the desert peaks awash in moonlight. "I've gotta tell you, bud. I'm not getting any warm fuzzies with this last-ditch effort."

"And yet you have no idea what events are in store, what magic experiences await. Remove the blinders, and allow the universe full command."

"Hoolie says you can't hack blockchain technology."

"Human inclination would dictate otherwise. The inventor, the person or persons we seek, is every bit human. They left a private back door. Accessible only to them, perhaps, but there, hidden."

"Man, I hope you're right."

"Not a matter of right or wrong. It simply is. It must wear you out."

"What?"

"The fretting and strutting on life's stage. Are your ecumenical learnings bone-dry? Do not lose heart. Outwardly we are wasting away, yet inwardly we are being renewed day by day."

"I could use some renewal."

"And you shall have it. A new dawn awaits. Go get some rest, amigo. Sleep easy."

Bo, who'd grabbed a blanket from the living room couch, wrapped himself and settled on a thick-padded patio lounger.

"You're sleeping out here?"

"Aye." He squirmed into a sleeping position. "There's a target on your back, my brother. I won't allow harm to befall you at this place. Nor on my uncle or ML or Marcus."

With that, he closed his eyes. Somewhere under the blanket was his Bundeswehr combat knife—the lone tool he required. Woe betide the killer who dared enter Richard and ML's sanctuary.

I cast a last glance upward, at the sky filled with stars, and said a quick prayer. And thought about an old expression—people sleep peaceably in their beds at night because rough men stand ready to do violence on their behalf.

Chapter 19

Richard and ML Dickerson, gracious as ever, offered coffee and breakfast. We declined the food but enjoyed hot java on the back patio as the morning's cool faded and desert heat nudged in. The day's mission was simple enough. Scour Slab City for someone or a group of someones called Red. Then I'd ask, beg, or cajole Red for help with a cryptocurrency transfer that used impossible-to-crack blockchain technology. Cryptocurrency pointed at Jordan and, maybe, a trail leading from Jordan to God-knows-where. Piece of cake.

Bo spotted desert bighorn sheep working their way down the nearest stark mountain.

"You still have eagle eyes, Bo," Richard said.

"And a lamb's heart," ML added.

True enough, unless battle emerged. And when battle emerged, a mongoose heart, perhaps, best depicted my best friend. We collected our kit and saddled up. As we gathered at my SUV, Richard shook hands with Marcus and me, and gave Bo a tight hug with an admonition to visit more often. He replied that such an event might occur and mentioned JJ's possible appearance with him.

"She's welcome anytime," Richard said.

ML hugged Bo and kissed him on the cheek, then repeated the gesture with Marcus. She repeated the goodbye with me, but ended it with a one-hand grip on my shoulder.

"I like you, Case. And believe I have more than a passing feel for what you do in this big wide world of ours." Her free hand patted my chest and her facial expression dropped all pleasant and sociable signs, eyes hard as flint. "You find that young lady. Whatever it takes. And when you find the people that took her, make them pay."

We exited the gated community and headed southeast. Ten minutes into the trip, as we hit the rural highway near Coachella—the venue for the well-known music and arts festival and another example of California-cool—Marcus, Bo, and I laid out semi-concurrent comments. Someone followed us.

"Do you believe the black SUV several hundred yards back contains friendlies?" Marcus asked. "Because they've been on our tail for a while."

Marcus rode shotgun and had maintained a side mirror scan.

"They pulled behind us after we left Richard and ML's community," I said, shaking my head. "My apologies, gents. They must have followed us from the airport, didn't want the hassle of getting past the neighborhood entrance guardhouse, and waited until this morning. I screwed up."

I had. It started with using my actual name for the charter jets, who filed flight manifests the same as commercial flights. There was an assortment of espionage agencies who could backdoor those systems and track me. The Russians. Or the Company. Oh, man.

"A moment, a time slice, filled with reunion and joy and reflection," Bo said. "And we each let our guard down. So be it."

"Bo's right," Marcus said. "We lost focus. Ignored the mission. A classic blunder."

"*I* lost focus," I said. "My mission."

"There's no 'I' in team," Marcus said. "The only adjustments for the mission will relate to what we do about them."

"Not them. Bogeys, my brethren."

Bo lounged along the back bench seat, one arm slung across the backrest, with glances toward our back trail and surrounding environment.

The rearview mirror displayed wild red hair, turning-wild eyes, and the genesis of a wolflike grin.

"You don't know that," Marcus said.

"Ye of little faith. There are four dour men ensconced within the vehicle in question."

Marcus pulled a cigar, the Zippo clacked, and the window cracked as smoke escaped.

"Point taken," he said, acknowledgment that when Bo assessed a situation, in whatever strange manner he chose, odds were high he nailed it. His crack eyesight discerned the number four. The dour part, well, neither Marcus nor I were in the mood to explore how he knew that.

"How far is this wreck of a place we're headed for?" Marcus asked.

"An hour," I said.

"I'm less than enthused about them entering our area of operation," Marcus said. "Is there some place we can stop and confirm intent?"

"Bombay Beach," Bo said. "A dozen miles before Slab City. I have enjoyed a digital reconnoiter of this area. An amazing tale, filled with nature's decree and man's folly."

"Okay," I said. "What's Bombay Beach?"

"A precursor."

"What the hell does that mean?" Marcus asked.

"A staging area, perhaps. A taste, to be sure, of our destination's texture."

Marcus sighed and shot me a hard glance. I shrugged a response. You either followed Bo down the rabbit hole or let it be. Marcus and I chose the latter. To no avail. As we passed irrigated agricultural land intermixed with stark Sonoran Desert, Bo treated us to a geography and cultural lesson.

Bombay Beach sits alongside the massive Salton Sea, California's largest lake, by far. Failed engineering created it when the Colorado River punched through a flood channel in the early 1900s. Water flowed into the massive Salton depression, well below sea level, for two years, until they plugged the breach. Voila, over three hundred square miles of lake in the desert. In the 1950s and '60s, life was grand. SoCal residents, including a fair share of celebrities, flocked there for water skiing, fishing, and grand parties. Lakeshore houses sprouted. Bo termed it "a golden era, a chronological snippet filled with endless possibilities." Marcus grunted in response and interrupted.

"While we're edified on crap I could not care less about, distribute weaponry. There's a chance the men at our backs could make a move. This is an isolated stretch of road."

Bo complied and continued his tale. He lifted rifle cases from the vehicle's back area, unlatched them, and handed two Colt 901 .308 caliber rifles to us front seat occupants, keeping one for himself. He distributed filled ammo magazines, and we entered the surreal. Bo filled us in on casual history while we slammed mags home and steel-on-steel clacks sounded, rounds chambered. Marcus performed lock-and-load duties for both his and my rifles and held the loaded weapons between his legs, pointed at the vehicle's roof.

But the environment outside had become surreal as well. We drove alongside the Salton Sea's north side, the lake stretching fifty miles into the distance with the Santa Rosa Mountains rising above the opposite shore. The sunlight was white-bright, the desert arid, and the lake's water brown. Something wasn't right—no boaters, swimmers, or beach walkers. No one around, few vehicles on the highway. You felt it in your gut. There was a weird not-right feel around us. Bo's tale explained why.

148

The Salton Sea has no outflow. Irrigation wastewater dribbled in, but evaporation provided a potent counterbalance. Salt levels trended up for decades, stocked fish died by the millions, birds by the thousands, and toxic algae blooms cast their brownish-sick color across the waters. The mass exodus of residents left abandoned houses and trailers littered along stretches of shoreline. They now stood, falling apart and collapsing, as stark reminders of good times long, long past. Where the highway passed close along the shoreline, fish skeletons bleached in the sun.

"Now that we're prepared for action, I'm thinking a man could acquire some beachfront property cheap," Marcus said. He spoke over the cracked-open window's wind noise, stared at the scene with slight headshakes, and monitored our trailing SUV in the side mirror. "You could establish Bo-world right here. An ashram for your kind. I'm sensing a golden opportunity."

"A potent musing, Bwana Johnson. Let's backburner that idea and consider another item. One of this little soirée's appeals includes the archeological element. We wander through the 1950s, frozen under a baking sun, and relish old-times-used-to-be. A rare opportunity, gentlemen."

"Let's talk bogeys," I said. "We pull off at this Bombay Beach place and assess. If they follow, let's plan next steps. I'm not sure a gunfight at the OK Corral is the best play. We *are* in the States."

"Are we?" asked Bo. "There's a potent pull from the time and space continuum that may well place us elsewhere."

"I would just as soon clean house before we reach our objective," Marcus said, ignoring Bo. "A search among the miscreants and malcontents at Slab City for an unknown Red is challenge enough without having to cover our butts against men who hold ill intent."

First, confirm they trailed us. Fifteen minutes later, Bombay Beach's ruins appeared as the trailing SUV maintained a discreet distance. I entered the cracked asphalt town entrance, marked with a faded, peeled billboard that displayed a vintage black-and-white photo of women in fifties-era swimsuits waterskiing. Rather than continuing along the main drag, I hung a left to circle the place and check the black SUV's intent. Before we disappeared into the shambled bowels of Bombay Beach, I halted and, along with Marcus and Bo, observed the SUV pull off the highway. It wouldn't enter the ramshackle environment and now waited, patient, for us. Not a good thing, and Marcus asked Bo to retrieve his binoculars. While he scoped the dark-tinted-window SUV, Bo offered a suggestion.

"Allow me ten or fifteen minutes," he said. "I'll approach them from the rear and enquire how their day is going so far."

No doubt he could, and would, do it. His weird cloak of invisibility would have him appear at the SUV's rear hatch window with a gentle tap, smiling. And a coin flip whether it would kick off a gunfight.

"No," Marcus said. "We stick together for now. You leaving our vehicle tosses too many variables on the table."

"Thanks, Bo, but Marcus is right. Let's keep it tight, at least for now."

I rolled forward. Intermixed with several lived-in trailers and shacks were burned-out structures, trailers, and rubble. I rolled at ten miles-per-hour, the road rutted dirt, and entered a strange and discordant wasteland. We passed the husk of an airplane, now turned into a metal-sculptured flying fish.

"A nearby area was once a military bombing range," Bo said. He leaned forward from the back seat's center, one arm draped over my right shoulder, the other across Marcus's left. His voice carried a timbre of excitement and awe. "I'm anticipating artwork with a post-apocalyptic motif."

"Oh, I believe the entire village has that motif covered, son," Marcus said, rolling his window down and taking it all in.

One collapsed shack displayed a fresh hand-painted sign that declared No Hipsters Allowed. Alrighty, then. There was a nose-down silver jet fuselage, its tail section canted upward at a forty-five-degree angle, highlighting a collection of object d'art pieces dangling from the tail against the desert-blue sky. Various other large art pieces stood scattered among the burned-out trailers and houses, most built from metal scraps. Several locals wandered about in flip-flops, shorts, and T-shirts, inured to any issues with their surroundings. We rolled past a half-buried lounger on the beach, surrounded by desiccated fish carcasses. A nearby doorframe and door stood upright and alone along the shore. The Bombay Beach Drive-In had a white-painted plywood screen with vehicle husks lined up in rows, waiting for sunset and the next Cary Grant or Bette Davis flick. Both Bo and Marcus had a point—the entire scene resembled a miniature post-apocalyptic Burning Man meets Mad Max.

I found it weird, it infatuated Bo, and Marcus was, well, being Marcus—a Montana rancher and former Delta team lead who held no truck with such foolishness.

But there was an undercurrent to the place, a sliver of clawback, as we passed small, concerted efforts to transform the place into an artists' community. If anyone could pull it off, it would be Californians.

"Stop here," Marcus said, lifting the binoculars.

I did, and he scoped the black SUV parked a quarter-mile away.

"Let's eat," Bo said. "And reconnoiter and weigh options and relish our here-and-now."

"There are plenty of fish bones you could gnaw on," Marcus said, the binoculars pressed against his eyes. "There may be some nutrient value left in those." He lowered the binoculars. "No change. They're stationary."

"Drive on, my Georgia peach. Both sustenance and more wonders await."

I continued down the main drag, headed back for the highway, the road still rough and broken. Near the village's entrance, a sign proclaimed the Bombay Bar and Grill. A waterskiing figure accompanied the verbiage. The parking lot held three vehicles—two current models and a 1970s Volkswagen Beetle. I pulled in and parked between two of the vehicles, using them as protective cover in case long-range shots were part of the bogeys' plan. With a head-turn, we had a decent view of the black SUV, now several hundred yards away. This was a solid play—we'd ascertained intent, or at least confirmed they trailed us. Now, with Slab City but twenty miles away, we could organize a plan.

I slid the Glock, resting between my legs, into the waistband of my jeans and pulled out my polo shirt's tail so it draped over my waistline. I asked Bo, who wore an untucked loose-fitting peasant shirt, if he was ready. His Glock's snick as a round was chambered sufficed as an answer. Marcus began opening his door.

"Marcus, we're below sea level. It's near ninety degrees already. Why not ditch the jacket and use your shirttail for cover?"

Marcus Johnson was a tall, slender, good-looking man and fastidious about his attire. He wore western boots, pressed jeans, a western shirt with pearl snap buttons, a clean straw Stetson, and a light jacket against a morning chill that had long disappeared. His .45 pistol hid in a custom jacket holster. He hesitated opening the vehicle door, considered for a half-second pulling his shirttail and removing the jacket, then continued to exit the SUV. I smiled at Bo, who returned the same.

"The man has style," he said.

"Yeah. Yeah, he does."

We didn't dally entering the building, our heads bobbing just above our SUV's roofline. It was cool and dark inside, the AC on full blast. The walls and ceiling were covered with memorabilia and ball caps and dollar bills, a middle-aged woman tended a cluttered bar with a prominent sign that stated cash only, two young tourist couples occupied barstools, and a wide back opening displayed a shaded area where a thin man sat alone, shaking his head and muttering at the tabletop.

"Like you always say," Bo whispered in my ear. "You can't beat a bar as a base of operations."

Chapter 20

"What can I do you boys for?"

The barkeep-owner smiled as she asked and wiped her hands with a dishcloth.

"How about three coffees and something resembling breakfast?" I said, also with a smile. She gave off a vibe that spelled instant like.

"How about three breakfast burritos?"

"How about eggs over medium with bacon?" Marcus asked.

"How about three breakfast burritos?" she repeated, her grin indicating a limited morning menu.

"Sounds great," I said and tossed a nodded greeting at the two young couples.

The barkeep poured three steaming mugs and delivered them across the bar top. I tilted my head toward the back opening and we strolled onto the warm deck. The shade awnings blocked sunlight, the walls were constructed of wooden slats and old timber, and featured more of what might loosely be termed artwork. We sat across the small area from the thin man who had stopped addressing the tabletop when we entered and now eyeballed us with a benign look. Or rather, one eye did. The other wandered a bit.

"We have to start with the premise they are, in fact, bogeys," Marcus said. He removed his jacket and hung it over a chair back. After placing it, he performed a dry run, reaching for the in-view .45. Satisfied, he continued. "Let's start with the enemy. Any thoughts on that?" He stared in my direction.

"Roll the roulette wheel. They could be anyone, although recent encounters suggest an Eastern Europe origin."

"Or our friends from Russia," Bo said.

155

"Yep. Could even be Company assets."

"Why would they be Company people?" Marcus asked. "Didn't they help you out in DC?"

"That was several days ago. Chess pieces move, strategies change. You never freakin' know until the dust settles and gun smoke clears."

"Great name for a metal band," Bo said. "Gun Smoke Clears."

"Let's go with affiliates of this secret group you talked about. That means Russians or Albanians or Romanians or one of those countries. Now, why are they following?"

"I've kicked a hornet's nest. All the players know I'm after the girl and on the side of Western clandestine services, which is beyond weird. The grand conspiracy views me as a thorn best removed."

We sipped coffee. An ashtray showed it was okay to smoke, so Marcus fired a cigar. The thin gent across the room fired a cigarette. The patio continued heating up.

"As in removed, hard stop?" Marcus asked, keeping the language vague.

"If the recent past is any indicator, yeah."

"Is it possible these bogeys know about Red?" he asked.

"I'd claim no way. They are here and now for one terminal reason. Me. A loose thread in their secret plan that requires snipping. And now I've exposed my blood brothers to my mess. Which plants this altered mission in the crapper."

"Stow the angst," Marcus said. "Bo and I are here to help deal with unknown contingencies."

"Bits and bytes and vacuumed debris from an honorable quest. Such noble efforts are *exactly* why we are here."

"And I appreciate it more than you guys can know. It's been a lousy effort on my part. I'm not used to failure." I sipped coffee and gathered thoughts. "This is a last-ditch effort. I mean, what are the odds this Red exists and has chosen a place like Slab City? But it's all I've got. Tomorrow, there's a good chance I'll make a call to parents in DC and let them know I've failed to locate their daughter. That sucks more than I can express."

"Dodging bogeys makes for a major distraction," Marcus said. "As I recall, there was DC and Jordan. Two run-ins with the enemy. Today's mission makes three. You haven't had an easy row to hoe, son."

"I'm trying, with lousy luck, to find a captured girl. All the rest is BS, occupying another world. And it pisses me off having to deal with it."

The owner arrived with a tray that held three burritos and a coffeepot. Refills happened, she asked if all was good, and after she received an affirmative, addressed the man across the room.

"Coffee, Sonny?"

"No, thanks. I could use a beer, though."

She shook her head and wandered off. Bo took a big bite of his burrito, scratched his scraggly chin whiskers while chewing, and addressed the matter at hand.

"Two birds, one stone."

Marcus had one bite of his burrito, called it good—indicated with his plate slid toward the table's center—leaned back, and sipped coffee.

"Handle the bogeys and find Red with one effort," he said, staring at Bo. "Let's walk through that."

We did. The question of sequence loomed large—address the hitters first or ferret out Red first or attempt both at the same time. Bo pushed for the concurrent approach.

"It allows a spatial approach, flow and swirl. Our situation resists the linear."

"I disagree," Marcus said. "Take on the bogeys. Deal with and remove immediate danger. Then search."

"Let's consider the upcoming setting," I said. "Is it really a lawless place? Do we whack these cats in broad daylight with residents watching from lawn chairs?"

"Not a problem," said a voice across the room.

I'd screwed up and used explicit language, now overheard. The thin man rose and wandered over.

"I'm Sonny Flute, beach preacher."

"Grab a chair, Sonny," Bo said as Marcus shot him a hard look.

Sonny slid a chair across the concrete floor and settled in next to Bo.

"You guys are talking about Slab City. I could use a beer."

Bo slipped him a fiver. Sonny stood and headed toward the interior bar.

"Recruiting assets, Bo?" Marcus asked, puffing the cigar.

"Accept the cosmic gifts, maestro. Insights and situational nuance may spill across the menu."

"Bo," I said, "be *very* careful providing details. This hairball we're dealing with doesn't need more players."

Sonny returned with a smile and a beer, plucked up his cigarette, and sat.

"How's the beach preaching business?" Marcus asked.

"It comes and goes. The important thing is to be there for people. Sometimes it's hard." His face grew despondent. "You know, I've got issues, sure. A head injury from years ago."

Marcus gently questioned his background and confirmed the man's unfortunate injury. The Montana rancher's demeanor changed to one of empathy wrapped around genuine concern.

"When's the last meal you ate, Sonny?"

"I'm not usually hungry."

"Chow down on this," Marcus said, sliding his burrito across the table. "Where do you live?"

"Here."

Sonny took a bite and washed it down with beer.

"Where's here?"

"My Volkswagen." The decades-old Beetle parked outside. "This is good. I've always liked eggs. You men are talking about Slab City, aren't you?"

"We are," Bo said, giving Sonny a squeeze on the shoulder. "Is it a place you're familiar with?"

"Us Bombay Beach folks don't rub elbows with that lot. I love preaching, though. Last week, this one woman came through the beach door. She was something else."

"A unique revelation?" Bo asked.

"I'll say. A full-length white mink coat. She stepped through and dropped the coat. Cast it out."

"Freed herself."

"Released. Yessir. I have it in my Beetle right now. It keeps me warm at night."

"A divine gift?" Bo asked.

"I see it that way."

Marcus and I glanced at each other, neither of us with the foggiest notion what the hell they were talking about. Bo sensed our confusion.

"The doorframe and door standing upright and alone and virtuous on the beach," he said. "She passed through. A spiritual awakening, casting aside material items. Prompted by Sonny Flute, beach preacher."

"I don't take full credit, of course. Good burrito," Sonny said, taking another bite. "Thanks."

159

"Of course. But well done, you. We"—Bo paused and waved a hand toward Marcus and me—"seek revelation as well. In Slab City."

Sonny swallowed, shook his head, plucked his smoke from the ashtray, and stared above our heads.

"Salvation at the mountain, sure. Yes. But past there, it is all ugliness and chaos." He lowered his head and locked his nonwandering eye on Bo. "I don't have the right to ask."

"Our cause is noble and righteous. You have my word."

Sonny took another burrito bite and edged closer to Bo.

"Do not be fooled at the entrance. No. Go deep into the bowels of the beast. Go there. No law, no salvation, no love. But," he said, shifting his gaze to Marcus, "be careful. Perform your duties. Slab City surrounds you with challenges."

"How big is this place, Sonny?" Marcus asked.

"Hundreds of acres. Hundreds. Go deep. A righteous cause, you said? There will be no consequences for your actions when deep."

The three of us shared stares and nods, the upcoming conflict's location confirmed. Marcus reached into his wallet and pulled a Benjamin. With one hand, he laid a gentle grip on Sonny's forearm. With the other, he slid it across the table. Fingertips kept it pinned.

"I want you to take this for food, Sonny. No beer, no smokes, no booze. Just food. I'll require your word on that."

Sonny Flute stared at the hundred-dollar bill, quizzical. Then he lifted his head toward the ceiling and scanned, then dropped his gaze toward Marcus.

"Nourishment."

"That's right, Sonny. Nourishment only. Do I have your word?"

"You have my word. Given with strength and appreciation."

160

Marcus released the bill, Sonny slipped it into a front pocket, and we finished our coffee.

"Alright," Marcus said. "We go deep and handle the situation. Then search. Then haul it out of there. We clear on that?"

"Roger."

"What an adventurous day! The situation in flux, strange ebb and flood tides surround, three brothers on a noble quest."

Marcus started a response to Bo, thought better of it, and instead made a simple statement.

"Let's ride."

Chapter 21

We turned onto the highway; the black SUV followed a quarter-mile back. One item stood clear—this conspiracy's showrunners, the Guardians, wouldn't quit until they planted my head on a stake. It smelled of classic Russian ops. Set the objective and keep coming until mission accomplished, nuance and subtlety be damned. It would stop, maybe, when I stopped my search for the girl, an act with strong possibilities. Or, maybe again, when I found Krystyna and her harrowing tale was revealed. But I knew all too well that either outcome was no guarantee the Guardians would back off. Russians held long memories, and "forgive and forget" wasn't part of their makeup. But I'd been on and off their shitlist for a while, so nothing new there.

"Sorry about this, guys," I said as we powered down the highway. "The whole hitters thing was always a possibility, but the prime mission remains connecting with Red. A mission you both fit into like a glove. So, here's my preference with these hunyaks following us."

"Stow that crap," Marcus said.

"It is so endearing when he does his Lone Ranger thing," Bo added. "A vibrant testament to our favorite goober's character."

I'd headed into "let me handle the bad guys" territory, but both blood brothers saw it coming and cut me off.

"Neither of you signed up for this," I said. "The menu never stated sanctioned killers."

"An ever-present side dish, my Georgia peach. A solid and continuous element. One we have dealt with often, and will do so again."

"It isn't a poor tactic having me handle those men while you two spread out and search," I said.

"There may not be any handling necessary," Marcus said. "We can't confirm their intent."

"I know their intent. So do both of you."

"Then we shall proceed as planned," Bo said. "The bravest are surely those who have the clearest vision of what is before them, glory and danger alike, and yet notwithstanding, go out to meet it."

"Socrates?" I asked.

"Thucydides," Marcus said. "Well put, Bo."

"I'm glad you two learned gentlemen agree, as long as you both understand those folks after us don't give a rat's ass about Thucydides."

"On that note, what's your best bet on their background?" Marcus asked.

"I'd put money on Bulgarians. The Russkies like them as proxies for wet work."

"Military experience?"

"Not necessarily. Thugs, killers for up close and personal applications."

"Good," Marcus said. "A wide-open area plays to our advantage."

"You'll want to turn off at Niland," Bo said. "Slab City is a couple of miles from there."

The small town of Niland had a grocery store, a diner, a gas station, and not much else. We took a narrow asphalt road leading northeast. After several miles, it petered out and turned into a hard-packed, rutted, dusty desert trail. The black SUV followed.

"They aren't subtle, are they?" Marcus asked, eyeballing the side-view mirror.

"Nope. Waiting for their opportunity and don't care that we're aware. And I'm okay with that. Since Niland, my pissed-off factor has ratcheted up. Way up."

As we traveled, two then three modern vehicles eased past, coming from Slab City.

"Slab City has tourists?" I asked.

"No, my inquisitive buddy. You will see."

We did. Couldn't miss it. On our right alongside the road, a massive painted religious folk-art mound with a white cross extended skyward. Over fifty feet high and a couple hundred feet wide, its surface appeared made from adobe. But it was the paint, the scenes and religious expressions that grabbed you. I slowed.

"Good Lord," Marcus said.

"I couldn't have put it better," I replied.

"Welcome to Salvation Mountain," Bo said. "Hence the tourists. You might remember Sonny's 'salvation at the mountain' comment."

The bright color mishmash was spectacular, eye-grabbing, unreal—set against gray and brown and scrub-brush-covered desert. Blue and white latex paint waterfalls and rivers cascaded down one section, joining a blue Sea of Galilee. "God Is Love," painted with shining red and pink. A massive red heart with hand-painted words within proclaiming Jesus's love. Huge green, aqua, white, and ocher patches—each adjoining another patch with figures and symbols throughout. A thirty-foot tree of life, biblical quotations, animals and fields, a painted pathway that led to the top. A technicolor religious art mountain, hand-created.

"We have to stop," Bo said. "A totem unlike any other."

"After the mission," Marcus said.

"If we're not pedal to the metal," I added.

A half-dozen sedans and SUVs sat parked at Salvation Mountain's base, and a dozen tourists climbed the mound while others wandered into a cavelike entrance at the base. We kept rolling. Several hundred yards down the road, a small outhouse-shaped structure, painted with bright colors and designs, announced "Welcome to Slab City." Alongside the structure, in the cast shade, an aluminum lawn chair claimed a spot. A woman in dusty T-shirt, shorts, and sandals occupied the chair, slumped over, either asleep or passed out. As we drove by, the rearview mirror showed the trailing vehicle hesitate, slowing. It wasn't hard to imagine an eastern European collection inside the car wondering what the hell was going on. Good. Come into this weird and dangerous playground, you SOBs. C'mon in.

A former US Marine Corps base, there were plenty of concrete foundations, or slabs, scattered about. Astride many were trailers whose livable level ranged from solid to falling apart. Intermingled were shacks constructed with pallets, tarps, plywood, and anything construed as a potential wall or roof. Solar panels showed on several structures. Latrines or outhouses—some three-sided, some four—sat at random intervals. Collections of stunted desert trees and oversized desert brush were spread across the place. We passed a community stage near the entrance where, I supposed, they offered entertainment.

No running water, no electricity, no sewer, with trash everywhere. Lighter plastic trash moved and shifted with the strong breeze, often snagged by strange artwork collections—created from junk—set at random places and intervals. Social areas dotted the place, marked with old sofas and chairs and benches, each item desert-bleached and disintegrating. Abandoned vehicles, decades-old and stripped of parts, sat painted and decorated with more artwork. They acted as a stand-alone piece or someone's home. Several residents meandered about, each with minimal attire as a head-nod to the heat. Others sat in shade and watched as we passed with neither friendliness nor malice. We simply *were*—a passing item noted and, perhaps, commented on. Our vehicle swayed in the ruts under a scorching sun, surrounded by a bizarre hardscrabble environment where powder-fine dust and trash and otherworldliness ruled.

The rutted track offered several offshoots, which led to more of the same. I turned right and stopped, the new track weaving among shacks, trailers, trees, and brush. Our enemy also stopped, a hundred yards back.

"Alright," Marcus said. "Let's take care of business."

"Not yet," I said. "I'll show, and let's see what happens."

"We all show," he said.

"In their world, neither of you hold high market value. I do. I'll go full display. We'll check their deployment."

I left our vehicle, strolled around the back, and leaned against the SUV's side, arms crossed, positioned between Marcus and Bo's doors. Both had rolled down their windows. Heat waves rippled; the black SUV was still. Then four doors swung open, and each released a man wearing a light coat and dark pants. The style and fit indicated eastern European. Jackets removed and tossed back into the SUV, they each filled a hand with a semiautomatic pistol and advanced.

After they'd made ten paces, removing any doubt as to intent, I addressed my teammates.

"Alrighty, then. Let's open the kimono."

I stepped forward and allowed both doors to open. Marcus handed me the Colt rifle, exited, and raised his to his shoulder. I did the same. Enough of this crap. These bastards, and the ones in DC and Jordan, were nothing but hindrances, obstacles. My pissed-off attitude changed, signaled by the soft metallic click of the Colt's safety flicked off. I threw the kill switch, now cold and committed and without a trace of remorse. Screw these hitters. Let blood pool on dust. It wouldn't be ours.

Bo's rifle remained in the back seat as he exited, but he pulled his Glock from under the peasant shirt and aimed down the dirt road. The four men halted. At the current distance, rifles swung the battle in our favor, a fact not lost on the killers. They scattered. Three dashed off, headed left, and entered the maze of structures, trash, and desert scrub. One sprinted in the other direction.

Marcus began issuing pursuit plans when a weathered voice sounded nearby.

"A word of caution, my fellows."

The voice arrived from a nearby pallet-and-plastic-sheeting abode, nestled under a scrawny and stunted desert tree. String-dangling symbols and artifacts hung from the tree as an old man rose from his rotted recliner with a grunt. Long white hair peeked from under a leather skullcap; he wore a full white beard, flip-flops, shorts, and an open shirt presenting a round belly. The cat looked like an outlandish desert Santa Claus. He held his pipe, a good two feet long, in one hand. He strolled our way, unperturbed by the weaponry on display.

"A cautionary tale prior to events," he said, firing his pipe. Between sucking puffs, he said, "I'm Gilgar. A shaman."

"We're a little busy, Gilgar," I said and held back the urge to ask him if he knew an Antoinette.

"Yes. Busy. But you may well run into children as your exploration progresses. I will assume those rifles carry great potency."

"They're positioning while we fiddle-fart around," Marcus said, irritated.

"He's got a point, Marcus."

The .308 caliber rounds could cut through a body and carry on with still-deadly energy. The pistol bullets, both the .40 Glocks and Marcus's H&K .45, would expend most of their power in the initial target. Marcus shot me a hard glance and walked to our SUV's rear hatch, opening it.

"Okay. Thanks, Gilgar," I said.

He closed his eyes and presented a slow bow, then returned to pipe-puffing and watching us alter plans. Bo and I joined Marcus at the vehicle's rear.

"Shithouse mouse, Case. You've offered up some weird-ass situations before, but this takes the damn cake." He removed his jacket, fished around in his duffel, and pulled a leather waist belt and holster. "Should we check with the shaman for further insights before we go get those bastards?"

Bo switched between scanning the environment and observing Marcus's prep.

"I'm loving this. Dust rises with each step, danger lurks from unseen places. Modern detritus strewn across a wild landscape. A shaman as counselor. It doesn't get any better than this, my brothers."

"Want to bet?" Marcus asked as he tightened the belt and filled the holster with his .45.

"Be stalwart of heart with your three targets. Avoid danger as best you can. I'll take the lone rabbit."

"Hold on," Marcus said, reaching again into his duffel. "Put these on."

He handed Bo and me earpiece communication radios, inserted his, and waited for us and a radio check.

"Copy?" he asked once we'd geared up.

"Roger" came back twice.

At that, Bo was off, no tactical instructions required. The killer who'd taken off on his own now faced a Bo Dickerson stalk. Dead man walking.

"Tallyho, fellow adventurers. Happy hunting."

He dashed away, each footfall raising dust, and disappeared into Slab City's mishmash. Marcus closed the back hatch, I locked the vehicle, and Gilgar watched, sanguine.

"Let's separate but take parallel tracks," Marcus said. "We may pincer these killers."

"Roger that."

Marcus, cautious as a field ops leader, wouldn't hesitate putting himself in harm's way. Beneath the taciturn demeanor and demand for operational clarity, he was still as badass as they came. He adjusted his Stetson, lit a cigar, rested a hand on the holstered .45, and strode, undaunted, into the bowels of Slab City. A black Gary Cooper in *High Noon*. Badass all the way.

I filled my hand with the Glock and edged right, closer to where the three killers had disappeared, then angled parallel to Marcus's track. Game on, you sons-of-bitches. Game on.

Chapter 22

They wouldn't cluster. Professional killers, in my experience, fell into two broad categories. The ex-military types prone to using long-distance hits with scoped rifles. And the seven-paces-or-closer types, the dark alley and catch you leaving a bar killer. The DC, Jordan, and now these hitters occupied the second category. They'd spread out a bit, sure, but wouldn't cluster.

I held the Glock with a two-handed grip as the sun beat down and the temp approached one hundred. Edged past a collection of shacks fashioned from timber and plastic tarps. One shack displayed doll heads dangling from strings. They shifted with the light breeze. I kept the pace slow, a stalk more than a walk, with all senses maxed toward a bizarre three-sixty-degree environment. Several concrete slabs, surrounded by head-high desert brush, sat unoccupied. One revealed a rectangular hole through the concrete. A former basement, filled with trash or acting as a latrine. I eased past a twin-engine airplane wreck on my left, the rear elevated with wood and metal and the entire fuselage covered with painted designs. Past the plane, I glimpsed Marcus, thirty paces away, doing his western shoot-out thing, cigar smoke lifting with the breeze.

Conversational voices, snippets, drifted within earshot as I passed. No alarms, no gasps or cries at armed men stalking, and, blessedly, no children. One thin dog trotted past raising dust, slowing in the hope I might offer food, before carrying on. I'd progressed fifty paces when a dilapidated trailer, one roof corner caved in, spit out a filthy shirtless young man in jeans who stumbled a few steps in the bright sun. Clearly a tweaker, he squinted, eyeballed me, and stepped in my direction. A good chance he'd ask for

171

money, but when awareness struck that I pointed a pistol, he halted and reconsidered.

As he stood still and scratched scabs along his side, I began passing him without acknowledgment, hyper-focused on my surroundings, scanning. It was a peripheral catch, but caught nonetheless. He froze his arm mid-scratch, eyes squinted toward my right rear. He'd spotted something, or someone, giving him pause. A hitter. Had to be. I swung my focus and the Glock in that direction, capturing nothing but a pallet-walled and orange-tarp-roofed house with discarded carpet as a front porch, situated against tall scrub brush. Plenty of hiding spots for a hitter. And plenty of surrounding obstructions for me to navigate and get behind the bastard. I quick-stepped right, past the tweaker, and circled his trailer, backtracking.

On a bare dirt patch stood a sculpted robot with junk steel legs, a gutted old console TV for a body, a smaller TV for a head. Past the robot, desert brush and the carpet-porched shack's rear. More conversation snippets floated in the air from a nearby small galvanized tin structure. I eased around the brush and halted, dead still. Pressed against the shack's side, a hitter. Short-sleeved, dark hair slicked back, slacks; he held his pistol with one hand and peeked down the trail I'd taken earlier. At ten paces away, pressed against the brush, I stood borderline in his peripheral vision. Kept my pistol raise slow and deliberate—no sudden movement to alert him—sighted, and squeezed the trigger. The weapon's sharp crack sounded across Slab City, the headshot clean.

There were no yells or screams from the surrounding structures, but a trailer door slammed and the conversations quit, the breeze through the brush the lone voice.

"Status?" Marcus asked through my earpiece.

"One bogey down."

"Roger that."

He went on hunting. Vigilance remained firewalled while I approached the body, scoped the immediate battlefield, and plucked up the killer's cell phone and documents, shoving them into my back pockets. I slid his pistol, a Bulgarian-made Makarov 9mm, into my waistband and continued in my original direction, now more separated from Marcus.

I skirted another bare patch, the display area for a vertical art piece, the base a six-foot wooden pole, the top littered with, well, hanging junk—much of which swung in the breeze with muted clangs. Farther on, a large desert tree, the most substantial I'd seen, shaded an old silver Airstream trailer decorated with several latex paint portraits. An older couple, unruly gray hair lifting with the hot air blowing through, eyeballed me with noncommittal stares. They sat around a wooden industrial reel on its side, repurposed as a table. The tabletop held a bong, a pack of smokes, and a half-dozen beer cans. They had consumed the beers warm, if not borderline hot.

I took a small track, which angled back toward Marcus's main trail on my left and captured movement between us two, headed toward Marcus. It fit. The three hadn't clustered but hadn't separated too far, either. I didn't have absolute confirmation with the quick sighting and said so.

"Potential bogey on your right, Marcus. Two o'clock."

"Roger that."

I approached a larger ramshackle structure, the hand-painted sign offering water and coffee and food for sale. Tossed-away bedsheets, knotted together and stretched between the structure and a nearby tree, offered shade. A single young woman sat there in a used-to-be white sleeveless undershirt, holding a squirming puppy. Two shots rang out, almost concurrent. My heart pounded, the gunfight's outcome unclear.

"Status?" I asked.

"Number two down" filled my ear, loud and clear.

Relief washed. This was my fight, and the thought of Marcus catching a bullet topped the list of things that would devastate me. As for Bo, who had provided no radio input, I held less concern. He would have stalked his quarry with predator efficiency. No gunfire from his direction meant little. Along with his pistol, he carried his Bundeswehr combat knife.

"Hey. We're trying to run a business, here."

A thirtyish white woman with hair in dust-filled dreadlocks and dressed only in torn bib overalls had appeared behind the younger woman and puppy, hands on the younger woman's shoulders. A fiery glare accompanied her statement. Combined with all-encompassing blue tats, including her face, and enough facial hardware to open a store, the admonition fit this time and place. Nothing about what the hell was happening or what's up with the shooting. A simple reprimand that our activities encroached on her life. I offered no acknowledgment and moved on.

More trailers and shacks, more junk art—one piece sat isolated in a dusty clearing and presented four upright humanlike legs planted in the ground, painted bright fluorescent-blue. They stood at least six feet tall, heels toward the sky. I continued angling toward Marcus, the heat oppressive, the air filled with the aroma of acrid dusty grit and, when passed, hand-dug outhouses. A dog barked in the distance.

Another shot blasted up ahead. It wasn't Marcus's weapon, the sound signature different. A second blast followed, then a third. I dropped all stealth and three-sixty focus and sprinted like a madman toward the sound, praying. Crashed through waist-high brittle brush and caught the sight of Marcus, his .45 in a two-handed grip, striding forward as a fourth bullet kicked up dust at his feet, ignoring the pistol shots aimed his way. I didn't, and continued a mad dash, slamming through a series of wooden art pieces that blocked my way. Rounding a tilted tumbledown trailer's corner, I located the source—three scraggly trees separated by packed-in desert brush. Hidden inside, the shooter, forty yards away. I began firing blind before slowing and sent hot lead into the vegetative jumble to draw his fire my way. It worked.

A bullet bee-buzzed past my head as I decelerated to a fast walk, still shooting. A deafening blast from my left signaled Marcus had added hot .45 hollow-points to the fray. We both strode forward, pistols booming, the target still unseen. I ejected an empty magazine and slammed a new one home without slowing forward movement, and continued blasting. I heard a fresh .45 magazine slam home on my left, followed with more Marcus trigger pulls. At twenty yards, the shooter's return fire stopped. Ours didn't. A few more strides, and the killer broke through the vegetation's back end, crawling on his belly, one leg limp and useless. There was another wound in his side, the blood bright against a now dusty white shirt. I stopped and took careful aim.

"In my sights, Marcus."

He ceased firing. I sent two more into the man's torso. He went limp; I advanced, still sighting on his body. At seven paces, I halted and put a round in his head. Just to be sure. Marcus approached from my rear. The surrounding area remained quiet—no screams or calls or frantic activity. Only silent stillness.

"Dammit, Marcus. You can't pull that crap anymore."

A Zippo lighter's clack answered me.

"You *know* I'm talking about all that western gunslinger bullshit."

I approached the dead man and rifled through his pockets, collecting a wallet, cell phone, and rental car key fob.

"Even some shithead up-close killer like this can get lucky. I swear. What the hell is the matter with you?"

"I wonder how Bo's doing?"

"I wonder why I don't get a heart attack watching you pull that off. What the hell, Marcus?"

Bo, lighthearted, came through our voice-activated ear radios.

"From the lively and adjective-laden conversation I'm hearing, I'll assume number three on your end has ceased to walk among us."

"Roger that," I said. "And I almost joined him because of heart failure. Marcus still thinks he's bulletproof."

"Speaking of gunfire," Bo said, "we may have entered a rip, a tear, in time and space. From where I'm standing, the Tet Offensive just took place in your area."

"What's your status, Bo?" Marcus asked.

"And on a side note, you both should be aware shooting classes are available at your local gun range."

"Status," Marcus growled.

"Mine has been resting peacefully for some time, now. Do you gentlemen require more bullets? I have plenty."

"We assemble back at the vehicle. Now."

"Another viable option for you both is a good optometrist."

"Get your butt back to the vehicles. Case and I will head that way."

"Negatory, steadfast leader. I'm on a quest."

I cut my hand through the air sideways at Marcus, emphasizing what he already knew. Bo was moving about, being Bo.

A brisk walking pace put us back at the SUV in short order. As we passed individuals and clustered Slab City residents, they observed us with nonchalance, perhaps glad we were exiting.

"We've got a body disposal issue," Marcus said as we walked, small dust clouds puffing up with each step.

"You think? And spent brass scattered about like Easter candy."

"I wouldn't sweat the brass. They'll be part of an art piece by sundown."

"I don't like this, Marcus. We're in the States, and we just hand-delivered four dead men, with witnesses out the wazoo."

"*You* don't like this? Really? Not to be redundant, but there are less strange places on other planets."

"Did you snatch your first guy's wallet, phone, and weapon?"

"Roger that."

"Hey, Bo," I said, and waited for a response.

"It is I."

"Did you grab…?"

"Done and done, my vision-challenged goober. Allow me tranquility. The trail is real and evident and filled to the brim with possibilities."

That was the one bit of good news within this entire freakin' mess.

Chapter 23

At the vehicle, Gilgar the shaman stood as we'd left him. He may have been asleep on his feet. Hard to say. As we approached, Marcus addressed him.

"We have an issue we could use some help with," he said.

Gilgar opened one eye.

"There are four dead men. Any thoughts on what we might do with their bodies?"

Marcus wasn't one to beat around the bush, a tactic well-suited for the current environment.

"We'll pay," I added. "You get five hundred as the organizer, five hundred per person for those that help."

The old shaman, both eyes open, straightened, inspected the bowl of his two-foot-long pipe, and fired it with a disposable lighter.

"My material needs," he said between puffs, "are few. Consider that word. Few. It has an Asiatic ring. But I am not a linguist."

"There must be some needs the money could help you with," I said.

"Yes. Needs." He puffed, staring at the ground. Marcus glared at me. Gilgar continued. "Jug water, certainly. This is an arid locale."

"We noticed," Marcus said, now squinting at the sky and shaking his head.

"Tobacco and herbs. Yes," the shaman continued. "And beans. Pinto, kidney, black, navy. Yes."

"What might the plan be?" I asked. "We need to get moving on this, Gilgar."

He smiled and pointed the pipe's mouthpiece toward me.

"Annie's old latrine. Yes. Her new one, after an appropriate ceremony, is ready. Deep and prepared."

"Sounds great. How deep is the old one?"

"How many bodies?"

"Four."

"This should not be an issue. A closing ceremony would also be appropriate."

"That's swell. There's five hundred in it for Annie. Can you get help? We need to move on this now, Gilgar. Right now."

He nodded and performed a sedate turn until he saw a young man shuffling past, shirt open, hair disheveled. Another tweaker. Gilgar waved him down; they approached each other and held a brief conversation. The tweaker glanced our way often, nodded at Gilgar's plan, and took off. Marcus and I deposited the dead men's documents and weapons in our SUV, and Gilgar signaled us to follow.

"Well," Marcus said. "At least he's found some quality labor."

"Limited choices."

"You're up to speed on this type of thing. What does an outhouse closing ceremony look like? Do we need to grab some incense? Eye of newt? Or should I ask Bo?"

I didn't respond, nor did Bo, who was ferreting about for the mysterious Red. Fifteen minutes later, moving at a snail's pace, we made Annie's location. She'd used stolen bales of hay and old tires as prime building material, the roof recovered tin. Multiple cords and strings emanated from the structure, seven or eight feet in the air and tied off at the surrounding brush, festooned with bits of bright cloth. They lifted with the scorching breeze. Annie failed to appear, although an older woman peeked out the doorway, once, before disappearing back inside. Gilgar joined her, exited, and

180

approached us. Annie wanted cash up front. Not a problem. I handed him five Benjamins for Annie, five for himself. I held back on labor payments until job completion.

A three-sided structure covered the new latrine hole, large mounds of fresh dirt piled around it. The old latrine, now an open hole, displayed hard-packed dirt and sand surrounding its opening. I wandered over and had a look. The bottom wasn't visible, a good thing from many aspects, and it would hold four bodies, no problem. The smell, which hit me during the inspection, would knock a buzzard off a gut wagon.

Our tweaker had recruited a friend, and they, moving fast, approached us dragging an orange tarp wrapped around what was clearly a body. They halted near the latrine hole and rolled the killer's body onto the ground, facedown. A single stab wound to his back had done the trick. A Bo signature move.

"So, like, there's three more, right?" a tweaker asked. "And we get five hundred each, right?"

"Right. When you finish the job," I said and began describing the other three locations.

He cut me off and said, "Yeah. We know. It's not like it's a big secret. Five hundred, right?"

"Right."

They dragged the dead man onto the latrine hole's lip and slid him in. The shaman, arms extended and face toward the sky, mumbled unintelligible words. Thirty minutes later, the fourth and final killer slid into his final resting place.

"Okay, five hundred each," the same tweaker said.

"The job's not done. Fill in the hole."

"Look, man."

He stopped speaking as I pulled twelve Benjamins and displayed them.

"An extra hundred each if you two fill that hole in ten minutes."

They got after it, grabbing two shovels from the fresh dirt piles around Annie's new bathroom facilities. It must have hit well over a hundred degrees, the breeze akin to a hot blow-dryer, but meth is a helluva drug and they worked their asses off. The result—a smooth bare dirt patch, unrecognizable from thousands of other bare dirt patches. I paid the labor, they took off to find more drugs, and I thanked the shaman. He bowed low and remained in that position. I turned to Marcus, who'd stood stock-still the entire procedure, one hand on his holstered .45, the other holding a cigar. I began decompressing from the firefight and burial stress. They'd asked for it. Taken a gig with murder stamped on it, plain and simple. Their ignoble burial didn't bother me. Taking life did, but weighed against either them or me, or Marcus and Bo, I halfway sloughed off the act. But still. More death. More disposed bodies.

"Well, that's that," I said.

We both headed back for the parked SUV.

"I'll admit it went better than imagined," he said. "Now, let's focus on the mission. Then get the hell out of here."

"Bo's on it, so we have that working for us."

"Yes, we have Bo. If you're suggesting we let him bird-dog this effort, you'll hear no argument from me. I wouldn't relish conversing with the neighbors."

The two SUVs stood out like sore thumbs within Slab City, but nothing we could do about that. I spoke, directed at Bo.

"Where are you, bud?" I asked.

"East Jesus."

"Which is where?"

"West of you."

"Of course it is," Marcus said.

"Alright, we're headed that way."

"Seek and ye shall find. I'll remove this device from my ear, but fear not. We shall connect before long."

I handed my ear radio over to Marcus who pocketed his as well.

"Let's drive," he said. "In the AC."

We did, and rolled west past more of the same. Marcus and I viewed, and felt, an Alice in Wonderland vibe, observing through our private tinted looking glass.

"I don't even know what to say, Case."

"I know. Weird."

"I meant the last hour. Think about it."

"I'm trying not to."

Marcus wasn't deterred. His perspective required airing out.

"Four hired killers, Bulgarian killers, followed us into a lawless Sonoran Desert enclave."

"Yep."

"A place filled, and I mean *filled*, with wingnuts, druggies, psychos, and, I guess, run-of-the-mill hermits."

"Yep."

"Plus at least one shaman. A geographic location where we performed some hallucinatory version of the OK Corral shootout."

"Seems that way."

"Where not a single resident gave two shits."

"Roger that."

"Then, with the local shaman's help, we recruited meth heads to drag carcasses through the neighborhood."

"Yep."

"And dumped said carcasses down a retired latrine."

"Pretty much covers it, bud."

He cracked his window and lit a cigar. Hot air blew in; I cranked up the AC.

"I can tell you view this as just another day at the office, son. I don't see it that way."

"I would have bet on that."

"And now we're looking for the East Jesus section of town as per Bo Dickerson."

"We are."

"Where we hope to find a person or persons who invented blockchain technology so they can track a Bitcoin transaction in the country of Jordan."

"Pretty good synopsis for a rapidly graying rancher."

"Thanks. I suppose I'm seeking confirmation this all really happened, and you didn't slip acid into my Bombay Beach coffee."

A half-mile later as we slow-maneuvered across deep-rutted desert tracks, I stopped and rolled down my window as a young woman approached. More heat poured into the vehicle.

"East Jesus?" I asked her.

Wearing an angelic smile, she turned and unfurled an arm westward.

"It is not far."

It wasn't. A tall wall of old TVs stood near an arched art entrance. Each TV displayed a hand-painted comment on poster board. Cheap plastic chairs stood sentinel, facing the TVs. The entrance arch, in metal, consisted of rusted wheels and junkyard artifacts. Near it, a large hand-painted sign. We exited the SUV and approached. A distinct feel permeated East Jesus. This Slab City neighborhood appeared less trashy and more organized.

The entrance sign covered a litany of directives under an East Jesus survival guide framework. Enter at your own risk. Why are you here and what do you want? Don't piss us off. If you show up after dark, you are trespassing and will stare down the barrel of a 12-gauge shotgun.

"I can't believe I'm saying this," Marcus said, "but I'm staring at the first thing I've seen here that makes sense."

"The East Jesus HOA states its position with little ambiguity. Shall we?"

We exchanged eye locks, Marcus sighed and shoved his Stetson down, and with tight nods we entered East Jesus under the artwork arch.

THE DC JOB

Chapter 24

It was an artists' dominion. Several trailers, well-kept, displayed professional-grade portraits painted along one side. The standing artwork, still produced from junk, at least held some personal appeal. Well, most did. There were pieces that defied, in my book, classification as art. Even so, the place was neater, more organized, with much less garbage strewn about. A dozen men and women worked on individual art projects. None gave us more than a cursory glance. It was apparent they didn't view us as a threat, no 12-gauge required. Clearly, they weren't up to speed on recent events.

"What do we look for?" Marcus asked. "Besides Bo, who might be inside a trailer talking Nietzsche with an artist or two."

"I'm working on it."

I scanned the well-built shacks and better-maintained trailers as we meandered. East Jesus had a semi-defined border, marked with larger artwork. A long wall built with mud and horizontal wine and liquor bottles acted as one marker. A pole line with streamers strung between them marked another. We passed a wrecked vehicle covered with glued-on plastic and metal bits, along with a human skull array, also in plastic. A fifteen-foot-long lizard, six feet tall, created from metal and papier-mâché and paint. Past the lizard, I halted.

"That's what we look for," I said and pointed toward a silver Airstream trailer mounted flush on a slab. The trailer was in solid condition, its roof covered with solar panels. Someone had arrayed two dozen large panels behind it. Solar panels weren't uncommon throughout Slab City, but this trailer had them in spades. What caught my attention most were three satellite antennae among the rooftop panels—two dome varieties and one dish type. Internet connectivity.

As we angled toward the trailer, a sizeable cloth awning that extended from the trailer's entrance side showed. It was supported with sturdy metal poles, a different and decent-sized fantasy creature perched on each pole's top. From our distance, it appeared they were created from duct tape. Lots of duct tape.

Bo came into sight first. He sat under the sunshade farthest from the trailer. His wild red hair lifted in sync with the cotton awning as the breeze blew. As we approached, another figure came into view. She sat in a rocking chair near the trailer's door and chatted with Bo, smiling. Nestled against the trailer's corner stood a small nativity scene, the figures created, at least the outer layer, from duct tape. Bo acknowledged our entrance.

"Red, these are my friends. Case and Marcus. Marcus is the good-looking one."

"Hi, Marcus."

"Ma'am."

"Nice hat."

"Thanks. Nice crèche."

"Thanks."

She turned toward me. A woman in her late thirties with a tight red afro, broad facial and body features, and freckles from stem to stern. She wore brown Carhartt work pants cut off at the knees, sandals made from an old tire, and a navy T-shirt imprinted with several fantasy dragons.

"You folks get out of the sun," she said with a pleasant smile. "So, you are Case Lee, a seeker of lost girls."

"Hi, Red. One girl, actually."

We shifted into the shade. I sat rock-solid on the incredulous side of facing *the* blockchain technology guru. It wasn't Red herself—she halfway fit. But the outlandish setting threw me. Here? Really?

"Why don't you fill me in on the details. Bo and I have touched on the subject, although other topics have gripped our interest as well."

"Red is a fellow sojourner," Bo said. "She owns a tight relationship with the cosmic breezes."

I avoided glancing at Marcus, which might have prompted a skeptical response from our team's senior member. Instead, I took in the immediate and captured details.

"Well, in some ways it's simple."

"Simple is good," Red said. "Simple is elegant."

"In other ways, it's a mess."

"Life is a mess."

She continued to smile. I returned the same. Nearby, two mini-refrigeration units hummed, tucked against the trailer. Small ACs. The trailer's door stood open, so Red wouldn't waste energy and cool the upstairs. Nossir. That cool air flowed elsewhere: the slab's basement, the entrance hidden by the trailer. Underground would be much cooler, but with an efficient AC system, it would be downright chilly. A requirement for computer servers.

I hesitated, unsure of how much to reveal. There was the Krystyna facet as a stand-alone issue. Then there was the whole kit and caboodle with conspiracies, political infighting, and state-sanctioned killers. I started small and tight.

"A client contracted me to find a diplomat's daughter. A Polish diplomat. Some men abducted the kid at Petra, in Jordan."

"That place is in an *Indiana Jones* movie, isn't it?" she asked. "I love those movies."

"Yeah, that's the place. Anyway, it's not a kidnapping, at least in the traditional sense. No ransom demands."

"Taken and killed? Life can be so brutal, can't it?"

189

"It can. But my gut says she's still alive. For what purpose, I can't get a grip on."

Past her head, a small plywood piece was wire-tied against a sunshade pole. Hand-painted with fluorescent white, it read: *Colour is Relative*. The British spelling of *color*. Red's voice was midwestern US flat.

"Bo insinuated a possible transactional trail is all you have at the moment."

"Pretty much. A friend explained that numerous dark transactions, deep web transactions, take place using cryptocurrency."

"So are millions of legitimate transactions," Red said, a touch defensive. "Us humans, at least a certain type, will always twist positive developments. They drag enhanced technologies kicking and screaming into dark abysses. I can't help that."

She couldn't help that. I raised my head and stared at the rippling shade cloth. It couldn't be. Yeah, Hoolie had sent me in this direction on rumors and deep internet scuttlebutt. But still.

"What be ye staring at?" Bo asked me.

"Cosmic breezes."

It took several seconds for reality to sink in and swab away the deep mental incredulity. Here, in this of all places, sat Satoshi Nakamoto—blockchain technology's inventor, Bitcoin's founder, multibillionaire, and duct tape artist. My last shot at finding Krystyna. My *only* shot.

I dumped the entire affair on her. The Guardians, the overall grand conspiracy for controlling internet information, political and spook warfare, hired killers intent on removing me from the equation—the whole enchilada. Why not? Nothing to lose, everything to gain.

Red waited until I'd finished, then asked, "Would anyone like water or tea?"

"Tea would be marvelous," Bo said.

"Peach or jasmine?"

Bo rubbed his chin.

"Peach. It would reflect well on our intrepid hero."

Red, sandals slapping, disappeared inside the trailer and closed the door. If the intent was cool tea, she headed downstairs for it.

"What do you think?" Marcus asked.

"I think I could kiss Bo."

"Other than that."

"I think Red is my only hope. It's come to this, the here and now. I've got no other cards to play."

"You've been dealt a few aces," Bo said. "Allow the game to marinate. Accept the universe's gifts. And chill, compadre. Chill."

Marcus fired a cigar and remained quiet, but did point a finger toward Red's trailer and raised one questioning eyebrow.

"Yeah," I said. "I think so."

"Unbelievable," he muttered, an acknowledgment that the enigmatic and long-lost Satoshi Nakamoto prepared us tea.

Red returned toting a large jug filled with ice and tea along with four glasses insulated with duct tape. Heaven knows what she had in the basement, or the size of her basement tech center, for that matter.

"Sit, sit," she said, lifting a chin at a bench pressed against her Airstream. Marcus and I did so while she poured the tea, rubbed Bo's head, and sat back in her rocking chair. The tea tasted peach-sweet and cold and perfect for the sizzling temperature.

"It's as if the desert breeze has blown an interesting tale my way," she said. "Can I talk a bit about the grand conspiracy you've laid out, Case?"

"Please do."

"I don't wish to sound pedantic, but digital information travels and flows. It just does. Think about it as existing in a gaseous state. Once released, recapturing it is nigh impossible. Oh, silly people will try, I know. But the genie has left the bottle and isn't returning."

"Good to know. I mean it."

She gulped tea, emitted an "Ahh," and continued.

"The clash between the political class and clandestine organizations fascinates me. Is this a regular occurrence?"

Brief concerns flashed, then dismissed. Satoshi Nakamoto, or Red, or whatever her actual name was, represented a potent force. A power backed with bleeding-edge technology and billions of dollars. What she considered acting upon with my spilled beans should have given pause. But the world at large was messed up, and the tiny subset of politicians and diplomats and spooks within that world—a subset often filled with not very bright people— messed things up even more. If Red held any thoughts about wading into that arena and stirring the pot, well, go for it.

"We, the three of us, have all experienced it back in our military days. But we're no experts, by a long shot. The button-pushing behind the scenes wasn't our concern. Since then, I still run into it. But again, not my concern. I try and maintain a narrow scope for my jobs. With this one, find the kid. Find Krystyna. I'm a simple guy and try to keep things simple."

"But it happens often?"

"Yeah. As I've learned from smarter people than me, these organizations, of whatever stripe, act as living organisms. Self-protection tops their concerns list. Power expansion comes in a close second."

"But their actions remain tempered so no harm comes to their home nation."

"I wish I could say so, Red. Maybe most of the time. Maybe. As you said, life is a mess."

She smiled and sipped tea. I downed mine. The last hour had drained me in more ways than one.

"I'll take a leap of faith," she said, "and assume the entire professional assassin thing is another regular occurrence."

"Not through my choice, believe me. But it happens, yeah."

"Then why do you continue doing what you do?"

"An excellent question," Marcus said.

"People hire our Georgia peach for what appear, on the surface, as straightforward jobs," Bo said. "because he's a straightforward guy and lacks universal spatial acceptance." Bo grinned my way. "But we love him and his simple ways, and love each other, and when any of us comes into harm's way, we gather as one."

"Deep concern from dear friends. I like that."

"Look, Red. I'm no thrill-seeker, and I'm sure no superhero. The killers who enter the fray are side-noise, hindrances, for the prime mission. In this case, Krystyna Kaminski."

"Why are you so committed to finding her?"

She and I locked eyes for several seconds.

"Because I said I would."

She flashed bright teeth surrounded with freckles, eyes crinkled, her smile heartfelt. She took a long sip of tea, pursed her lips, and threw me a lifeline.

"Blockchain was designed as the most secure transactional system in the world," she said, matter-of-fact. "It is the technology cryptocurrencies use. Such as Bitcoin."

"That's what I've been told."

"If there *was* a backdoor crack"—she paused and scratched a freckled calf—"it would provide limited information."

"Which beats anything I've got now."

"No individuals, no institutions like banks, no specific locations." She paused and cocked her head. "Regional identification only. A geographic swath. Perhaps as finite as a country. Perhaps not."

"Country location would be a godsend."

"Hmm."

"Our intrepid scout, unleashed onto alien turf, the quest clean and pure," Bo said. "A brave knight, rough and rusty around the edges, but undaunted and stalwart of heart."

"It brings me no pleasure stating this," Marcus said, "but Case is damn good at what he does."

Red drained her glass, an internal decision made.

"Do you have encrypted communications?" she asked.

"256-bit."

"Why don't you give me your number? Who knows what might appear within the ozone?"

I did. We rose while she remained sitting.

"I can't thank you enough, Red. Honest to goodness, I'm swirling the drain. Anything you can do comes with a truckload of heartfelt gratitude from me."

"I understand. It has been a pleasure. Bo, stay in touch. I do stray from East Jesus occasionally. Perhaps I'll venture in your direction someday."

As we left the awning's shade, I paused and dug into a pocket.

"Oh. There's a black SUV parked out there. The rental company will come for it in a few days, using the vehicle's GPS. But until then, it's available."

"Ah. There are several items I should pick up in LA. Thank you."

No doubt high-tech supplies and buried-deep technology, provisioned outside normal vendor channels. Fine by me. I tossed her the fob for the killers' SUV. She caught it. And returned a wink.

Chapter 25

We rolled from Slab City as the SUV swayed along the deep ruts, and the denizens cast an occasional unconcerned glance. We stopped at Salvation Mountain where tourists parked their vehicles. The day baked, and the mountain with its bright colors stood in stark contrast against the arid environment. Near the pathway that led into and up the structure was a three-sided shed where two young women, Slab City residents, sat and played with two kittens. A brochure was available, and Marcus picked one up.

A lifework from a fellow named Leonard Knight, twenty-eight years in the making. He'd constructed it with hay bales and adobe and discarded tires and discarded windows and automobile parts and fallen desert trees. And half a million gallons of latex paint. The painted color patchwork covered the entire structure, the palette determined by whatever paint was donated on any particular week. Leonard kept with a biblical theme throughout, the message clear and based on "God is love." As for transgressions, we three may have toted a fair amount onto the premises.

We wandered inside the mountain, then ascended the outside painted path toward the top. If there was such a thing as a folk-art masterpiece for laypeople like us, this was it. Even Marcus was bowled over.

"Twenty-eight years. That's commitment and mission focus," he said, eyeballing the artist's handiwork. "An admirable effort."

"There's a unique energy here," Bo said. "Ancient and new, grounded and spectral."

"I'm agreeing with you more and more, Bo," Marcus said. "It worries me some."

"Cast your worries on something higher."

We had a bird's-eye view of Slab City and a distant peek at the Salton Sea. We stood silent for several minutes. The road ended here unless further intel came my way. I thought about the upcoming call with Jakub Kaminski. The conversation would entail a nebulous final lead, hope slim. I felt drained, empty.

"Where's your head, goober?"

"Feeling semi-worthless, with a sprinkle of bizarre hope."

"Don't start," Marcus said. "You slide into the blues too easy."

"Yeah, well, it's a well-greased slide." I laid a hand on their shoulders. "I can't tell you what it means having you two here. Help with the hitters, sure, and you, Bo, ferreting out Red. Remarkable stuff. But there's a lot more to it than that."

"It's the bond, my brother," Bo said and placed a hand on mine and squeezed.

"There I go again. Agreeing with Bo."

We stood quiet for another minute. The hot breeze blew Bo's hair around, several tourists joined us, took in the view, and left.

"Slab City," Marcus said. His Zippo, windproof, clacked open and fired a cigar. "Hollywood couldn't make that place up."

"Can't say I'll miss it. But from a larger perspective, it's the type of place Red would hide out." I rubbed my head and let out a big exhale. "Man, that was unreal running into her."

"As real as it gets, my main street amigo. People with lofty means might try to hide from everyone, but end up among others of lofty means. You gotta go mundane."

"Slab City is way, way down the mundane totem pole, bud."

"Still, prime turf for escape."

"The duct tape art threw me," Marcus said, "but I liked her."

"Me, too. Down to earth, unpretentious."

"And makes an excellent glass of iced tea," Bo added. "Although I'm unclear on her other culinary arts."

"You think she'll come through?" Marcus asked and then addressed two tourists with the temerity to tell him the mountain was a no-smoking area. "Don't worry. I have special permission. From Leonard."

"Leonard is dead," one said.

"Exactly."

They exited the mountaintop under Marcus's glare. He continued.

"I sensed the backdoor crack she mentioned is genuine enough."

"Yeah. Me too. The caveats about geographic scale bothered me, making any intel she provides a wobbly nail to hang a hat on. But better than nothing."

"Wobbly contains potential, goober."

"I can't tell that to Jakub and Anna Kaminski."

"You can explain that the trail, while amorphous, exists. Because it does. How fruitful the path, well beyond our abilities. Your new bird dog has mad skills, my brother. Mad skills. Allow her to work the fields. And this fretting you commit to, without cease, is tiresome."

He had a point. But in the non-Bo world, linear time existed, and the clock continued ticking. And with each tick, my odds of success lowered. I delivered a heavy sigh.

"You're not working through the dead body thing again, are you?" Marcus asked.

"No. But now that you mention it, there's no shortage of those."

"Murderers, son. They came after us. They came after *you*."

"Yeah, I suppose. Still."

"Let's get off this adobe mountain and hit the road," Marcus said. "Mission accomplished; further success is far removed from our hands."

"Sound advice," Bo said. "Movement, not static reflection, is the immediate order. Now, cow whisperer, instead of you scratching your side, a key dry-skin indicator and expected in the current environs, you should try a special body butter well-hidden in my rucksack."

"No, thanks."

Bo was a body care aficionado, another affectation that made Bo who he was.

"It contains jojoba and other essential oils."

"No, thanks."

"And sufficient rose oil for an alluring scent."

"Let's vamoose," Marcus said. "Time to hit the road."

Marcus, Bo, and I each stuffed a Benjamin into the Salvation Mountain donation box—made from quarter-inch steel, welded to a thick metal pole, and sunk into deep concrete. The box displayed a professional-grade padlock. Its construction stood as a simple reminder we stood near Slab City. Marcus drove as a logistical phone call or two topped my near-term agenda.

"Bo," Marcus said, "dig in my rucksack, a side pocket, and find the flask of bourbon."

He did and passed it forward, then availed himself to a bowl of weed. Marcus took a small sip. I swallowed a hefty slug. On standby for Red—a simple and singular tactic. I'd wait and hope and, at some point, call it quits. Man, I hated the thought. Admit defeat and let the Kaminski parents know their daughter remained lost in the abyss. How long to wait? I didn't know. A day or two? Longer?

First, I called Mossad. They owed me. Aubrey's number rang a dozen times, never cutting over to voice mail. So much for that. They had relegated me to bit-player status. Pinging Jules was another option. But she would have contacted me if her intel spiderweb had tingled. Same with Marilyn Townsend. Well, not the same, but I wasn't prepared for acceptance as a second-class asset from her.

With minimum enthusiasm, I called Jakub Kaminski. I explained a thin, thin trail still existed and that I'd give it a few more days.

"You cannot quit," he said. "I have received nothing from the clandestine world. I have asked both your CIA and Mossad for information, twice now, since I revealed everything."

"Yeah, Jakub, that turned out a futile effort. I'm sorry."

"There is nothing for you to be sorry about. At least you are trying. You appear as the *only* person trying. You cannot quit, Mr. Lee."

I committed to several more days and signed off, knowing full well I'd committed to nothing more than sitting on my hands.

"You finished with tactical calls?" Marcus asked as Bo spoke softly on his phone from the back seat.

"Yeah." I downed another slug of bourbon. "Finished."

"Don't bother with flight plans for me," Marcus said.

"Why? You hitchhiking?"

"I'll rent a vehicle in Palm Springs and drive."

"That's at least a twenty-hour drive."

"A bit more. I'll take back roads and make it a three or four-day trip."

Marcus Johnson was a man of the West, and folks with big sky and empty asphalt in their veins found long, isolated drives all upside. I got it.

"You sure? I'm happy to charter your aging rear end a jet."

"There are several spots 1 haven't seen in a while. I'll scoot through Utah, check out Bryce and the Wasatch Range again. Then up into Idaho, making sure the Tetons haven't moved."

Simple travel plans helped lift me—grounded, real, doable. His and Bo's uncomplicated presence lifted me as well.

"I hear they're prone to do that."

"I may cut through Yellowstone. The tourists have thinned out now. Rent some kit and go fly-fishing. There's something about casting dry flies on the Madison as a buffalo herd crosses downstream."

"About as good as it gets."

"Roger that. As good as it gets."

I'd head for Charleston and family and the *Ace of Spades*. Thoughts about hanging it up—the whole wild and wooly contractor thing—squatted like an ogre on my life path. Maybe it was time.

"I, on the other hand, would appreciate an Albuquerque aerial whisking," Bo said, finished with his phone call. "JJ has asked how my visitation with Uncle Richard and ML worked out. She also requested information about the activities of one Mr. Case Lee as it relates to my well-buttered hide. Enquiring minds, don't you know."

"What'd you tell her?"

"The truth. Albeit from a high perspective."

"How'd that work out?"

"Her prime concern, as I understand it, is whether she'll get fired from the FBI if she shoots you."

"A legitimate career-path consideration."

"Fear not, my rugged and angst-filled compadre. Our quest has been noble, a potent salve for her disquiet. Plus, you can drop me off and stomp the accelerator. A jet during takeoff makes for an iffy target."

I arranged an afternoon charter for Bo and me. Once we were airborne, I'd contact Mom and let her know I'd drop in but spend the night on the *Ace*. She'd stuff me with food and concern and love. I could use the last one now.

As we approached the interstate highway, I asked Marcus to pull over near an agriculture field. I deposited the hitters' four cell phones and their Bulgarian documentation inside a thick weed patch alongside an irrigation canal. I'd made the mistake of leaving expired combatants' cell phones, their GPS likely activated, on China Jim mountain during a Nevada job. I left these phones on as well, with purpose. Whoever organized the Slab City hitters' parade could track their latest round of killers, minus the killers, alongside a farm road near Palm Springs. They could scratch their heads and figure that one out.

At the airport, I gave Marcus my SUV for turn-in at Billings, Montana. Not included with the rental agreement, they'd be pissed and charge out the wazoo. Fine—a reimbursable expense. My Zurich client never complained.

"Keep me informed," he said as Bo and I bailed at the private air terminal. "I have a vested interest in the outcome."

"Will do, bud. Thanks again."

We shook, and he pulled me close.

"Heed the late great Yogi Berra's words. It ain't over till it's over. So chin up, son. If you get word—and I don't doubt it will point toward some godforsaken part of the world—I know you'll do the right thing. Saddle up and deal with it."

I missed him before he blended into traffic. The charter jet made an uneventful stop in Albuquerque. JJ wasn't around. Bo and I hugged, twisting, and exchanged a few false punches.

"Are you up on your Dostoevsky?" he asked.

"Afraid not."

"To live without hope is to cease to live."

"Did old Fyodor have a timeline for this hope? Because the sand is about empty in the hourglass."

"He did. Perpetuity."

"We'll see."

"Be grateful, be of good spirits, have faith."

"Who said that?"

"Bo Dickerson. Love you, bud."

"Love you too, Bo."

Acknowledgment that two such friends blessed me beyond any expectations lifted my spirits and draped me with comfort.

Chapter 26

Mom pulled out all the stops for supper. Chicken and dumplings, green beans simmered with fatback, buttermilk biscuits, mud pie. I provided two bottles of Prosecco Extra Dry, served over Mom's disapproval, which vanished once we'd coerced her into having a small glass. Peter and I winked, and even CC received a small amount. We ate on the screened-in back porch with Tinker Juarez in backyard exile. He stood at the screen door and stared with white-hot intensity. It was dark, my arrival late, and fireflies blinked in the yard as shadowy Spanish moss, hanging from the old oak tree, swung with the faint breeze.

"It is *so* good having you back," Mom said. "I hope you plan on staying a spell before taking off on your next contract."

"Well, I'm still on this job, waiting."

"What type of job is it?" Peter asked.

He allowed for a vague answer, knowing, or at least suspecting, my engagement types.

"It's pretty cut-and-dried. Find a girl who went missing in the Middle East."

"Now, when you say the Middle East, where are you talking about?" Mom asked.

"Jordan."

"As in the River Jordan?"

"One and the same."

"Did you stop at Jerusalem?" she asked.

"Didn't have time." Or an option, as Mossad had been plenty clear on my approved route. "But I was where Moses saw the Land of Milk and

Honey. And visited a place called Petra, where Moses struck the rock and a spring flowed. It still does."

Mom and Peter both enquired in great detail about the biblical landmarks. The tales enraptured CC as well.

"You know, Mary Lola, we could visit those places, along with Jerusalem. People do it all the time," Peter said, serving first Mom, then CC, then himself more chicken and dumplings. I'd scarfed mine down, but refused seconds, having eaten more than my fair share of the beans and buttermilk biscuits.

"Where they snatch young girls away and take them God-knows-where? I would love to visit, but heaven knows where we'd end up. No, thank you." She turned my way. "The poor thing vanished into thin air? Good Lord."

"It's been pretty frustrating. There was a lead in California. Marcus and Bo joined me and helped out."

Mentioning my two friends provided an off-ramp from job details, and Mom took it, asking at length about both. She wrapped up with a relationship question, her forte.

"I have a hard time seeing Marcus and Bo work together. When y'all were in the military, well, that's one thing. But now, they are hardly two peas in a pod."

"Opposite ends of the stick, for sure. But it works, I think, because of mutual respect."

Mom also expressed amazement that JJ still put up with Bo, and that Marcus, working Montana's wild lands, still hadn't been eaten by bears.

"Does my wild child still drag a donkey through those New Mexico mountains?" she asked.

"He has been, but Jezebel isn't feeling well, so Bo's on standby status with the gold prospecting."

"Jezebel?" she asked.

"His donkey."

Mom shook her head.

"Let him know I haven't given up on him. He's in my prayers every day. So is his well-employed lady friend, who must be a remarkable person putting up with a man who drags donkeys around. Jezebel. I swear."

"What I'm hearing is you're on standby status as well," Peter said. "How long do you think that will last?"

"Sixty-four-dollar question, Peter. At some point, I'll have to throw up my hands unless the California lead delivers."

The conversation settled into talk of friends and neighbors and births and deaths and marriages. Peter weaved a great and funny tale from his insurance days. The wandering topics were real and present and filled with humanity. I reveled in it. The customary pause before dessert arrived, so Peter and I cleared Mom's fine china and hand-washed them. CC let Tinker in then joined me in the kitchen where we exchanged donkey calls, laughing and giggling. Even Peter brayed once or twice.

The mud pie was excellent, CC went off to bed, and Peter headed home. Mom and I sat on the porch, the neighborhood still and quiet as the light breeze from the Atlantic added an early autumn tang.

"I'll pray for that girl," Mom said. "And ask why you're so down about the entire affair."

"I'm the parents' only shot at finding her. They're counting on me, and I'm failing."

"Do you believe the child is still alive?"

"I do."

"What a horrible thing for a parent. The not knowing."

"I can't imagine. I'm running out of time, Mom, and further search is liable to be for her remains."

"There are some things that some people might consider worse than death," she said, her voice soft and pain-filled. "I won't think about those things. But I know my son." She laid a gentle hand on mine. "There's not an ounce of quit in you, honey. This hasn't always been a good thing, and it has worn on me from time to time, but if anyone can find her, it's you."

Then Mom entered a place I'd never experienced from her. Driven, I supposed, by visions about an abducted teenage girl lost in a strange part of the world among kidnappers and killers and conspirators.

"When you find her, and you will, be aware you deal with evil." Her unblinking eye lock said it all. "Pure evil. Do not hesitate delivering justice."

With matters such as this, an innocent and family abused, you wouldn't want to mess with Mary Lola Wilson.

Late night found me draped on the *Ace's* foredeck throne, Gray Goose in hand. Charleston lights reflected on the water, the city quiet. A tug and barge exited the Ashley River and crossed Charleston Harbor, the tug's low rumble carrying across the water. I checked again for communications. No messages or emails or calls. I slept belowdecks as the mild breeze tugged the *Ace* against the tie-up lines and dreamed about desert lions and sandstorms and far-off cries.

I performed routine maintenance on the *Ace* the next morning, movements dull and my mental focus lacking for the tasks at hand. The dock owner's office contained a small and limited grocery store, although his fresh sandwiches never disappointed. I spent lunch on the throne with a pastrami on rye and chips and a beer, opening the laptop and checking email again. Nothing, nada. I folded it shut and set it on the deck. Almost as an afterthought, I dug for my phone somewhere among the throne's padding and duct tape. I had a message. Encrypted, there was no identified sender, no hint of who sourced it. Red. Had to be.

Cyprus-Jordan-Mauritania

I shot upright, spilling the beer. The money trail, terminating in the northwest African country of Mauritania, on the Atlantic coast. If Red had stood with me at that moment, I'd have grabbed her and twirled her in a bear hug and delivered wet smacks all over her freckled face. A legit trail, not red-hot, but damn sure warm. It was enough. It was everything.

I'd never mucked about in that African neck of the woods, but had performed ops farther south in the Congo and Angola, so Mauritania wasn't a complete unknown. I remembered it defined backwater, renowned for two things: old rusted ships—freighters and tankers—driven onto the beach as refuse.

And the most active slave trade on the planet.

Chapter 27

Pieces fell together. The old Bedouins outside Petra nodding in agreement when they identified the kidnappers as tajir. The word *tajir*—merchants, shopkeepers, traders. Slave traders. My Arabic wasn't good enough for added nuance and clarity. What a screw-up. Mom's "things worse than death" tied right in. If you wanted to make an example of a person who bucked a geopolitical conspiracy, have his daughter auctioned off as a slave and whisked away into an insular country's interior that not only condoned the practice but also lived it. Several choice photos distributed among certain conspiratorial players as well as the parents would prevent any more defections. It all came together. Oh, man.

Gotta move, gotta kick this into high gear. Flights. Start with flights. Three charter jet calls produced a top-of-the-line Learjet that could get me there with an eight-hour flight time. They asked me whether the destination was Nouakchott, the capital, or Nouadhibou, the other spot in Mauritania that resembled a city. I didn't have a freakin' clue, so told them the capital. I could change the destination later. The jet wouldn't arrive at Charleston until six o'clock. I had six hours' wait time. A quick mental calculation translated into wheels-down at eight in the morning, Mauritania time. Gotta move, the clock was ticking.

I paced the *Ace*'s foredeck. It could still be too late. They may have auctioned off Krystyna already. It didn't matter. Well, it mattered a helluva lot, but I'd located a hunting area, a fresh scent. My blood rose. Tighten your jockstraps, you SOBs. I'm headed your way. If she was already a slave for some tribal head or clan elder or wealthy merchant—either in Nouakchott or Nouadhibou or a smaller village out in the boonies—I'd find her. Yeah, I'd find her and bring her home. And make people pay.

211

Intel. Man, I hurt for intel. Not Red—bless her and her strange ways and her delivered money trail. Cyprus as the starting point for the blockchain money transfers wasn't a red flag. The island state was renowned as a banking haven. Hell, I had an account there. As for on-the-ground intel, I'd start with Jules. I considered the Company, who'd offered help. But the Clubhouse first because Jules had better gritty underworld contacts. Much better. And I trusted her, big time. Townsend not so much, and for sure not the CIA as a whole. I took a deep breath, settled, and shot the Clubhouse a message.

Urgent. Next slave auction—Nouakchott or Nouadhibou or Other? Departing in six hours. Also, fixer?

She'd glom onto the context and meaning in a heartbeat. Then crack the whip and unleash her intel bloodhounds. Time was short. Nothing I could do about that, and I'd left my timeline angst in Clubhouse hands. The fixer was more problematic. Whether Jules had one in Mauritania was an iffy proposition. An isolated and seldom-heard-from country in the Sahara wasn't prime Clubhouse turf. But she'd amazed me more than a few times.

I decided on holding off contact with the world's top spook until I had feedback from the Clubhouse. I'd message her for on-the-ground help once I'd confirmed the destination. There was a US embassy in Nouakchott, and she'd have assets either there or nearby. Senegal bordered on the south. She'd have field operators in the Senegalese capital, Dakar, for sure. If Jules pointed me in the right direction, and her fixer could get me through customs with my weapons, I'd ask the Company for evac possibilities. A long-range chopper or rough-terrain-capable airplane to haul Krystyna and me out of there.

Gotta move. Let's go, people. Flights, check. Intel in progress. Operational framework, unknown. Except for a major parameter—trust. True and tight defined my perspective, trusting no one but Jules from here on out. Everyone else, including Townsend and the Company, were suspect. Either with me or against me, and the solitary individual planted firmly in the "with me" camp worked from an office above a Filipino dry cleaner in Chesapeake, Virginia. I was fine with that.

Calm down, Lee. Tie up a local loose end. Perform research. You've got several hours.

I called Mom and let her know I would take off soon after the girl. I didn't provide a destination, and she didn't enquire.

"I understand. I'm glad to hear the fire back in your voice," Mom said. "Wherever you travel, know that CC and I love you and expect you back healthy and smiling."

"Will do. Love you, too. Kiss CC for me."

Laptop open, I breathed deep, settled down, and focused on Mauritania. Four hundred thousand square miles, ninety-plus percent Saharan desert with sand, arid plains, several mountain ranges, and scattered rock outcroppings throughout. A hard, hard land, and a country almost twice the size of Texas. Four million Mauritanians, most in either the Nouakchott or Nouadhibou areas, both coastal towns. A thin stretch near the Senegal River toward the south held the lion's share of people not in Nouakchott or Nouadhibou. A swath known as the Sahel, where North Africa's endless deserts transitioned south into grassland savannahs. Mauritania's deep interior held few people, most clustered around small villages, isolated and seldom visited.

Arabic was the official language, although with Berber words tossed in the mix, it created a challenging Arabic dialect. French was also widely spoken, as Mauritania and Senegal and many other North and West African countries were former French colonies. The official religion—Sunni Islam. Atheism was punishable by death. A series of coups marked the government, one general after the other taking charge.

A major Mauritania industry was scrap steel. Abandoned ships littered Nouadhibou's beaches. Freighters, tankers, cargo ships—once they'd lived their useful life and aged beyond repair, ship owners had two choices. Go through the vessel decommissioning hassle, dry-dock it, and cut it apart. An expensive proposition. Or, with sufficient money placed in the appropriate Mauritanian official's hands, they stripped an old ship of anything valuable, loaded it with sufficient fuel to make Nouadhibou, and ran full-steam onto sand bars and often the beach. Then they'd walk away, having added to the largest ship graveyard in the world. The locals would salvage sellable steel, acetylene torches busy at it, while toxins like bunker fuel and oil and grease sheened the coastal waters. You'd want a hard talk with your travel agent if sent there for vacation.

Mauritania was the last country on earth to outlaw slavery, pressured through economic and diplomatic channels. The new law meant nothing. Mauritanians believed slavery a part of the natural order, reflected with twenty percent of their population, or eight hundred thousand souls, living as slaves. Slavery was generational, with children born under the condition doomed to live their lives as their parents did, housed with owners' goats and sheep. Skin color identified the two classes, with the lighter-skinned Berber bloodlines owning the darker-skinned people from the Sahel—with Senegal to the south a prime raiding locale when demand for slaves outstripped supply. Open slave markets were not uncommon. They had dragged Krystyna Kaminski into this world. I would get her out, come hell or high water. With that thought, I headed belowdecks and assembled a weapon selection. Whatever armaments a Mauritanian fixer could provide me wouldn't do. A vehicle and supplies and local intel, sure. But for items that went bang, I wanted my own kit. Beyond any doubt, I'd need them.

A Colt 901 .308 caliber assault rifle, with an Elcan Specter scope wired for night vision—my prime weapon. Four extra filled magazines and an additional hundred rounds, boxed. An H&K M762 rifle, also chambered in .308. The bullet interchangeability between the Colt and the H&K kept it simple. The H&K came equipped with a fine Leupold scope in 3X-9X magnification for long-range work. Three extra loaded magazines for the H&K. Two .40 caliber Glock pistols with four extra loaded magazines and an additional rack of ammo. A twelve-gauge Mossberg pump shotgun and a box of double-ought buckshot. For up close and personal work.

A large duffel bag accepted the arsenal, with multiple towels packed around, between, and among the weapons and extra ammunition. It kept the damage and clank factor down. I felt uneasy, under-armed, with the selection. A dozen frag grenades would have been nice. I salved my concern by dropping in more ammo for the Colt and H&K.

I still had several hours before arriving at the airport, time spent pacing and fretting with an occasional perusal of my laptop for more local research, more local intel. It was slim pickings. I returned belowdecks and packed my rucksack. It would get cold at night in the desert, so I added a lightweight jacket. I resupplied my field first aid kit and added extra wound wash and bandages and sutures. Toiletries, clothing, a dozen protein bars, and a field water purification filter found their way into appropriate locations, along with a roll of Benjamins that could choke a mule. I had no aversion to bribing my way out of a tight spot, in particular with a teenage girl in tow. Tossed in a small tool kit with wrenches and screwdrivers and a wire cutter, along with a small roll of baling wire and a roll of duct tape—Red's medium of choice. Then small diameter nylon rope, a lighter, waterproof matches, and a small fire-starter kit. And minimal extra clothing besides the jacket. I thought again how frag grenades or even a Claymore mine or three would have been sweet—sufficient room remained for them in the rucksack or duffel. Acutely aware I'd land as a one-man army—and I had no problem with that—I knew the more firepower I had the better.

I exited the *Ace* and paced the dock. Upon landing, I'd require the fixer to have greased the customs and immigration skids, allowing me safe and unmolested passage with all my kit. Then a vehicle, supplies, and maybe a fast boat. Escape via sea was a potential option. Air evac as well, although a Company jet or chopper might be a pipe dream. I'd see, unsure how the Company would play their hand. And again, trusting no one but myself once I'd made feet-on-the-street.

Exit time approached, and I entered the Uber vehicle, toting both the rucksack and duffel. No word from Jules. It wasn't a showstopper. I was headed in. Worst-case scenario: land and have the pilot taxi toward a runway section adjacent to a jumbled neighborhood. Then bail and haul it, with a fifty-fifty shot that a Mauritania shantytown would offer sufficient cover for escape. Not a good start, but beggars, choosers. One issue loomed—where to land? Nouakchott or Nouadhibou? I had eight hours of flight time for figuring it out. Or flipping a coin.

The Clubhouse message arrived as I boarded the Learjet. Halle-freakin'-lujah. It had taken Jules six hours, and heaven knows what levers she'd pulled and threats she'd delivered digging up the intel. She provided a name and contact information for the fixer, plus:

Nouadhibou. Customs clearance only, plus vehicle. Do NOT pack light. Godspeed.

Chapter 28

Jules's note showed how in sync we were. She'd ID'd the next slave auction's location, Nouadhibou. Her fixer could slide me and my tools past customs and immigration, and provide a vehicle. Weaponry wasn't available, hence the red flag about packing light. Jules was nothing short of miraculous.

I messaged the Nouadhibou fixer and confirmed my arrival time. I also enquired about the possibility of a large fast boat that could carry me to Senegal without refueling. It was a tall order—six hundred miles along the coast. But options, baby. Always a good thing. After arrival, I'd ask him for the slave market's exact location and pick his brain for its staging. I acknowledged, again, that Krystyna might not be there, held in reserve for another auction. Or already sold off. Either way, I'd be in the mix and hot after it.

I considered the Marilyn Townsend message. I'd have a vehicle, and the fixer might also provide a fast boat. Air evac would cover the bases.

ETA Nouadhibou 0800 local. Subsequent schedule unknown. Air evac on standby appreciated.

She responded within ten minutes.

Understood.

Which didn't mean jack. She now understood my mission focused on Nouadhibou and understood Krystyna might be there. And understood my request for evacuation help. The Company's subsequent actions were now a crapshoot. So be it.

My confidence level ratcheted up, a target location identified, Clubhouse support structures established, and a smooth flight before active hunting. I informed the pilots my destination was now Nouadhibou. The last six hours had brought a dramatic turnaround, and I was jacked. Several hours later, as the jet engines hummed, I'd calmed down enough for sleep.

I woke as bright sunlight streamed through the plane's windows, the African coastline stretched across the horizon. Stark desert abutted coastal waves. No palm trees, no vegetation other than the occasional Saharan scrub brush, and no sign of life. Until we circled Nouadhibou on our landing approach. The small city sat on a spit—a slender peninsula extending southwest—creating a natural harbor. The steel hulls of rotting ships flecked the bay in every direction. Every cargo-carrying ship imaginable sat decaying, some atilt as they sank into the sand bottom and others more nestled, more resigned to the inevitable effects of saltwater and waves. It made for a post-apocalyptic scene. Scattered nearby were fishing vessels by the hundreds. Smallish open boats driven with outboard motors. None would do for an escape south. The seas this day were rough and the distance too far for them. I considered, as a last option, escape over the much closer border with Western Sahara. But southward toward Senegal offered refuge, civilization. The international community hardly recognized Western Sahara as a country, a lawless no-man's-land where next steps, once inside that place, became a lethal roulette game. Any sightings of us, inevitable, would focus on killing me and taking Krystyna. From the skillet into the fire. But first things first. Find the girl.

Wheels down, the landing smooth, and we taxied toward a smaller concrete block out-building that acted as the private plane terminal. As the engines shut down, I collected my things. One pilot opened the cockpit door. He wasn't smiling.

"We've got a problem."

Military personnel or cops—hard to tell which in many countries—rushed the aircraft's left side that faced the small terminal. A military-type vehicle rolled and stopped at the front landing gear as a smaller cop car wheeled behind the advancing troops. Automatic weapons pointed our way. Anger and betrayal coursed. The fixer, had to be. Someone or some group outbid me for his services and procured intel on my arrival.

"Let me see what's going on," the pilot said.

The second pilot joined him, and they lowered the doorway, exiting with hands raised. The cops snatched them up and shoved them into a small police car. Shit. The troops advanced toward the door hatch. A shoot-out had no upside. They had me trapped, the lowered door the plane's single entrance and exit. Yeah, I'd take a bunch with me if firing started, but at the end of the day, I was screwed.

I also exited, hands up. They swarmed, cuffed my hands behind my back, gave me a thorough pat down, and shoved me into the military vehicle's back seat alongside two armed cops. As we drove away, I viewed four or five men enter the plane's interior. Where they'd find my rucksack and duffel full of goodies. Not good.

The drive through town revealed what I'd expect. A few, very few, half-modern two-story buildings. Multiple mosques, their minarets by far the tallest structures. All the rest was comprised of shacks and mud-brick or adobe huts and ramshackle lean-to markets and dirt roads filled with litter and trash. The place smelled of open sewers and sweat and desperation.

The cop station, a mixed concrete-block-and-mud-brick two-story building, sat situated among more shanties and hovels. Three men escorted me inside. There was no booking process or fingerprints taken, and no point offering bribes. They had my rucksack, so the Benjamins were already part of the haul. A large central room occupied most of the building's first floor, with scattered desks and file cabinets and a table with hot plate and dishes.

Through a doorway and into a smaller room with a whirling fan, an old metal desk, open window, and two more cops. The jailers.

"This is the guy," a cop with a firm grip on my handcuffed hands said. "Keep him separated. We are told he is dangerous."

"He doesn't look dangerous," a jailer said. "He looks like a tied-up chicken."

They laughed. I remained silent.

"What about the pilots?" another cop asked.

"It is too early for knowing," the jailer said and pointed at the desk phone. "The General may want the plane."

They'd inform the General, or current president-for-life, about the prize, and he'd make a decision.

"We should ask the chicken what he thinks."

They laughed again, a jailer joined my little troop, and we started up very long, very narrow steps. I glanced back through the doorway and viewed my rucksack and duffel placed on a central desk. A cop with ornate epaulets on his uniform, clearly the head knocker, had unzipped the duffel bag. The next sixty seconds afforded the best opportunity for escape. Strike early, strike quick, strike sure.

The guy with my cuff key remained behind me, the jailer in front with his set of jail cell keys, one more cop as tail-end Charlie. Three unsuspecting men. The magic moment would arrive when taking off my handcuffs. If they performed the act before I stepped into a jail cell, Katy, bar the door.

A long concrete aisle separated two rows of windowless jail cells, ten on each side. The pilots had beaten me there and stood together, silent. The first cell on the left, empty and next to the pilots, was mine. The jailer unlocked and opened the cell door, then stood aside. At my back, the cop shoved me forward. I faked a stumble toward the cell but stopped at its entrance, stock-still and hangdog with shoulders slumped.

"Aren't you going to take these off?" I asked meekly in Arabic, pulling my wrists apart as an indicator, back still toward them.

Both cops wore sidearms; the jailer did not.

"The chicken speaks Arabic," the jailer said. "That should help during the years you rot in here."

Several chuckles among the crowd, and go-time popped. One wrist free, the cuff dangling from the other, I whipped around and, using momentum, cold-cocked the SOB with a right cross. As he collapsed, unconscious, the other scrambled for his holstered weapon. Too damn late, hoss. I flew the few steps his way and delivered a body slam, my left hand capturing his right on the weapon's still-holstered grip. A right-hand punch plowed into his throat, and a knee to the nuts took the fight out of him. His hand released the weapon, I snatched it from the holster, and aimed at the jailer's forehead who, on his knees, attempted to wrestle his unconscious compadre's pistol from its holster.

"Stop."

He did and raised his hands, eyes wide.

"Remove this handcuff," I said, extending my hand. "Then take off your belt and empty your pockets. Now."

He complied and stood with hands shaking. The handcuffs clattered as they hit the floor. He turned his pockets inside out, empty. The other inmates, a half-dozen and scattered among the other cells, started a small ruckus, asking for release. I pointed the weapon in their general direction and said through clenched jaws, "Shut up. Shut up or I will, by Allah, shoot each of you." They quieted down.

221

I addressed the quaking jailer. "Get in," I said and pointed the pistol's barrel at the empty cell. He did. I pulled the unconscious man's pistol, slid it into a pocket, and turned for the other cop who held both hands at his neck, sucking air. "You, too. Belt off, empty your pockets."

He returned a hunched-over glare. The man I'd knocked out began stirring, and the jailer that remained in the jailer's room far below called up the stairs. Jeez, Louise, gimme a break.

"Bewba. Is there a problem?"

The hunched-over cop attempted to call out, but the throat shot he'd received created a hoarse croak. Before he could try again, I lashed out with a kick to his solar plexus. He crumpled to the ground.

"You. Bewba," I whispered to the jailer in the cell. "Answer your partner and tell him your key isn't working. One wrong word and you die. Do it. Now."

He did, my pistol aimed at his head. Grumbles drifted from downstairs, along with slow shuffling footfalls headed up. Gotta move. Too many shifting pieces, too many men to cope with. I placed my active pistol on the ground, straddled the unconscious man as he came to, lifted his torso with my left hand, and delivered another knockout punch against his jaw. The footfalls from the climbing jailer sounded louder. I retrieved the pistol and bolted for the man I'd kicked, who now leaned plastered against the wall, sucking air, and I spun him around. I applied a sleeper hold, right hand still gripping the weapon, and cut off blood flow to his brain. It took five long, long seconds before he passed out. He slid onto the floor, and I pressed against the wall next to the doorway. Just in time for the second jailer's entrance. The scene with his partner inside the open jail cell, one cop stretched out at the cell's entrance, and the second cop passed out along the wall should have created an alarm cry for the men downstairs. My pistol's barrel pressed against his temple kept things quiet.

"Off with the belt. Empty your pockets. Everything on the floor. Now."

He complied, eyes wide, nostrils flared with fear.

"Now this guy," I said, directing him at the choked-out man who now stirred. "Belt and pockets. Move. If you or anyone else makes a noise, you will all die."

I aimed toward the jailer still inside the open jail cell.

"This one," I said, nudging with my toe the unconscious man I'd leveled twice. "Same thing. Belt, pockets. Now."

The guy at my feet reacted to my foot nudge and began coming around.

"Hurry," I said, directed at both jailers. "You have five seconds or expect a bullet."

They hustled.

"Now, get everyone inside the cell."

The two men pulled and dragged, and soon enough four men were inside the jail cell, the hallway floor littered with belts and jail keys and loose change and car keys and several small pocketknives. I closed the cell door, and the old lock mechanism latched shut. I gave it a hard pull just to be sure, then waved the pistol once again toward the other inmates and reiterated the only two options—shut the hell up or catch a bullet. I added extra spice and explained I'd shoot them in the balls first, then the head. My Arabic didn't contain any Berber words, but they got the message and shut up.

"Which is the master key that opens all the cells?" I asked both jailers while holding up one of their belts with an attached keychain. "Remember, balls first, then the head."

They pointed out the correct key, and I unlocked the adjacent cell with the two pilots. They'd remained silent the entire time except for one who had exclaimed, "Whoa, whoa," and a final, "Whoa!" while I'd administered our escape's first phase. I had an obligation to take care of these guys. I'd dragged them into this shitshow, and I'd see them off to safety. One pilot strode from the cell and nodded my way. The other stepped slowly as he exited, eyes as big as saucers.

I ran a quick mental status. Upstairs in a Mauritanian jail with four captured cops and jailers, two pilots in tow, a group of armed cops downstairs with my weapons and rucksack, no place to go but into the lion's den, no transportation, and no clue about the slave market or Krystyna. Other than those few items, things were going pretty doggone well.

Chapter 29

"Alright," I said to the pilots, "I'm getting us out of here."

"How?" asked the hesitant one.

"Working on it. I'll be right back. You may hear shooting. Don't worry."

"I don't know about this," he said. "Let's call the US embassy."

I asked their names. They knew mine. Mark was the freaked one. Rick stood cool.

"Mark, there's two things wrong with the embassy tactic. They're in Nouakchott, a couple hundred miles away. And our phones are downstairs in the main room. I'm not gonna waltz in there and ask for them. Besides, the General may take a liking to your Learjet, and he won't care what our diplomats say."

I didn't mention that the last thing the US embassy and its diplomats wanted was a call from two pilots locked up in Nouadhibou. Two citizens associated with Case Lee.

"Can you get us back on the plane?" Rick asked. "I'll fire it up and take off in minutes."

"Good plan," I said. "Let's work that direction."

"Do you need that one?" he asked, pointing at the pistol in my front jeans' pocket.

I handed it over, and he had the wherewithal to pull back the slide and ensure a round was chambered. Rick would fight. Mark, not so much.

"Right. Keep everyone up here quiet. I may send more upstairs. Again, you might hear shots. Don't freak."

"Got it," Rick said.

Mark remained silent. I crept down the stairs. The jailer's small room remained empty, the doorway into the main room off to the side. I peeked through the jailer room's open window. Four cop cars, old Renaults, sat lined up, nose-in. Good. I inched toward the main room's entrance, a quick glance revealing the head knocker with his epaulets staring at the tabletop loaded with weapons. My weapons. He hadn't started on the rucksack yet. He stood on the table's opposite side, facing me while looking down. Four other cops stood around, pointing and chatting about the weapons. They were all armed. The front double doors, wooden, were closed but clearly unlocked. I strode in, pistol raised, and aimed at the head guy.

"Everyone stays still, and hands in the air. No one will get hurt."

I continued a fast pace for the table. One moron failed to register the message, slapped his holster, and began pulling the pistol. I dashed for the table, dove, and rolled underneath it as a shot rang out. The blast deafened within the enclosed space. He fired a second time at the tabletop as I tumbled underneath it and popped out the table's other side, rising alongside the head honcho. I pressed against the chief's back side, who stood with mouth open at the frantic violent action, and jammed the pistol's barrel against his head. He transitioned from head knocker into my personal shield and ticket out of here.

"Guns on the floor!" I yelled.

"Put your weapons on the floor!" the chief screamed.

The man who'd fired twice kept his weapon pointed toward us two.

"*Now!*" the head guy said, screaming louder.

They complied, the guy who aimed at us doing so last. I pulled my shield's pistol, stuffed it into my jeans, and called loudly for Rick. He hustled downstairs and entered, pistol raised, prepared. Working together, we collected all their weapons. Then belts off, hats removed, pockets emptied. While Rick guarded them, I dashed to the front door, threw the deadbolt, and lowered an old-fashioned four-by-four timber section into two brackets set on either side of the doors. Then I hustled for the six windows, three on each side, closed them, and threw the latches. It wouldn't take much effort breaking through those, but my intent was more for noise containment. They'd holler their heads off from the upstairs jail cells once a minute or three had passed.

We marched them up the stairs and into the cell where they'd jailed the pilots. I lied and explained we'd be downstairs the next thirty minutes, and if I heard any ruckus from the jail cells, I'd run back up and start shooting. Starting with the head guy. Mark, Rick, and I collected all the keys we could find, both upstairs and down.

"What's next?" Rick asked as we assembled downstairs.

"Everyone grab a cop hat," I said, stuffing my weapons and towels back into the duffel. I tossed the captured pistol into the bag as well, pulled my Glock, and chambered a round.

We shifted into the jailer's room. I hefted the duffel and rucksack onto the table, then removed and pocketed my phone from the latter.

"Hand me anything that looks like a car key," I said. "Put the rest in that bag."

A ubiquitous plastic grocery bag with a jailer's lunch sat on the desk. I poked my head out the small window, wearing a cop hat, waited for a single pedestrian's passing, and crawled out, selecting the nearest Renault cop car. Inside, it took the third car key attempt before it started. I signaled, and Rick exited the window first. He waited until Mark passed him my duffel and rucksack, then got in the front seat with me, depositing my gear in the back. Mark, still freaked, jumped in the back. I reversed out, drove fifty feet, and turned down a dirt side street.

"Okay. I'm not taking any paved roads," I said, driving fast. "Rick, use this and guide me to the airport."

I pulled my phone, entered the security key, pulled up the GPS function, and handed it over. I checked the rearview mirror. No pursuit. But Mark had taken off his hat.

"Hat back on, Mark. It's all we've got for disguise. Rick, I'm looking for a spot well away from the terminal. Ideally a packed neighborhood near the taxiway."

"On it."

"How are you set for fuel?" I asked.

"We can make Dakar, Senegal. No problem."

"Mark, hand me the plastic bag full of goodies."

He did. I tossed it out the window. The side-view mirror reflected keys and wallets and loose change scattering as the bag hit the dirt and split open. There were sufficient locals walking the dirt street who'd collect everything. It would all disappear into the neighborhood, never to be seen again.

I crept toward intersections with paved roads, scanned for cops, then shot across. Rick guided me with the GPS. We received nonstop curious looks from pedestrians, but high odds their relationship with the Nouadhibou police weren't positive. They'd stare our way, sure, and chatter among themselves, but wouldn't relay any details to the police. I wove through small market areas filled with donkey-pulled carts as vendors set up shop on the hard-packed ground, and made frequent turns down rutted dirt streets. The sun beat down from a cloudless sky.

Fifteen nerve-racking minutes passed as we approached the airport. Rick had me turn at what was little more than two ruts that terminated at a half-fallen-down slat fence, four feet high. A hundred yards past the fence, the narrow taxiway. I nosed against the fence and jumped out. Rick joined me.

"Good," I said. "Good. The terminal is a quarter-mile away. Your jet is sitting there, no other aircraft."

"And no air traffic as well," he said, scanning the skies. "So what's the plan?"

"Help me push this fence down."

The section we pushed collapsed, a few slats broke, and the rest fell like dominoes.

"Alright," I said. "Bold as brass, calm and easy, works best in these situations. I'll drive along the taxiway toward your jet and pull up at the plane's door. A lone cop delivering the Learjet's two pilots. People watching will assume some deal was made, and they've released you."

"What if they don't assume that?"

"I'll handle it. You guys fire it up and get going. How long is warm-up for the engines?"

"With this heat, I can roll in five minutes."

"Roger that."

I eased the Renault over the broken-down fence, across the hardpan surface, and onto the taxiway. Then rolled at a sedate speed for the terminal and parked jet. Across the runway, opposite us, the Atlantic Ocean and Nouadhibou Bay.

"Take off your cop hats, gents. You're pilots again."

I kept mine on and asked Mark to produce the Colt rifle from the duffel and lay it on the back seat. Heat waves shimmered across the entire area, the sky light-blue, the ocean azure, the terminal bright-white. As we approached, it was clear no flights were scheduled for the immediate future. Not a soul wandered the tarmac. I extracted the Glock from my pocket and placed it between my legs.

"You want this pistol back?" Rick asked.

"Nope."

"Good." He paused and presented a tight smile. "I want you to know we're still available for your next little adventure. I'll chalk up this Nouadhibou delay to a contaminated fuel issue, which caused the Dakar diversion. You on board with that, Mark?"

"I suppose."

"He's on board," Rick said. "I would appreciate one little thing the next time you and I fly, though."

"What's that?"

"A minor request. Keep my butt out of jail."

We both chuckled. The jet's hatch stood open, the step-stairs no doubt a welcome sight for Rick and Mark. I parked nose-in near the hatch, the terminal at my back. People inside the terminal couldn't identify my features but could see the identifiable cop hat. Rick shook hands and smiled.

"You don't need to hang around, Case."

"I'll wait until you're ready to roll, then scoot."

He and Mark exited, climbed into the jet's cabin, and closed the hatch. Within sixty seconds, the engines fired. I waited through the warm-up, sweating, a keen eye on the rearview mirror. It took a long, long time for five minutes to pass. Then, through the small cockpit side window, Rick gave me a thumbs-up. Ready to roll. I backed away, turned, and headed down the taxiway ahead of them, moving fast. Back through the slat fence line, still with no pursuit. I stopped, exited the vehicle, and watched the jet turn onto the runway and goose it.

After takeoff, the Learjet turned over the ocean. In a strange move, he continued the turn and circled behind me at a low altitude. Rick roared the jet right on top of me and waggled the wings as a salute and goodbye. Then kicked it in the ass for Senegal.

Alright. Knock a couple items off the issue board. But a quick glance at the distant terminal added one. A military-style vehicle hauled it down the taxiway. I didn't require cue cards to understand who they were after. I started the old Renault and drove it deep into the adjoining neighborhood, turned often, wove among narrow dirt paths, and considered next steps. A few operational challenges aside, Krystyna Kaminski's trail lay here and now. And I was on it.

Chapter 30

I could find someone in the current neighborhood who would guide me, for a price, to the slave market. No sweat. And I'd handle activities once there, even if Krystyna wasn't on the auction block today. They'd know her whereabouts. And they'd talk—I'd see to that. But the Mauritanian government now wanted my head on a platter, and escape options once I'd found her constituted my major concern. I rolled to a stop. There was no other traffic, a few folks meandered about, and no sign the military vehicle tailed me. I texted Townsend—not with a specific request or cry for help. A simple tickler, a gentle nudge. It was early a.m. in DC, but she'd be up.

In Nouadhibou.

It would suffice. Now, ditch the cop car and get another ride. I cruised with caution, an eye peeled for the appropriate vehicle and driver. Several turns and ten minutes later, I spotted a man leaning against an eighties Mercedes-Benz. The vehicle had passed through multiple hands in multiple countries before landing here in what would be its final resting place. Typical for this neck of the woods, it had no headlights or taillights or bumpers. No windows. Two quarter panels with different colors, and the driver's side mirror hung limp, dangling from a cable. Perfect. It would blend in with most other Nouadhibou vehicles. I parked behind him, removed my cop hat, and exited the vehicle when my phone pinged. Townsend responded. I smiled and waved at the man, and checked the message.

1630 local. Meet asset.

As for the location, she supplied specific geographic coordinates. I entered them into my GPS as the man leaning against his old Benz watched and smoked. A spot, a coffee- or teahouse, on the town's north side. Fair enough, but the timing was weird. Not the meeting time. Her response time.

She knew I had landed at 0800 and could have delivered this information long before now. My gut rumbled with mild concern, but I was dealing with shadow players. Who knew what background machinations rumbled?

I approached the thin man as he stared my way without alarm or friendliness. I expected the former. I had arrived in a cop car. A foreigner in a cop car.

"As-Salaam Alaikum," I said. Peace be with you.

"Wa-Alaikum-as-Salaam." And peace upon you.

"What's your name?"

"Razak."

"Razak, I have a business opportunity for you."

He nodded in response.

"Can you drive me to an isolated place in Nouadhibou? A place where no one will find me for a few hours. And the police cannot see me as we travel. I will pay one hundred US dollars."

He returned a half-smile and a nod.

"Do you have a phone?"

"Yes."

"When I call you in a few hours, pick me up and take me to a place on the city's north side. For this, I will pay one thousand US dollars."

He returned a full smile.

"These things can be done. But first, you must move your vehicle. I do not want it near my home."

"Of course. Are you ready to go?"

"Yes."

I'd learned years ago that time schedules presented an issue in many countries and now addressed it.

"Are you ready? This minute?"

"This minute?"

"Yes. This minute. One hundred dollars. US."

He tossed his cig and entered his vehicle. It took a while for his old Benz to start, belching smoke when it did. He pulled away and signaled out his window to follow. Several blocks later he slowed and again signaled. We were still within his neighborhood, but he'd created a satisfactory distance between the soon-to-be-abandoned cop car and his home. I retrieved my duffel and rucksack, placed them on the back seat, and rode shotgun.

"No police," I said, reiterating the chief points.

"No police."

We drove on sand and hardpan and gravel roads for two miles, near the coast.

"I know such a place. You will not be disturbed."

"Thank you, Razak. That would be most excellent."

We turned onto the beach, drove north, and passed dozens upon dozens of rusted beached and abandoned ships. Several had sun-bright dots onboard—acetylene torches at work as men cut steel under the blazing sun. The ships thinned out, and Razak pointed toward an ancient freighter canted thirty degrees, rust-covered and partly salvaged. Locals had cut steel from it in various places, leaving a Swiss-cheese appearance.

"You will not be bothered in there."

"Excellent."

I could access a hole-cut entrance, would wind my way inside, establish a defensive position, and remain unseen. We exchanged phone numbers after I paid him. As I pulled my kit from his back seat, I wormed a hand into a rucksack side pocket and, using feel, peeled off ten Benjamins. I displayed them as if holding a card hand and reiterated the schedule.

"I will call you at four o'clock. I expect you here no later than four fifteen. Understand?"

"Salat al-'asr is near this time."

Late afternoon prayers, the third of the day. The Adhan, or Islamic call to prayer, would ring out from the mosques sometime around four o'clock. I'd work around it.

"I understand. But to receive this," I said, displaying the Benjamins again, "you must be here soon after I call."

"And I will, inshallah."

God willing.

"If you do, inshallah, you will receive this money."

As Razak pulled away, the old Benz spewing exhaust, I shouldered the rucksack, lifted the duffel, pulled the Glock, and stepped into a cavernous shadowed maze of steel, rust, and scattered useless equipment. It smelled like sea and salt and a general funk. Footing was treacherous—rusted steps and jagged edges. Rusted-through valves and pipes and pumps littered the dubious flooring. It was perfect.

I made my way toward the four-hundred-foot vessel's stern, ascending when possible. The thirty-degree list and random missing bulkheads and hull sections made for an M. C. Escher-like environment. I parked it under an overhang at the stern, away from the seabird poop littering the open spaces, and set up shop for the hours-long wait. A protein bar and an apple—the fruit taken and stashed when I'd boarded the Learjet in Charleston—provided breakfast and lunch.

I sent a quick message for the Clubhouse about the fixer. Not as admonishment, but feedback for her future reference. Fixers were an iffy proposition around the world, and Jules would want to know if there were issues.

236

Fixer compromised.

I used the small binoculars and scanned both the immediate and distant areas. Small fishing boats came and went among the abandoned ship carcasses, desert met sea with little vegetation in the mix, and Nouadhibou squatted on hardpan surface, shimmering with heat waves. Salat al-zuhr, the midday call to prayer, delivered by a muezzin or crier through loudspeakers, washed across the landscape from mosque minarets. Traffic in town and on the beach slowed and stopped. With prayer rugs placed on the ground, the faithful performed their five-times-a-day ritual. The sea breeze blew, gulls circled and called. And a reply from Jules arrived.

Fixer expired.

Bad news. Someone within this hairball's inner workings had whacked my guy. Russia's SVR a possibility. Or someone from a diplomatic corps who was intimate with Nouadhibou's underground could have hired a hitter. Or— and this possibility, real enough, raised alarms—the Company did it.

I avoided wading through those waters. Keep it simple, stupid. Find the girl. Get her out of here. "In it but not of it," as Bo, using an ecumenical reference, had once told me. But still. I would meet with a Company spook about the slave auction agenda. He could smooth out a few road bumps, such as the auction's location and timing, and if Krystyna was or had been for sale. Although I could, through my own contacts such as Razak, suss that intel on my own. All it took were sufficient Benjamins and bullets.

A vehicle for escape would help, an airlift via chopper even better. But I could work around those, too. I'd observed several decent Toyota Land Cruisers in town and, with cold cash as the incentive, could acquire one. Cover from the local authorities would benefit me—the cops at the jail were now, for sure, released and pissed. The Learjet departure would have pissed off others. So, yeah, aid in the keep-low department would be helpful. But I was prepared to go it alone if necessary, a sound approach on any gig. I was well-armed, well-supplied with cash, and well aware that the lone critter I trusted on the ground sat, at the moment, inside the husk of an old freighter. Fair enough.

As the afternoon dragged on, my head kept revisiting Krystyna. If she was in town now, a big if, what must she be thinking? Did she have hope, or was she crushed, resigned, hopeless? I prayed not.

Hold on, kid. I'm no superman, but smart money seldom bets against Case Lee.

Chapter 31

The day's third call to prayer sounded near four o'clock. I gave it twenty minutes and phoned Razak. At four-thirty, his decrepit Benz rolled down the beach toward me. I'd be fifteen or twenty minutes late for the meeting with the CIA asset. Not bad for this part of the world.

We wove down side streets as I guided him with my GPS. We entered the town's original section where low mud-brick architecture and small, ancient open plazas dominated. Townsend's GPS coordinates placed us among a tight row of shops, eateries, and coffeehouses. I exited the Benz, stood alongside, and told Razak to keep the engine running. It didn't take long.

"Mr. Lee. It's good seeing you."

A man in his thirties approached wearing traditional garb. A light blue long, loose robe-type shirt with white, airy, light cotton pants. His turban was black, his accent northeastern US, his skin and features Arab-American.

"I am Amir." I wouldn't learn his surname. This was a CIA field operator, a man who worked Arab countries across North Africa and into the Middle East. "You won't require a driver anymore."

I leaned through the Benz's passenger window and handed Razak his thousand bucks and whispered I might call him later for another ride. You never knew. I pulled my kit from the back seat, Razak rumbled away, and Amir said, "Let's get some coffee."

We walked thirty paces along the shops and ducked into a tiny coffeehouse. Within this ancient section of town, everyone wore traditional garb. I stood out like a sore thumb. My duffel and rucksack alongside our table, we ordered coffee. Amir, after asking if I was hungry and receiving a negative, ordered a fish and rice dish. His Arabic contained several Berber words, unknown to me. This cat knew the North African turf.

"You have created quite a stir here," Amir said, smiling. "I understand this is your standard operational mode."

"I'm a little surprised we didn't meet earlier today. Like when I landed."

I ignored the operational mode BS, a standard CIA all-seeing-eye statement.

"I was certain you had made other arrangements. Arrangements that must have gone awry."

"Yeah, there was a bump or two in the road today."

"And, from what I understand, a bump or two on a few policeman's heads. On a positive note, we've learned something, and have added jail escape to the Case Lee list of attributes and abilities," he said with a grin. "Also on a positive note, the cops don't visit this old section of town. Families, clans, and tribes keep the peace."

I got down to business.

"Why don't I require a vehicle and driver?"

"Nearby is a rather decent Land Cruiser. It's yours."

"Thanks." I meant it. "And thanks for whatever help you can give me regarding Krystyna Kaminski."

"You are welcome."

The coffee arrived along with a half-dozen dates on a small plate. The coffee was thick, sweet, and gritty.

"Speaking of Krystyna," I said.

"You are in luck, Mr. Lee."

My heart jumped. Jaw clenched, nostrils flared, I said, "Tell me."

"The auction starts in less than an hour. And I'd like a talk with you about that."

"You confirm she's here. Right now."

"That is the situation."

The proprietor arrived with Amir's dish. I let out a puffed-cheek exhale and stared out the tiny establishment's doorway. Jumbled raw emotions flooded me. Relief, massive relief. Draining relief. Soon replaced with excitement. Anticipation redlined, the girl within my grasp. After all those freakin' miles and dead ends and dead bodies, she was here. Now. And anger didn't take a back seat—people had tried killing me, and my friends, over a bullshit conspiracy where spooks and diplomats played musical chairs while pain and horror and death whirled. Screw them, and screw everyone involved.

"This is quite good, Mr. Lee." I turned my head and observed him hold up a fork with fish and rice. "Are you sure you don't want some?"

I shook my head and returned to staring into the big lost out the doorway. Wipe it clean, Lee. Contemplate all the crap back on the *Ace* with a vodka on the rocks. Focus. Get the girl and haul her to safety. Anyone and everyone who impeded that single aim was the enemy. It didn't matter if violent actions stretched from here to Timbuktu, I'd get this done.

First, deal with the trust factor. As a Company man, the trust factor with Amir sat at the bottom of the well. And I required intel. Valid, actionable intel. As in right this freakin' minute. Nothing against the guy—but he was a clandestine player, and I had drawn multiple painful lessons from past encounters with them.

Oh, man. She was here.

Hang in there, kid. Hang in there.

"How long have you been in Nouadhibou?" I asked.

"I arrived before dawn."

That checked. The Company couldn't find her until I'd let Marilyn Townsend know my destination, a trigger point for them to scramble an asset. I shoved aside pride, knowing I'd scooped them. The CIA didn't have Bo or Marcus. And they sure didn't have Red. I had a flash visualization of the latter sitting under the awning with Bo. He'd found her, connected with her. And her money trail message for me came with an implied quid pro quo. Get the girl. Above all, get the girl.

"How'd you know about my jailbreak?"

"Local scuttlebutt. I have been busy, Mr. Lee, gathering every informational scrap available."

Something about his statement smelled tainted. Not unusual when dealing with espionage actors. He remained at the bottom of the well.

"Now, about the auction—" Amir said.

"How often do they hold these?"

"As I understand it, not often. Every two or three weeks."

"How many do they sell each time?"

The words felt like acid on my tongue. How many do they sell. People.

"It depends. One thing is certain—your young lady will be the prime attraction. They will hold her until last."

"I'll handle the auction. What about air evac?"

"No can do. The vehicle is as far as I, and the Company, can go. It really is. We can't have any fingerprints on this."

That part I believed. God forbid they positioned themselves at the forefront of this rescue attempt.

"Fine. Tell me about the market's layout. And describe the before and after picture."

"Again, this is hearsay. They hold the auction—no big surprise here—at the old slave market. I have driven past it several times." He took another bite. I stared, unblinking, and waited. "It's a single-level stone building. My local asset has informed me there is a wooden platform. A stage, I suppose, where they display the unfortunates by lot. Some are single individuals, others are family members sold together."

"Your local asset knows a helluva lot about this."

He raised an eyebrow.

"That is his job. And mine."

"Where do they keep these wretches before the auction?" I asked, my lip curl involuntary. I still had trouble talking about it. It was too horrific and too damn matter-of-fact.

"Behind the building. You will find a semicircle of vehicles—owned by both the slavers and likely buyers. It's an ugly scene, I'll grant you, but a standard process. The people for sale stand around inside the vehicle semicircle, hands tied, as prospective buyers wander among them and check the goods, while the slavers expound on each one's benefits."

"Who are the buyers?"

"According to my asset, well-off Nouadhibou residents will make up half the crowd. The other half will be well-off clan and tribal leaders from the hinterlands. They make their money through trade and, often, raids on other clans. Also, the transactions at the auction, the sales, are conducted in gold. Only gold."

And cryptocurrency, bud. Which I wouldn't mention. My gut wouldn't quit roiling. This cat, and the Company, played this. The slave auction involved the Company somehow and in some way. To what extent, unknown. But they had a hand in it, and the hand was filthy.

"What about after the auction?"

He finished his plate, sipped coffee, and popped a date in his mouth. The proprietor came over and cleared the dishes. Amir ordered another coffee. I declined.

"They gather again out the back, inside the vehicle semicircle. That is where the gold changes hands. Then the successful bidders load their slaves, and everyone departs. Except for the vehicles, nothing has changed for centuries."

"That's it? Just the buyers and sellers?"

"Well, no. And that is another item I'd appreciate discussing."

"I'm all ears."

"The Nouadhibou residents, the successful buyers, will have an armed guard with them at all times. It's a different story with the desert clansmen."

"Tell me."

"They arrive and depart with a decent contingent of fellow clan members. All are well-armed. They travel this way because, well, most are raiders. And memories run deep. Opposing clans, including those who have been raided, may also arrive for the auction. As I've been told, there's a strange equilibrium with all the parties armed to the teeth. A mutually assured destruction play, if you will."

"So what?"

"I, we, don't want you upsetting that equilibrium. A massive gunfight in Nouadhibou will draw too many eyes and too many questions. So keep it cool. Okay?"

Keep it cool, my ass. But his descriptive was helpful. The obvious strategy—wait until they loaded Krystyna up and follow her. Take out the new owners once they left the slave market, be that in downtown Nouadhibou or out in the boonies. Either way, didn't matter.

"I'm cool as a cucumber, Amir."

"Just as long as we understand each other."

"Yeah, we understand each other."

"I am well aware you are focused on rescuing the girl. That is fine. Just keep in mind there are other players to consider."

"Don't give a shit about other players. Where's that vehicle?"

He raised his eyebrows, shook his head, and soon after we strolled down a dirt street toward my escape hatch. He'd parked it down a side alley. Ten or fifteen years old, with two spare tires and two gas jerry cans strapped on the roof. I loaded my gear into the back next to five gallon-sized water jugs.

"Is there fuel in the jerry cans?" I asked.

"They are full."

"Is the gas tank full?"

"Almost." Amir removed his sunglasses and inspected them for dust. "Tell me about your plans if you rescue the girl."

"Listen up, Amir." He halted his sunglasses inspection, and we locked eyes. "There's no if in this situation. Let's be damn clear about that."

Chapter 32

"Alright," he said. "Tell me about your plans *after* you rescue the girl."

I'd keep things nebulous with this guy. My trust in him hadn't ratcheted up during our sit-down. His arrival before dawn pointed toward some touchpoint with my arrest. The sit-down with him, timed for less than an hour before the auction, didn't bring any warm fuzzies either.

"Two options," I said, "since air evac appears too much to ask." He ignored the gibe. "Western Sahara, which makes for a quick border crossing, or Senegal."

"Senegal is four hundred miles south."

"Yeah."

"It seems like a straightforward choice."

"Yeah."

End of discussion. Western Sahara, a massive land area with only half a million residents, had been on the United Nations list of non-self-governing territories—whatever that meant—since 1963. It was one thing departing Mauritania, and another to find you've landed in a worse spot.

I didn't share my thoughts with the Company man, who clearly preferred I head toward Western Sahara. He had his reasons, which he'd never reveal. What he failed to mention, and I damn well knew, was pursuers wouldn't respect the ill-defined border between Mauritania and Western Sahara. They'd be on my trail regardless of lines on a map. Senegal didn't offer my soon-to-be enemies that option. Another former French colony, Senegal was relatively stable. Yeah, Mauritanian raiders crossed the Senegal River occasionally for slave-capturing runs. But they went after defenseless people. I was far from that, and any thoughts they might hold about tangling with me on Senegalese turf would be met with hot lead. And I wouldn't have to watch my back in Senegal, unlike Western Sahara. Once we crossed the river, I was confident I'd get Krystyna to safety. It wouldn't be a cakewalk getting there, but what else was new?

"Alright," I said, climbing behind the wheel. "Let's roll."

Amir rode shotgun and added a final admonishment. "Remember, you will be the only westerner there. All eyes will note that, so you will be under extra scrutiny."

"Fine. Which way?"

"One other thing. There will be several unfriendlies there."

"Oh, there'll be a buttload of unfriendlies once I grab Krystyna."

"I meant professional unfriendlies."

We held a brief eye-lock. Yeah, I understood. Other clandestine players. Players who'd had a hand in this abduction and who were card-carrying conspiracy members.

"Got it. Which way?"

"One last thing. I will not remain once they auction the girl. I will not linger. Now, turn left."

He directed me along dirt roads, past stone and mud-brick structures both ancient and just old. The Land Cruiser drove well, the engine smooth-running, the steering stable. The gas tank read three-quarters full. Ten minutes later we entered a hard-packed dirt plaza, surrounded with single- and two-story structures. A semicircle of vehicles—Renaults, Benz's, and a surprising number of Land Cruisers—corralled the rear of a wide single-story stone structure. The slave market. Among the sedans, a recent washing was evident. Thick dust covered the Land Cruisers. I parked at the plaza's edge, thirty yards from the buyers' and sellers' vehicles.

"Why don't you lie low until it's over?" Amir asked. "This puts you right in the middle of activities."

I didn't respond and exited the Land Cruiser, pocketing the keys. The Glock remained tucked in the waistband of my jeans, hidden by my knit shirt's tail. I opened the Cruiser's back hatch, unzipped the duffel, pulled both the Colt rifle and Mossberg shotgun, and laid them alongside the duffel within easy reach. Hatch closed, I donned sunglasses and strode toward the vehicle collection.

"Hey, Case," Amir said to my back. "This isn't a smart move."

I halted, turned, lifted the shades, and made eye contact.

"With me or against me, Amir. There's no neutral ground here."

He just stared back. I lowered the shades and continued on. Fifty or so men, in turbans and traditional garb, milled around inside the semicircle. They chatted, smoked, and pointed toward the still-hidden center of attention. At least half were armed with old AK-47s, M1 Garands, bolt-action Mausers, as well as modern Belgian FN FALs and German G3s. They wore pistols of every make and model outside the flowing blue, white, and black robes. Fifty men—daunting but doable.

I eased toward the semicircle and drew plenty of attention. Too bad. I remained expressionless and sought a view of the product display area. An older man, dark-skinned with gray hair, stood with head hung down, hands tied behind his back. He drew little attention, although a few potential buyers passed, paused, and looked him up and down before moving on. One exchanged words with the seller who stood at the man's rear.

I shifted left, closer to the building's wall. Two young girls, ten or eleven years old and dressed in bright-patterned Senegalese robes, stood side-by-side, sniffling as tears tracked down facial dust. Sisters, I'd bet. They, too, were dark-skinned with hands tied. They drew a fair amount of attention as the seller and potential buyers pointed out respective attributes and potential defects. My emotions churned with an overwhelming otherworldly sense, but it was all too real. I choked back bile and focused on maintaining a benign expression.

Across the enclosed space, a Senegalese woman held a one- or two-year-old child. She kept her eyes on the ground as she softly bounced the child, whispered to it, and kissed its tiny head. She, too, drew decent attention. A mother and child combo—a desired commodity. More haggling, more seller and buyer interchange.

The sun, low in the sky, was blocked from the area, which smelled of unwashed bodies and tobacco and ancient travesties. I shifted again and pressed against the stone building at one end of the semicircle. And there she was, the auction's star.

Her blond hair was pulled back in a ponytail, the same as her photographs. A teenage girl's soccer team hairstyle. They'd dressed her in a just-below-the-knee skirt, which displayed her lower legs and bare feet—a major source of interest for the men in a women-remain-covered society. She also wore a navy-blue knit shirt that displayed her youthful body. Hands tied behind her back, she stood upright, rigid, with eyes that flashed across the crowd and sought help, salvation.

Several turbaned men lifted and felt her hair. They rubbed it between their fingers and commented. One middle-aged man grabbed her upper lip and had a look at her teeth. She struggled against the affront, even aiming a kick at the guy while observers laughed at the tussle. Krystyna still had fight in her. Excellent. One tough kid.

Discussions, arguments, and spoken attributes swirled around her, much of it focused on her value as a concubine. I doubted they'd sexually assaulted her—a fourteen-year-old virgin held greater market value. I remained focused on her face, waiting. As she scanned the crowd with understandable desperation, she spotted me standing at the crowd's edge, the lone westerner outlined against the building's stone wall. I lifted the shades and tossed a brief smile and quick wink her way. Hang in there, kid. The cavalry has arrived. Her eyes flashed with acknowledgment. Then the fleeting contact was lost as milling men interfered with our line of sight.

The brief connective moment meant everything. For Krystyna, hope. A glimpse that her nightmare might end. And hope fulfilled that she was still loved and efforts toward finding her hadn't stopped.

For me, the moment shined as affirmation and an anchor point for my given word. And a white-hot incentive for making the rescue happen, dangerous obstacles aside. You and me, Krystyna. It'll be alright.

I backed away from the crowd and sought Amir. He was holding a sincere chat with a local. His asset. I took the opportunity and sidled back to the Land Cruiser. Using it to block views, I dropped onto the ground and had a look at the vehicle's undercarriage. Five minutes later I stood and rejoined the crowd's periphery.

Old thick double wooden doors swung open to the outside, as did a smaller single door farther along the stone building's wall. The crowd still chattered and haggled and argued, and began filing through the double doors. I observed the participants press inside as the sellers poked and prodded their human wares toward and through the smaller door. Krystyna searched over her shoulder and shot me a last glance as they shoved her inside. Her expression conveyed a simple message. Please, let's do this. I returned a grim nod.

Chapter 33

Amir appeared at my side and we filed into the dim, expansive room. The heavy wooden double doors closed behind us, darkening the interior even more. Stacked stone columns throughout the space provided roof support. The ancient floor, flat stones worn smooth over centuries, lay sprinkled with dirt and sand. Shuffling footsteps from the crowd kicked up dust, highlighted by shafts of setting sunlight through small, square, elevated windows. A small wooden platform, the display stage, pressed against the wall we'd just entered through. The crowd's volume decreased as clans huddled, bidding strategies discussed. Amir and I stood at the rear alongside a stone column.

An auctioneer mounted the stage, announced several platitudes aimed at the crowd and the quality products soon to be sold. The captives remained hidden behind a small cloth screen. They brought the old man, head still hanging, shoulders slumped, onto the stage. The auctioneer kicked off a terrible, sad, and ancient tradition. I couldn't help but feel thrown back into antiquity. Babylon, Egypt, Greece, Persia, Rome—the immediate setting would fit them all, and many, many more.

As I watched, several in the audience—and they looked like locals, but who the hell knew?—pulled cell phones and took photos, Amir included.

His action triggered clarity, or at least as much clarity as I'd find in shadowland. I observed him snap a few photos as the bidding began and considered my immediate reality—one drenched in clandestine logic and gamesmanship.

I'd been the Company's bird dog, plain and simple. Sure, they'd tried finding Krystyna, but held me as a hole card. I'd pointed toward Mauritania. Toward Nouadhibou. Pointed out their objective. My usefulness ended there.

Amir shot another photo, the bidding price low, the bidder's voices low-key, almost uninterested. The auctioneer harangued the crowd, got nowhere, and he announced the winning bidder. They led the old man off the stage and back behind the cloth screen. The auctioneer began a brief speech on the quality of the upcoming offerings.

The Company wasn't here for help with a rescue attempt. Nope. They'd sent their guy to capture photos of the horror, with Krystyna the glam shot. Leverage. It was all about leverage. While the other side would take photos for leverage against Jakub and Anna and members who thought about bolting the Guardian's conspiracy, the Company would use similar photos for leverage against the conspiracy. Head games, global chess, raw clout. The photos Amir now took replaced me as their new hole card. There was no proof, and I'd never know for sure, but I'd bet good money on it.

The two young sisters were next. My pent-up rage bubbled, and I fought hard, damn hard, to keep the cork in the bottle. Heartrending, brutal—while I stood within a crowd inured to such a scene. I just didn't get it. A way of life in Mauritania, I'd read. No, there were no excuses. The lack of humanity around me was crushing.

The bidding became lively, and I did my best to shunt the entire scene aside. Either that or traipse outside, grab weaponry, reenter, and clean house. Given half the occupants were well-armed, such an action wouldn't have helped the odds with Krystyna. Still, the desire remained, burning.

I shifted gears, a distraction, and considered the morning arrest. The Company had set it up. Unleashed in Nouadhibou, I was liable to disrupt their photo op. So they organized my arrest and detainment. For how long? A day, a week, ten years—I'd never know. If I put a gun against someone's head, I'd likely hear the plan involved releasing me before the auction. Maybe. Maybe not. And the "not" got under my skin, big time. Krystyna auctioned off and whisked away to a living hell while they captured the right images, the right evidence.

Amir and others took more photos, this time the two young girls. They stood together, frightened out of their minds, as men in a strange language waved hands and yelled bids.

The best the Company could do, once I'd escaped, was dangle a meeting and keep me on ice until near auction time. The vehicle? A Marilyn Townsend gesture. Without her, I wouldn't have it sitting outside. Small recompense for screwing me over with the arrest. But I could hear her ordering people down the CIA food chain: "Provide him a vehicle. It will present him a decent chance." Bottom line—they'd played me like a fiddle. So I focused on the immediate, the prime mission, and left the mental garbage behind.

The two young girls cried, hands tied behind their backs. The younger one leaned into and nestled against her older sister's neck. As the auctioneer worked the crowd, bids rang out. It was at that moment the prime mission changed. I stood there consumed with cold fury, eaten up with disgust. I'd had enough. The smart move was to stay with the original plan. The right move—the small voice that ignored the odds—said otherwise. It took me sixty seconds to develop Plan B.

They announced the winning bidder, the girls shoved offstage and back behind the curtain, and the scenario repeated with the mother and child combination. Again, the crowd became animated, the bidding active, and the auctioneer worked the audience. As they awarded the mother and child to the highest bidder and moved them offstage, the crowd became more intent. The big item was next. I sidled closer to Amir, who had his camera at the ready, and positioned myself behind his left shoulder.

They brought Krystyna on stage. Clearly frightened, not quite shaking, she still maintained an undercurrent of feistiness. And hope. She searched the crowd, found me within the gloomy setting, and locked eyes. I lifted a forefinger near my face and moved it, along with my eyes, toward the crowd. A simple signal—don't focus on me. She got it, and shifted her attention onto the audience. Amir snapped more photos. I spoke into his ear, voice low.

"You think you'll find a market for those photos?"

"I would well imagine."

His eyes were bright, on the job, performing his assignment.

"You didn't need to whack my fixer. Or did your local asset kill him?"

He shot me a brief, hooded look over his shoulder.

"And for the record, I tossed the GPS you planted on the Land Cruiser."

He lowered his phone for half a second, then resumed taking shots. I wouldn't allow him, or the Company, to track me. One perspective, which I held to be false, was I had cut my lifeline. No Company rescue if things went sideways. Another perspective, one I'd bet on, was I'd lowered the odds of them further messing with me. A jaundiced worldview, but I'd rather fly solo, on my own, than roll the dice with them.

The crowd became raucous, the bidding hot and heavy. The auctioneer took a handful of Krystyna's hair and emphasized the rarity of this prize. As the crowd agreed, the bidding escalated. She maintained a certain stoicism. I admired her grit. One slice of good news—the wary eyes cast my way as the lone westerner diminished as the auction started and were nowhere to be seen by the time Krystyna made the stage.

"By the way," I said, "and consider this a friendly tip, that whole equilibrium thing you mentioned? Not so much anymore. Shit will hit the fan sooner than expected."

Amir was a pro and kept snapping photos while he asked, over his shoulder, "What does that mean?"

I ignored his question and continued as the bidding hit a fever pitch.

"And those unfriendlies you mentioned? They're going to be highly pissed once I kick off this little fandango."

He shot a quick glance across the room toward players I hadn't identified as clandestine. Fine, play your games, boys. But buckle up. You're about to be introduced to the world according to Case freakin' Lee.

I didn't wait for the figurative gavel to fall on Krystyna and edged around the crowd, headed for the thick double doors. The crowd was too frenzied to notice. I cracked open one door, slipped through, closed it behind me, and dashed through the vehicle semicircle for my Land Cruiser. Back hatch opened, I stuffed an extra Glock magazine in one pocket and a handful of shotgun shells in the other. Then pulled the Mossberg pump shotgun—my personal crowd-control device—and ran back into the soon-to-be killing floor.

I focused on Land Cruisers that created the semicircle but were not parked bumper-to-bumper. One had ample space at its rear. I jumped in the driver's seat, put the manual stick shift in neutral, then with both feet planted on the ground, shoved like hell backwards while turning the wheel. It clipped the sedan's headlight behind it, creating noise, but at the moment I was alone on the dusty plaza. That wouldn't last. I continued shoving and turning the wheel, lined up with the double doors, and jumped back in. I'd created enough momentum and eased the brake on when I felt the door's resistance against the vehicle's rear. I shifted it back into gear, pulled the emergency brake, and pulled my lock-blade knife. I drove it into the sidewalls of two tires then dashed among the other parked Land Cruisers and punctured a tire on three more. Gotta move, gotta fly. It would get ugly, fast. I sprinted back toward the stone wall.

The small door for the newly minted slaves had remained opened. It swung outward as well, but the wrong direction for my position. Screw it. I pressed the shotgun against my outside leg, partially hiding it, and strolled past the opening. A quick glance inside captured the auctioned-off man, woman, and children huddled behind the cloth screen, surrounded by their sellers. The sellers didn't notice me pass, focused on their wares. Past the opening, I pressed against the wall and eased the door a quarter shut, allowing me a brief hiding spot. I slipped behind it. The sun was low, the shadows long, the noise from the inside poured through the open door. The auctioneer bellowed for a final offer, silence returned, and the winning bidder was announced. Then the aftermath chatter picked up.

The world outside the immediate ceased to exist, emotions tamped down, and an ice-cold assurance filled me. Without hesitation or remorse or doubts, I heeded Jules's words and allowed no mercy to course through my veins.

Chapter 34

They shoved the old man stumbling out the door first, followed by a handler. Next the two girls, the woman and her child, and Krystyna. Sellers and handlers prodded them into the open area. Three armed with pistols, two others with rifles. Inside, voices changed, filled with concern. The change coincided with the large double doors thumping against the parked Land Cruiser's rear bumper. Rattles from the double door drew the handlers' attention. I had five in the shotgun's magazine, one in the chamber. Six shots before reloading. It would more than do.

I slammed the smaller door shut and yelled, "Get down!"

Krystyna, wide-eyed, spun, saw me, and dropped. The two young girls watched her hit dirt and followed suit, as did the mother and child. The old man stood dazed. As the five collapsed, the handlers whipped around, and two pulled weapons. They went down first. The shotgun's explosive roar told the crowd inside and out that the fun was over and payback had arrived. At seven paces' distance, I took headshots. The well-lubricated slide mechanism clacked again and again on the heels of each trigger pull, sliding a fresh shell home, the weapon glued against my shoulder. The concussive booms echoed across the plaza. At the short distance, the buckshot devastated. It was over in seconds. Not a one fired back, all dead before they hit the ground.

I leapt toward Krystyna, pulled the lock-blade, and cut her hand cords as she lay on the ground. The small door flew open at my back. I whipped around and wielded the shotgun with one hand, slapping the trigger. The buckshot blew back two men and bought me a few seconds.

"Take the knife. Cut the others' hands free. Then get everyone in that Land Cruiser."

I pulled her upright and pointed toward my vehicle.

"Now, Krystyna! Move fast!"

She scrambled. I pulled the Glock and blasted several rounds into the door opening while sprinting toward it. As they returned at least five shots, the bullets sounding their violent buzz as they zipped past, I slammed the door shut again and moved with well-honed practice—Glock back in a pocket, shotgun ammo retrieved from the other, and shell after shell slid into the weapon. Bullets pounded the door's interior surface, and wood splinters erupted from my side, their firing almost but not quite penetrating. I chambered a round, slid away from the door, opened it a crack, cut loose with three blind blasts into the interior crowd, and slammed the door shut again.

As I shoved my last three shells into the weapon, I shot a glance at the double doors down the wall. They'd given up their attempts at opening it. Damn. I'd hoped they'd pound on it longer. The men inside, armed men, would exit a doorway at the ancient building's opposite side. It would take them less than thirty seconds to circle and enter the plaza, guns blazing. Gotta move, gotta fly.

My Land Cruiser stood with one back door open, the mother and child and two young girls on the back seat. Krystyna pulled the old man toward the open door. No time, gotta fly.

"Let go of him, and open the back hatch!" I yelled, sprinting toward them. "Then get in the front seat. Now!"

My yells signaled enemy action. The wooden door flung open again at my back, slapping the stone wall. I slammed the brakes, boots skidding on the hard-packed surface, and turned. Three men exited, one with a full-auto FAL battle rifle, the other two with pistols. I focused on the guy with the FAL who shot from the hip and sprayed bullets my way, several pounding dirt near my feet. I fired, pumped, fired again. At that distance the buckshot spread, and the first shot staggered him. The second put him down. I fired a third time at the two with pistols as they stood close together, hitting both men. Neither fell, but their pistol aim would now suck. I turned and dashed for the vehicle.

I tossed the shotgun through the open driver's window, across the dashboard, and swept alongside the vehicle. Snatched up the old man and flung him into the back alongside my duffel and rucksack, slamming the hatch shut. Back in the driver's seat, I started the Cruiser as more men exited the small doorway, firing. A bullet popped against my door.

"Down! Everyone down!"

Krystyna curled onto the floorboard and yelled as well.

"Descendre! Descendre!"

Thank God she spoke French. I slammed into first gear and stomped the gas pedal. As we leapt forward, tires spinning, I checked the rearview mirror. The good news—everyone in the back seat had hit the floor. The bad news—a horde of armed men who'd exited via another door had circled the building and now flooded the plaza, gunfire blasting our way. Bullets popped windows and punched into the Cruiser's body. One blew through the rear window and exited the front windshield while another slapped and broke the passenger-side mirror. The engine howled, redlined, as I shifted into second gear and left the collection of slave dealers and buyers and handlers behind. Two last bullets thwacked the Cruiser's rear. They'd be on us again soon enough, but we'd cleared the gunfire.

Oh, man. My adrenaline meter stayed maxed out, but relief also flooded. Two minutes of unleashed hell, the odds slim, death pounding at the door. We'd made it. Oh, man.

"Alright," I said. "Krystyna, you and everyone can get back on the seats. Tell them. And ask everyone if they are okay. Do it now. I need to know if there are any injuries."

She translated, and they responded they had no injuries and crawled onto their seats. The elderly man in the far back spoke. I asked Krystyna what he said.

"He is fine but would prefer to remain down. Tell me, who are you?"

She spoke English with a slight Polish accent.

"Your parents sent me."

She smiled and asked, "What is your name?"

"Case Lee."

"Thank you, Mr. Lee. Thank you."

She laid a hand on my arm and gave a gentle squeeze. Her thanks and touch hit me hard. A personal human connection at last, or massive relief that this mission phase had succeeded, or simple words and a gesture that offered more than sufficient reward. Hard to say.

"We're still in a great deal of danger. But so far, so good. Where are all these folks with us from?"

"Senegal."

"Well, that's where we're headed." We locked eyes. "It won't be easy, but we'll make it. You have my word."

First, get the hell out of Dodge. Nouadhibou sat on a narrow strip of land that protruded into the ocean. While I tore down dirt roads, headed north off the spit of land, our adversaries would be on my tail, searching, as others changed flat tires and alerted the police. Fifteen miles of lousy paved road lay ahead before we exited the Nouadhibou peninsula and turned south on the Nouadhibou–Nouakchott highway, the lone major highway in the country. We wouldn't be on it long. As the prime artery for the country, we'd travel ten-plus miles either side of it and avoid roadblocks while working through gravel plains, rock outcrops, and sand dunes.

Sunset approached, as did evening prayers. We'd join the few vehicles that didn't pull over and lay their prayer rug along the roadside shoulder. Guaranteed our pursuers wouldn't stop either. I cut through a neighborhood and found the paved road headed north, off the peninsula. Pedal to the metal, I flew past slower vehicles. At Nouadhibou's northern edge I half-expected a police roadblock, but they hadn't scrambled fast enough. Farther along the highway to Nouakchott would be another story. I had a long list of pissed-off Mauritanians who'd be on my trail—cops, military, slave sellers, slave buyers, plus well-armed clansmen of all stripes who would join the chase on general principles. I was a popular dude.

"Are we being chased?" Krystyna asked.

I shot another look in the rearview mirror. A half-mile back, several sets of flashing red-and-blue lights. Cop cars. Multiple sets of headlights lagged behind them, shining in the desert dusk.

"We are. It's okay."

"How far is Senegal?"

"Four hundred miles."

"That is a long way."

"It is. But we'll be alright."

She relayed the information to the back seat occupants. Sixteen plus hours at twenty-five or thirty miles per hour cross-country. The only viable option. Fuel would become an issue, but first things first.

The mother settled her crying infant with a gentle song, the two young girls huddled together wide-eyed, and the old man remained stretched out in the far back. Our tires whined on asphalt, and the engine's rpm remained redlined. My Land Cruiser wouldn't last at this pace and the cops, in their old Renaults, were gaining ground on us. Not good.

I made the turn east, hauled it one mile, and backed off the pedal. Deep dusk had arrived, darkness our friend. The half-moon would soon enough light up the flat terrain, so maintaining distance was critical. But first, lose the cops. A soft right turn, and I eased off the paved road and onto the hardpan desert. Hard-packed gravel, sharp rock patches, and sand ribbons greeted me. I lowered the speed to thirty miles per hour. A flat tire would be deadly at this point. But the maneuver worked.

Two cop cars stopped cold where I'd turned off, aware they drove on near-bald tires. A third eased off-road, cop lights flashing, and drove less than a hundred yards before it returned to pavement. I wove along, avoided jagged rock patches, climbed small sand ribbons, and stuck to smoother hardpan. The pursuing Mauritanians from the slave auction arrived where the cops had halted and didn't hesitate. They followed, headlights on. I kept mine off, although the approaching moonlight would highlight our vehicle, especially when we topped fingers of sand. They would drive faster than me and risk a blown tire. If they lost a vehicle or two, others would continue the pursuit. Best to strike early and set basic ground rules. Rule one—I will blow your ass away.

I topped a small dune and drove four hundred yards past it, turned the vehicle at an angle, and stopped. Chatter erupted from the back seat.

"Why are we stopping?" Krystyna asked.

"To send a message."

Krystyna translated while I snatched the shotgun from the dashboard, circled our vehicle, and opened the back hatch. The old man sat up. I reloaded the shotgun, shoved it into the duffel, and pulled out the M762 rifle with its 3X-9X scope. My long-range weapon. Light was poor, but the Leupold scope would draw in sufficient light for accurate shots. I'd switch to the night-vision-equipped Colt when full-on darkness arrived. I also grabbed several towels from the duffel. The old man nodded my way and smiled, the first positive emotion he'd exhibited.

"Merci beaucoup," he said, thanking me.

I returned a grim smile.

"Merci de tout mon coeur," said the mother from the back seat.

"She thanks you from the bottom of her heart," Krystyna translated. "We all do."

"Tell everyone they are welcome and that it's going to get loud."

She translated. The old man said something else, but I had already moved toward the vehicle's front. I rolled up several towels as bench rests, laid them on the hood, and chambered a round. I adjusted the scope to 7X magnification and aimed toward the small sand dune I'd traversed. It didn't take long.

The enemy's first vehicle crested the dune and flew down our side. A tough shot, but the sand was smooth, the vehicle stable on its descent, and I squeezed the trigger. The rifle boomed, the blast rolled across the desert, and the children and infant in the back seat screamed. The bullet blew through the windshield and hit the guy in the chest. Adios, asshole. As the vehicle swerved, driverless, and the man in the passenger seat tried to regain steering control, I put another round into the radiator.

A second Land Cruiser, then a third, followed on the first one's heels. I pounded another bullet into the second vehicle's driver. The loose sand, with no hand on the wheel, drove the vehicle at a cross-slope angle downhill, as the passenger struggled to regain control. Too late. The Land Cruiser rolled twice and settled on its side.

The third vehicle's driver, quick to react, angled away down the dune on a less steep incline. I didn't have a decent shot and refocused on the first vehicle I'd hit. It rolled along, slow, as the passenger crawled across the dead driver, opened the door, shoved the body out, and took his place behind the wheel. Once he'd quit squirming and settled into the driver's seat, I put another round through the windshield and hit him, too, in the upper chest. The Cruiser rolled to a stop.

The third one, after angling away, hauled it back over the dune. I had no solid intel on the number of vehicles in pursuit—five, six, or seven a best guess—but knew this cat would halt their progress on the dune's other side and let them know bad things happened when they crested. Good. Message delivered.

I hustled for the back hatch, slid the rifle back into the duffel, and pulled the Colt with its night-vision scope along with an extra magazine. Before slamming the hatch, I produced several protein bars from the rucksack and grabbed a gallon water jug. Krystyna and the mother were comforting the three kids with soothing words and hugs. Back in the front seat, I handed Krystyna the food and water jug, then wedged the Colt into my lap, the front stock resting in the crook of my left arm and the barrel sticking out the window. Engine fired, we hauled it south.

"Break those bars into pieces, and hand them out. And pass the water jug around."

As she prepped the protein bars, I considered the trailing enemy. They'd split up and flank me, driving faster. It would take them an hour or so, but it was inevitable. I couldn't risk the flat tire. The stretch of desert we traversed was only twenty miles wide between the Nouadhibou–Nouakchott highway and the ocean. At some point soon, I'd cut east, cross the highway, and enter mile after mile of isolated and empty Saharan desert. My highway south. I had a solid and surprising wingman with me. Krystyna had proven levelheaded, fearless, and carried through with direct orders. Pretty doggone amazing for a fourteen-year-old kid.

As she passed the broken-up protein bars and water jug back, the mother and old man spoke in unison. Krystyna pressed them, but they were adamant.

"What's going on?" I asked, focused laser-like on the terrain, headlights off, the half-moon now shining.

"They insist you eat and drink first."

"Tell them I'm fine."

More protests as the mother reached forward and grabbed my shoulder as she spoke.

"They insist. They will not eat or drink until you do. You are a hero."

I gave a long, slow exhale and shook my head. I was a far, far cry from hero status. A beat-up ex-Delta operator who found himself immersed in situations where doing the right thing was hardwired, with little conscious choice involved. Besides, heroes sought injustices. I stumbled into them.

I took a small piece of protein bar, and Krystyna passed the food and water, opting to wait until the others had taken their share. Awesome kid. The two young children smacked their food and exchanged low whispers. The old man emitted an appreciative grunt as he chewed, and the mother breast-fed her infant while eating. Stars appeared from horizon to horizon, the night cooling. Four hundred freakin' miles. I cast a quick prayer toward the incredible vastness spread above me.

Sixteen hours. Please, just give me sixteen hours.

Chapter 35

As we continued south, out of immediate danger but aware that could change in a heartbeat, I asked Krystyna the names of the Senegalese. We made introductions.

"The mother is Awa. The infant is Abdou," Krystyna said. "The young girls are Mariama and Rokhaya."

I got a giggle out of the youngest with my pronunciation.

"The man in the back is Mamadou."

I raised a hand as greeting, and the mirror captured a white-toothed flash from the far back.

"Okay. I'm Case. Krystyna, please explain to them we are still in serious danger, and I need them to do as I say if danger arrives. That's important. And let them know we are headed for Senegal."

A brief conversation ensued. Awa, the mother, reached forward and patted me on the shoulder as she spoke.

"She says they will do as directed," Krystyna said.

"Bon," I said toward the rear, hitting the limits of my French. "Très bon."

Miles passed, and my vigilance and awareness never wavered. I asked Krystyna about her travails, including my personal warped curiosity regarding the CIA's involvement.

"At the slave auction, did you notice the man I stood next to?"

"Yes. He used his phone and took pictures."

"Was he one of the men who took you in Jordan?"

"No. They were different men."

Good to know. The news didn't open a fallback position of love and kisses between me and the Company, but it reaffirmed my speculation over their role. Gamesmanship, leverage—the usual BS. I asked her how she was transported from Jordan.

From Petra, the kidnappers drove her to the Gulf of Aqaba and jailed her on a small freighter. It sailed for the Gulf of Suez and up the Suez Canal where they put her on another freighter at Port Said, Egypt. Then a slow boat west through the Mediterranean, past Gibraltar, and docking at Nouadhibou.

"How were you treated? In general terms."

Detailed abuse didn't fall into my wheelhouse of interest—she'd deal with that herself or with parents or professional help. A broad-brush descriptive would suffice.

"I was not molested, if this is what you are asking. They beat me several times but provided food and clothing. I do not speak Arabic, so what they said around me was unclear."

"How many languages do you speak?" I asked, moving on. I wouldn't imply the boat trip was a blessing in disguise—though it had provided me time, a precious commodity when chasing an obscure trail.

"Polish, of course. And English, French, and German."

A diplomat's daughter. Her linguistic skills didn't surprise me. I tried shifting the conversation to lighter topics—her soccer playing, school, other interests. A quick chat with a nice young lady, but she circled back to our situation, and me.

"How did my parents find you, Mr. Lee?"

"Call me Case. They approached my Swiss client, who contacted me."

"Then they did not know you?"

"No. I've met them, though. They are both good people."

"I miss them very much."

"I'm sure you do. But it won't be too long before you're back in DC."

"Is it possible for me to contact them?"

Man, I was an idiot. Of course she'd want to contact her parents. Good grief. I pulled my satellite phone and checked cell coverage as well. It was solid. Sprinkle enough tall cell towers across this flat terrain and you would cover a lot of turf. That wasn't good news.

"Before you call them, I want to emphasize we are still in a great deal of danger. This won't be a cakewalk."

"Cakewalk?"

"It won't be easy."

"What is our situation?" she asked. "You can tell me, Mr. Lee. I am not afraid."

There was no point hiding our current status from someone who'd exhibited as much maturity and moxie as she had.

"I believe they split up and travel faster than we are. I'm avoiding a flat tire, which would place us at a cold stop for thirty minutes or so. That's a long time to sit still right now. I would bet one group of them"—I pointed to our right—"is circling us from that direction. The same on our left."

"Do you have a plan for this? And you should know, I can shoot. My father has shown me how."

I had to smile. I couldn't foresee Krystyna blasting away at the enemy, but it was another signal she was one tough kid.

"We'll turn left, east, soon. I'm hoping that puts us behind the enemy on our left as they continue south. We'll cross the main highway and continue into the desert, heading southeast. Toward Senegal. It's big, empty country, and we might lose our pursuers out there."

I didn't mention the gasoline issue. We wouldn't make it to Senegal without refueling, but I'd cross that bridge once we'd shaken off the enemy.

"What is our greatest danger, then? My father will wish to know. I wish to know as well."

"That we run into the people chasing us when we turn east. Plus, they have cell phones and will communicate with each other out here. If we run into them."

"I understand. And I believe you can lead us through this situation."

"The good news is, the farther we travel, the better our odds. At some point, they'll give up. Fingers crossed, Krystyna. Fingers crossed."

I handed her the phone in satellite mode. I wouldn't chance cell phone triangulation if authorities tried locating us. She spoke Polish, her voice excited, and tears flowed. I could overhear first her mother's voice, then both parents as they switched to speaker. I heard "Mr. Lee," several times from all three parties. After five minutes, she handed the phone back.

"My father wishes to speak with you."

"Hi, Jakub."

"Mr. Lee, I, we, cannot thank you enough. It is a miracle! Although I understand you are not out of danger. What can I do to help? Anything, Mr. Lee. Anything."

"There is something. Research the Senegal side of the river. I don't know where we'll cross, but I need a few things."

"Anything. Please tell me."

"Locate NGO camps and small airstrips."

NGO—nongovernmental organization. Across the world, NGOs helped poor countries. Mercy Corps, CARE International, and many others. There were two reasons for this request—they'd care for the five Senegalese with me. And most established NGO camps had an airstrip. A gravel, dirt, or grass airstrip, it didn't matter. What mattered was a quick way to Dakar, board a charter jet, and get out of the region. Small towns also often had airstrips. With that option, the seven of us could fly to Dakar and the five Senegalese transported from there. I explained this to Jakub.

"Should I ask my country to engage the Senegal military?"

"No, Jakub. We don't want any military involvement. It's too far for a chopper until we get close along the border anyway. But use your diplomatic status wherever you can. It could be helpful."

The last thing I wanted was the hassle of another country's military. I was armed to the teeth. Goodbye, Mauritania jail; hello, Senegal jail.

Jakub and I signed off, and Krystyna held a conversation with Awa in the back seat.

"We should stop soon. The baby needs a new diaper, and everyone could use the bathroom. And she asks if she might use the phone."

"Of course. Do any of the others need to make a call?"

Another brief conversation.

"No. They are all from the same village. Word will spread."

Awa made a call, Krystyna entering the numbers for her. More passionate discussions, more tears, more flooding relief. It reaffirmed my Plan B, big time.

Once the call ended, I said, "It's time to head east. We'll travel that direction and find a rock outcrop so people can have some privacy."

Krystyna translated, Awa patted my shoulder, and we turned eastward, toward the Nouadhibou–Nouakchott highway fifteen miles away. It became more than cool, and I discovered the Cruiser's heater wouldn't function. I thought about the available clothes in my rucksack, and fuel. And kept my eyes peeled on the horizon for headlights here in the middle of nowhere. Under the moon and starlight, a large outcrop jutted skyward. I altered direction and headed for it. As we approached the jagged castle-like structure, the Land Cruiser ran across a sharp-edged stone field. Not the end of the world, but I'd been so focused on the horizon, my head swiveling and checking the rearview mirror, that I hadn't explored alternative routes for accessing the outcrop. As we approached its base, a change in the vehicle. Subtle, but there. We were losing air in a tire. Well, it was bathroom-break time anyway, and in thirty minutes I could have us back in action.

I switched off the vehicle's interior lights so open doors wouldn't kick them off, and we all left the vehicle. I rummaged around in my rucksack. Krystyna got my sneakers. Her feet weren't near as well adjusted for bare and rocky ground as the Senegalese. The mother received the light jacket as a blanket for her and the infant, as well as a T-shirt as a new diaper. A sweatshirt would work for the young children. The two, skinny as rails, could burrow together inside it. Krystyna received another T-shirt after refusing the long-sleeved bush shirt, which I gave to old Mamadou. We were set. We'd be cold, but we were set. Handing over the long-sleeved shirt, I performed another horizon search.

As a terrible stalking night predator, slow-moving headlights a half-mile away crept right, then left, searching. Another headlight pair appeared behind it. Then a third.

"Everyone into those rocks. Now!"

Oh, man, oh, man. They moved with stealth, on the hunt. Hunting us. There was a chance they wouldn't spot us. Their direction wasn't straight our way, approaching at a forty-five-degree angle. But our vehicle's dark shape, more rounded and smoother, would stand out against the jagged upthrust alongside us. Oh, man.

I grabbed the weaponry-filled duffel bag and headed into the upthrust. Fifty-plus feet high and a hundred yards across, it loomed under the starlight as a Tolkien castle with irregular toothed turrets and deep crevasses, black against the night. We scrambled up a rimrock section, and I asked everyone to assemble farther in, at my back within a steep depression. I carried the Colt and switched on its night-vision capability.

Three vehicles, at least two men in each. But they angled away, all on a slow serpentine prowl, seeking with headlights and eyesight. Then one slowed to a crawl. Whether they saw our vehicle's out-of-place outline or moonlight glinted off a reflective piece of the Land Cruiser, I'd never know.

It turned and halted, the headlights pointed our way. I knew the routine. Using cell phones, they'd communicate, not only with each other, but with the other contingent farther west. It wasn't long before the three vehicles lined up, an arrowhead in our direction. At five hundred yards, they remained still and waited. Waited for their fellow hunters.

THE DC JOB

Chapter 36

I called for Krystyna, and she scrambled up the rimrock and joined me. There was no point sugarcoating the situation.

"That's the enemy out there. They will kill me and capture or kill the rest of you. Now, please look at me." She stopped gazing at the three sets of headlights and turned her head. "You, and the others, must understand something. I've been in these situations before. We'll be okay. You have my word."

"What if there are many of them?"

The moon and starlight lit up wide eyes that showed a trace of fear. I realized for all her attributes, she was still a kid. For a brief second, I considered dancing around the appropriate words. I'll handle it, or take care of it, or some other words that lacked hard reality. I went with the definitive bare truth.

"It doesn't matter how many. I will prevent them from doing you or the others any harm. If that means killing them all, then that's what I'll do." I let the words sink in before continuing. "I'll scout our position. Keep an eye on them, and call me if there are any changes. Don't worry about making noise and yelling for me. That doesn't matter now. I'm counting on you, Krystyna, and I'm sorry to put you in this situation. Be we'll do this. Together."

Her eyes narrowed as she returned a tight nod. It may have been her experiences leading to this point that had hardened her, or it was part of her makeup. Either way, her jaw muscles worked, and she focused across the desert. She was all in.

I scrambled down and hand-signaled the others. Stay put. Then took off. Jumbled boulders, sharp jagged spires fifty feet high, and leaning sandstone slabs twenty feet in the air filled the hundred-yard diameter upthrust. I scoured the area, moving fast. Near the center, a decent sanctuary for the noncombatants. At the inside base of a massive tilted stone slab was an area surrounded with smaller uplifts and large boulders. Protected from above and on three sides, it would do. I didn't have a problem battling the slavers and tribal clan members, but protecting the others presented a challenge. I continued rapid movement, scrambling, and noted spires as landmarks, marked distances, becoming familiar with the rock maze.

Fifteen minutes later, Krystyna called for me—first with a moderate voice, then a loud yell. I came running and ascended the rimrock at the upthrust's edge. Two more sets of headlights arrived from the west, far distant. They took their sweet time crossing hardpan and joined the other three. They savored the moment, discussing plans. Fine, you SOBs. I had a few plans of my own.

"Come with me."

Krystyna followed, we collected the rest, and scrambled into the rock castle's center. At the tilted stone slab, I situated everyone and unzipped the duffel. I pulled the spare Glock and handed it to Krystyna.

"This is loaded. You pull the trigger, and it will fire. You can keep firing until it is empty. Understand?"

"I understand."

"You do not need to shoot anyone, Krystyna. But use the weapon and keep the other men away. They will duck and hide. That is sufficient. I know the sound signature of that pistol. When I hear it, I will come running. Do *not* get in a shooting fight with these men. Understood?"

"Yes. I will shoot."

"And I will come for you. Whatever I ask from you, stay behind rocks. Do *not* expose yourself. Is that clear?"

"Yes. It is clear."

Old Mamadou spoke. I waited for the translation.

"He says he is familiar with one of your weapons."

I squatted down alongside the duffel. He did the same. The huge overhead stone slab blocked the moon and starlight, making sight difficult, but he reached inside the duffel and lifted the shotgun. I reached over and clicked the safety off. Then confirmed, through Krystyna, that he understood it was ready to fire and loaded with six shells. We stood and locked eyes. Mamadou spoke again, his voice filled to the brim with resolve.

"He says he will protect his fellow villagers. He says not to worry."

I returned a tight nod, a critical hole in our defense now buttressed. If he could, in fact, shoot the weapon and pump fresh rounds. A chance I'd have to take and a helluva lot better than nothing. I snatched two extra magazines for my Colt and shoved them in pockets.

"Tell them to stay here. There will be shooting. Stay here until you or I come get them. Tell Mamadou that is the danger point," I said, and pointed toward the one unprotected area of their hiding spot. She gave brief instructions, and I said, "Now come with me. Hurry."

We hauled it back to our rimrock sighting spot, the oversized sneakers flapping as she walked. Man, we were one motley crew for a firefight. But I had zero expectations anyone but me would engage the enemy. Krystyna, maybe, but only a few blasts for alerting me about their locations. I wanted everyone kept safe. I'd handle the killing.

The five vehicles remained still. It wouldn't last, but my gut said one reason for their hesitation was the sand dune whack-a-mole they'd experienced earlier. They knew I could shoot, with the result a hesitancy among them for direct assault. Yeah, well, boys, it gets worse. I've got a night-vision scope on my Colt and will flat light up your asses when the time comes.

"Alright. They'll make a move soon. Now this is critical, and I really, really need you to understand." We were belly-flat on the rough stone, and I used a forefinger to indicate a large circle on the rock. "This is us. You and me." I pointed at twelve o'clock on the simulated circle. "That's twelve, just like on a clock face. Understand?"

She nodded back.

"Okay. This is three o'clock. Point for me, Krystyna, where that would be for this rocky area."

She did, lifting her hand at a ninety-degree angle and pointing toward the three o'clock position of our circular fortress.

"Excellent. And six o'clock?"

She got it, and I went through several more positions.

"Okay. That's how you will tell me where they are. Do not say over there, or to my right. Use the clock. You and I will move around. But every movement they make is in relationship to the clock we just went over. No matter where we are within this rock area, the clock doesn't move."

"Yes, Mr. Lee. Yes, I understand. This is a very good system."

"They will probably split up when they come. That's when you're to run like a rabbit and find out where they are on the clock. Don't go all the way to our castle's edge. Climb a large rock so you can see them. Do not get close to them. Yell loud so I can hear you."

She nodded back and said, "They will know where I am when I yell."

"You will run like a rabbit after you yell. They will only *think* they know where you are. If you have to shoot, do it to make them duck and hide. I'll come running for you. Understand?"

"Yes."

"After you scout their positions, go back to the center with the others."

With wide eyes, she nodded again. Man, I was asking a lot from a fourteen-year-old kid, but options were limited. Once she'd ID'd their positions, sanctuary waited under the tilted slab with the others, including Mamadou and his shotgun. I'd take it from there.

Several minutes later, movement from the enemy. Two vehicles started and peeled left, keeping the five-hundred-yard distance as they circled. Another performed the same maneuver to the right. The remaining two roared straight toward us, their Land Cruisers bouncing and swaying as they charged.

"Now, Krystyna. Go now." I grabbed her upper arm with a firm grip. "I'll meet you back at the middle with the others."

She scooted down the twenty-foot incline and took off, pistol in hand. The two vehicles headed for me beelined toward our Land Cruiser below. My rifle's sight displayed why they rocked back and forth as they traveled. They didn't avoid rough patches because both drivers and the passengers had ducked below the dashboard. The drivers would shoot a quick peek often enough for a general direction, but not long enough for me to aim and fire. They'd learned.

My only emotion was concern for the six people with me. Otherwise, the surety of cold termination ruled the moment. It didn't matter if they numbered ten or fifteen or twenty. They'd all lie dead within thirty minutes.

Both kicked up a dust trail, evident in the moonlight, as they approached. The first one on the scene slammed the brakes ten yards from our disabled Cruiser, and a single passenger flew out the door, headed for our protective vehicle. He didn't make it. I drove two bullets through his upper torso, double tap, and he collapsed. The muzzle flash revealed my position above them as the driver leapt from his seat, an automatic battle rifle blazing. Bullets whined off close-by rimrock as he stood and ripped bullets my way.

You don't stand still in the open during a firefight, dumbass. I put a bullet in his head.

I swung my sight at the trailing vehicle, now also skidding to a stop. They were smarter, and angled close by our Cruiser before they halted and dove out, keeping low. Our vehicle blocked my visibility of the driver and front seat passenger, who crawled and scrambled behind our Cruiser. A third man from the back seat also dived and scrambled. But our Cruiser didn't block him from my view. Two quick shots, sharp cracks in the night, another one killed. Three down, two left at our twelve o'clock.

I fired a warning shot at the remaining two, emphasizing I was still there, then slid backwards and flew down the rimrock into our rocky warren. The two I'd left would be uncertain whether I remained up top. They'd stay put for a while, buying me time.

If you're wondering, assholes, I'm off to hunt your friends. But I'll be back. Oh yeah, I'll be back.

Chapter 37

I hadn't gone twenty paces when a cupped-hand teenage cry bounced and echoed across the jumbled terrain.

"Nine o'clock! Two at nine o'clock!"

I dashed that direction for thirty yards, stopped, and began a stalk. Rifle against shoulder, both eyes open, right eye sighted through the night-vision scope. Quick glances downward, checking footing for noise and stability, then repeat. All senses maxed, I listened for boots-on-rock or whispers. A light cross-breeze, the sky cloudless, no wildlife noises. Two soon-to-be dead men ahead in the darkness among cold stone structures.

Cloth scraped stone. Ahead, hidden from view around a narrow spire. A quick scope up the structure showed no climber, so I edged around the spire's base as the Elcan scope turned night into day. The enemy worked his way through a rock jumble, assault rifle in one hand. Somewhere past him, his partner. I had this guy dead to rights, so I waited for his friend's appearance.

My spare Glock rang out—one shot, then another. Damn. No time to hunt his partner. I snapped aim back for the man who'd made the mistake of noise and fired two rounds in him, then a mad dash toward Krystyna's position. The calculated stalks I'd planned once she'd ID'd locations flushed down the toilet. Welcome to typical battle plans.

I flew past the tilted stone sanctuary, remained silent, and hoped Mamadou wouldn't rip buckshot in my direction. I scrambled around boulders and over rocks with second-long halts for scoping. The third stop, I saw her, crouched behind a stone shelf below another spire.

I kept my voice low, but loud enough so she'd hear. "It's me. Case."

Her head turned in my direction; I advanced, and squatted beside her.

"Are you okay?" I whispered.

"I am fine. There are three men."

"Where?"

"Four or five o'clock. One almost ran straight toward me. I became frightened and shot."

"You did fine. Just fine." She huddled in a tight ball, the Glock too large for her two-handed grip. The sight hammered me—I'd asked too much from her. She'd performed as a star, but there were limits, and she'd hit hers.

I'd left one enemy at nine o'clock and two at twelve, behind our Land Cruiser. Four dead. Four to ten more, somewhere among this rock maze, each advancing in the darkness. I'd get Krystyna back under the giant tilted stone slab with the others. As they remained hidden, I'd continue to stalk, hunt, and pick off the enemy one by one. A workable plan. First, get her back to sanctuary.

Then the infant howled and cried. Awa tried her best, the sound muffled, but they could still hear the baby across the entire upthrust in the dead-still night. A noise beacon, signaling. The enemy would draw tight, like moths to light. Oh, man. New plan, new plan, gotta move.

"Follow me. Four paces behind me. Close, but not too close. We'll move fast. Close, but not too close. Understand?"

She returned multiple tight nods, head bobbing, terrified.

"Yes. Yes, I understand."

Cold and calculated out the window, replaced with redlined adrenaline and fear for the others and all senses in hyperdrive. We scrambled around boulders with no time for scoping. I checked several times and ensured she remained on my tail at four paces. I was the lead target. Any fire, I prayed, would come my way and not hers. We worked through a tight small crevasse. When I spit out the other end, single shots fired in rapid succession met me.

Weapon on shoulder, target acquired, two chest shots—actions so well-honed it took place in less than one second. He crumpled, dead.

"It's okay. Come on."

She followed, hunkered down, wide eyes scanning. The baby's muffled cries continued. Twenty quick-time paces later, another single shot past my head. It ricocheted off stone, chips blown. I felt a sting across my left cheek, ignored as I attempted target acquisition. Nothing. The enemy had fired and ducked back down. Gotta move, gotta fly.

"Come on, come on. Keep moving."

Another thirty paces, and we approached the giant leaning slab's back side. I edged around it and called out.

"Mamadou! Don't shoot! It's me."

No time for translation. I counted on him understanding the lone English-speaking male approached. I rounded the corner. It was darker within their three-sided sanctuary, but I could make out Mamadou, shotgun aimed my way, standing in front of the mom, baby, and two young girls who laid pressed into the semi-cave's farthest reaches.

"C'mon, Krystyna."

I added a hand signal as reassurance. She joined the others, who whispered and rubbed her back and arms. The baby continued crying.

You've got everyone in deep shit, Lee. Something's gotta change in our favor.

Guiding my six people toward an outer edge, hard against the desert, limited our enemy's attack vector. They wouldn't scoot around us on bare ground, where I'd have a clean shot at them—they'd learned their lesson about that. But I couldn't have a human train follow me, given the last few minutes where the SOBs popped up like gophers and fired. My people would get shot and killed.

Think, you idiot. Think.

I knew where the enemy would focus, where they would all head. No guessing there. Alright. Alright, then use it. Make the best of it. I signaled Mamadou over and showed him what I wanted. Large rocks and small boulders lay scattered near the open entrance. I set my weapon down, lifted a bowling-ball-size rock, and placed it in the center of the entrance. Then went back for another. Mamadou got it instantly and joined me. Together, we rolled a decent-sized boulder into our Maginot Line. As we began rolling another one, grunting with the effort, Awa and Krystyna joined us, Awa having given her crying baby to the young girls.

We worked like whirling dervishes as the enemy approached, deadly bullets aimed our way any second. But the enemy had experienced my return fire, the lone reason they crept toward us instead of charging. The bastards would soon enough experience a truckload more return fire. In under two minutes, a decent twenty-to-thirty-inch-high barricade stretched across the narrow entrance. It would do. It had to do.

I had everyone but Mamadou stretch out flat, tucked within the farthest sand patch under the enormous slab, deep in darkness. I asked for Krystyna's translation as I spoke.

"Stay flat. Do not stick your head up. Stay flat. Mamadou will position behind the rocks we just moved. Stay down, please."

Krystyna asked, "Where will you be?"

I pointed past the rock line.

"Out there. Don't worry. I won't let them get you."

"You are hurt," she said. "Your face."

"It's fine. Please get back down. Lay flat. Let me have your pistol for Mamadou."

I still wasn't convinced Mamadou could chamber another round after he fired. With the semiautomatic pistol, he could keep pulling the trigger. I could have asked him to fire the shotgun into the night and prove it, but it would have eliminated the element of surprise. At the moment, the enemy remained unaware a third person toted a weapon. They hadn't tasted buckshot here in the desert.

"No."

We locked eyes in the deep night shadow. I didn't see an itch for battle or a come-and-take-it attitude. No, I saw a fourteen-year-old gripping a lifeline, holding tight to an artifact that might help her escape this continuing horror show. I nodded, squeezed her shoulder, and let her keep the pistol, knowing full well Mamadou, the gate's guardian, might represent a one-shot wonder.

I signaled Mamadou, and we scrambled for the miniature rock wall. I got him belly-flat with a solid firing angle from between two small boulders and patted his arm. The old man twisted his head and smiled my way. He tossed in a thumbs-up for good measure. I stepped across the barrier, entered the killing floor, and faced an unknown number of enemies hell-bent on my death and the others' recapture.

One thing was certain. The one thing that mattered. I'd walk my people out of here past nothing but breathless bodies.

THE DC JOB

Chapter 38

Ricochets were a concern as bullets could slap the leaning slab's interior and rain down onto the five hiding below. But hell, everything was a concern. With Mamadou manning our Alamo's gates, I'd circle close and tight around the massive slab and go after the enemy, intent on bringing the fight to them.

Rifle pressed against shoulder, with cautious steps I moved forward, hunting. Three at our five o'clock. The ones Krystyna shot at. Two at our twelve o'clock. Whether they'd left the Land Cruiser's protection and entered the battle zone, unknown. My last kill may have been one of them. One at our nine o'clock, his buddy dead. And two or three or four somewhere between six and nine o'clock—the fifth vehicle.

I went left and hunted the lucky bastard whose buddy had scraped too loud against stone. Crouched, slow and steady movement, the scope a godsend, lighting up my vision. A foot scuff sounded, and I moved quicker, keeping inches from rock and stone, preventing a visible outline. At thirty yards, boulders sat jumbled at a stone mound's base. The mound's top afforded direct fire down into the sanctuary, under the protective slab. The man had ascended the boulders and slipped once, making a noise. He now climbed on smooth rock, cautious, gaining elevation up the mound. The crosshairs locked on his head, trigger squeezed. With my rifle's sharp crack, his body tumbled backwards and down. Before he hit the stones below, bullets ripped from an automatic rifle and peppered the large boulder I pressed against. I spun away, kept skin-tight with smooth stone, found another firing angle, and scoped upward. The bullets had come from above me.

The idiot sprayed my former position again, giving away his location. He'd halfway climbed a spire, now twenty-plus feet in the air, forty yards distant, and outlined against the night sky. No place to run to, baby, no place to hide. Another headshot, and he and his weapon cascaded down, the automatic rifle clattering against rock as it fell. Seven down. I ejected the magazine and slammed a fresh one home, stuffing the used magazine in my back pocket, eight bullets still available in it.

Mamadou's shotgun blasted, the concussive boom distinct from a rifle's sharp crack. On its heels, two joyous sounds. The click-clack of a pump shotgun chambering another round. Good for Mamadou. And an enemy's screams and cries as the buckshot wounded but didn't kill. I took off along my back trail, now moving quickly with long strides.

I extended my trail farther away from our Alamo's entrance to a position behind the attacking SOBs. The wounded man's hollers acted as a location marker, and I went deeper into enemy-held turf. Here the terrain became more broken, flat ground a rare commodity.

Twenty yards ahead, a vehement whisper instructed the wounded man to shut up. My legs spanned a narrow crack, one foot higher than the other, as I performed a silent awkward straddle-walk forward, scanning with the scope. Close quarters stuff, split seconds deciding life or death. The baby continued crying as the wounded man moaned and cursed. Moon and starlight reflected off smooth stone surfaces, the air borderline cold. An occasional eerie squeak or groan sounded as stone structures cooled from the day's heat. A hellscape, a Dante's world. With more killing on the way.

The enemy who'd instructed the wounded man to shut up about a little buckshot, now ten paces away and still hidden, spoke in another loud whisper, the message still the same. Spit curses returned from the wounded man. Pebbles shifted, sounded, as the hidden man crawled. His rifle barrel appeared first, my scope keyed on its owner. More shifting noise, his head peeking from behind a boulder at ground level. He aimed toward the injured man. I remained frozen, crosshairs on his temple. He ripped a ten-bullet string into his cursing companion, who fell silent. I squeezed the trigger and ended the shooter's life. They may have been from competing clans or members of hated families. I'd never know. Nine down.

I continued a methodical stalk, silent, scanning, easing among spires and smaller upthrusts, crawling over large boulders like a snake. Ten minutes, then fifteen. Perhaps they recognized my Colt's sound signature during the battle and assessed the situation, or somehow counted heads. They may have even texted each other and disliked the odds. Whatever it was, two voices, seventy paces away, made plans for a hasty retreat and called loudly for each other. I positioned alongside a head-high boulder and listened.

So did the enemy on the boulder's other side. He couldn't hold back and screamed curses at the two men planning their escape. Our boulder nested against a vertical rugged uplift on one side, a similar-sized boulder on the other. One way to get to the bastard. Over the top. As he continued screaming a litany of curses that insulted the escaping men's families, I set the Colt on the ground and pulled the Glock. His vocal howls covered the gritty noise as I scrambled upward. Arm extended over the boulder's top, pistol pointed downward, I emptied the weapon, firing blind. The yelling stopped after the first three rapid shots, replaced with cries of pain. Three more shots, and he fell silent. The next nine shots in rapid succession were both insurance and a mindset indicator. I'd had enough.

I slid back down, ejected the magazine, slapped a fresh one home, chambered a round, and shoved the pistol back in my waistband. Picked up the Colt rifle and hustled ten paces farther, finding a gap where I could crawl through and make visual confirmation of the blind firing. He was plenty dead.

A vehicle started far in the distance. I was twenty paces from our battleground's edge and covered it with a fast scramble, aware the two planning a hasty departure might not represent the final combatants. A ten-foot drop put me back on desert flooring, and a mad dash around the upthrust's circular edge brought into view a slow-rolling Cruiser, the driver yelling out the window. Within seconds, a man left the stone fortress and sprinted toward the vehicle. I pressed against a rock wall, steadied my aim, and set the crosshairs on the running man a hundred yards distance. He tumbled with the first shot, lay dead with the second.

The driver saw the action, stomped the accelerator, and turned his vehicle's tail toward me. I took steady aim and put a round through his back window as a final statement—you assholes messed with the wrong guy.

I worked along the wall, treading sand, until a slope afforded reentry. It wasn't over until I'd scoured the battleground and confirmed all enemy combatants had their ticket punched. I performed a methodical hunt and covered the entire castle area. Forty-five minutes later, I had full confirmation. It was over.

"Don't shoot, Mamadou! It's me. I'm coming in."

Krystyna confirmed my message in French. I entered the old man's line-of-sight and stopped, repeating, "It's me." He stood and waved a hand. During my forty-five-minute recon, Awa had gotten the baby to sleep. It approached midnight, the desert wilderness silent, temperature chilly, the stars sprayed across the sky with unreal clarity. The five emerged from their dark recess and approached me and Mamadou.

"Is it over?" Krystyna asked.

"It's over. Let's get out of here. We have a long drive."

They peppered me with questions in both French and English until I held up a hand and said, "Later. We need to get going."

I turned and led them from our fortress and back to our Cruiser. A viable option presented—we could take two now-unoccupied Land Cruisers, later models, and leave our original vehicle, flat tire and all. I asked, through Krystyna, if either Mamadou or Awa could drive. The old man answered in the affirmative but explained he was sticking with me in the vehicle I piloted. Oh, well. Back to one vehicle.

I chose one with good tire tread, lower mileage, and a roof rack with two spares. I asked for help collecting jerry cans and strapped six onto our new ride's roof. It would get us to Senegal. We transferred my rucksack and duffel and water bottles to the new ride and topped the fuel tank from an extra jerry can. Mamadou created a back-space nest for himself, although he refused to give up the shotgun. We had a minor argument—I wasn't comfortable with him and his loaded weapon bouncing around—and reached détente when he agreed to let me empty the chamber so that he'd have to rack a round before it would fire.

We piled in and started rolling. To everyone's relief, the vehicle's heater worked, but rooftop supplies rattled, so I stopped and rearranged items. Silence was golden for the rest of the trip. Before we continued, Awa shifted her baby over to the young girls and exited the vehicle. I was already back in the driver's seat. She marched around the Cruiser, opened my door, reached past me, and flipped on the interior lights. I immediately flipped them back off, wondering what the hell she was doing. She turned them on again and slapped my hand when I reached again for the switch. Then she grabbed my head, inspected my face, and, through Krystyna, asked if I had medical supplies. In short order, she removed my field kit from the rucksack and plucked sharp rock shards from my head's left side. Awa wiped each puncture with wound wash and delivered a running soliloquy in Senegalese that, I supposed, both praised and scolded me.

Her head ministrations complete, she ran her hands first over my legs then my torso. When I winced as she rubbed my right side, she pulled me halfway out the door, lifted my shirt, and inspected what turned out to be a flesh wound from a ricochet. It hadn't penetrated, tore up a chunk of skin, and would, no doubt, leave an ugly bruise. More wound wash, a bandage applied. She straightened me back up and kissed me on the forehead. Then back to her seat, closed her door, took her baby back, and said something to Krystyna in French.

"She said you can turn the light back off now."

We rolled forward. The shotgun discussion with Mamadou prompted Krystyna's transfer of her Glock back to me, a seminal moment. She, and the rest, now held on to a sense of the possible, a light at the end of a terrible dark tunnel. Heartening to sense and see, but we were still a long way from relative safety.

We continued east and hit the Nouadhibou–Nouakchott highway. I halted a hundred yards away and waited. For miles in both directions, nothing. No headlights, no roadblocks, no discernible movement or activity. I rolled the dice, took the highway south, and made up lost time, still driving with the headlights off. Fifty miles later, I figured I'd pushed my luck enough and eased off the highway, headed south by southeast, deep into the Sahara.

Chapter 39

The miles and hours rolled past, people slept. I never relaxed, a keen eye toward a three-sixty horizon. We skirted two campfires, miles apart, and avoided sand dunes. There was no sign, no indication of pursuit. We stopped twice before dawn for bio breaks and refueling, and ate the remaining protein bars. I had head time aplenty, and couldn't shake the mission's weirdness, the long strange search for a kidnapped teenage girl, filled with hitters, spooks, global conspiracies, techie geniuses, and tribal clansmen. Red, in particular, stood out. She'd provided the critical piece, the trail. Her and Bo under a shade cloth, a duct tape manger scene nearby. Dots connected, a picture formed, clandestine players in the shadows—opaque brushstrokes on a wild and wooly canvas. DC and Jordan and Kansas and Slab City and Mauritania and soon, God willing, Senegal. Jail breaks, slave markets, and dead men scattered across the landscape. The entire thing spinning out of control from the get-go. Weird. So damn weird, and I wondered if there was something about my aura or style or attitude that brought it on.

But a safe arrival in Senegal opened a wide door for positive emotions— a sense of accomplishment, a do-the-right-thing affirmation. I had never desired pats on the back or attaboys. End results, if solid and honest, were more than sufficient reward. I carried those action-oriented testimonials within my heart, and they supported me, buttressed my actions. It wasn't a bad way to live.

Sunrise on the Sahara. A dim horizon glow on my left, changing to vivid pinks and reds and, for a brief time, violets—colors that framed empty desolation. A short time later I ran into old tracks, vehicle scars, at random intervals and patterns. I followed one south. It dawned on me what I tracked—remnants from the famous Paris–Dakar Rally. An off-road race held for decades through this part of the world. In the late 2000s, they cancelled the race and shifted it to other locations around the globe. The rally organizers had listed security threats in Mauritania as the prime reason. Yeah, no kidding.

Krystyna stirred with the dawn, yawned, and gave a half-smile. Awa and Mamadou rustled as well. We spoke in low, soft tones.

"Are we close?"

"We're getting there. It will be midday when we arrive at the river."

She scratched her head and yawned again.

"Can we stop?" she asked.

"Sure."

I adjusted course for a large boulder field where folks could have privacy. Everyone piled out, stretched, and smiled. Dawn greeted—they'd made it through the night. A new day and closer to home. It took twenty minutes for everyone to take care of business. I rooted around my duffel and pulled several towels, cutting them into thirds. More diapers for the baby. Mariama and Rokhaya, no longer wide-eyed with fear, smiled and chatted with Awa. Everyone sipped water from a jug. Mamadou, stiff and walking with a slight limp, lifted his face toward the sun. His peaceful countenance highlighted his personal sun salutation. I stretched a bit as well, although the side wound barked back, limiting movement. I would have paid a king's ransom for a cup of coffee.

As we rolled again, the Senegalese chatted with soft voices in their local language, and Krystyna addressed me.

"I have been thinking."

"What about?"

"I have been thinking I may never return to normal."

Thin ice on two fronts. We weren't out of the woods yet. She, and the others, through both voice tone and facial expressions, assumed we'd made it. In Case Lee's book, we'd made it when the Senegalese were back in their village and Krystyna and I landed in DC.

On the Krystyna personal front, I was more than unsure about the right words for addressing a return to normalcy. Psychiatrists and psychologists had specific tools for a teenage girl to handle life-changing trauma. My best bet, my only bet, was personal honesty.

"Oh, I don't know. You'll go back to school, play soccer, hang out with friends."

"Yes. But everything will be different."

"Maybe in some ways."

"How do you deal with such events, Mr. Lee? How do you return to normal?"

Hoo, boy. I wasn't a poster child for normal, not by a long shot. Besides, this was about her, not me, although I could draw on lifetime experiences and address possible perspectives. Otherwise, I was out of ammo.

"I don't know the best way for handling it, Krystyna. But I know this. It happened. There's no point pretending it didn't, no point shoving it into a dark space hoping you will forget."

She remained silent, perhaps waiting for more Case Lee pearls of wisdom. The well was pretty much dry on the normalcy topic, but I couldn't end the conversation without highlighting the obvious.

"You should also remember, for the rest of your life, one big thing."

"What thing?"

"When faced with terrible, horrible circumstances, Krystyna Kaminski kicked butt."

She cracked a half-smile.

"So maybe it's best you acknowledge and accept it all happened and move on with life. Get back to normal. But never forget—when you faced evil, you spit in its face. That makes you one tough little badass."

I glanced her way. She displayed a broad smile, staring out the windshield. I offered up my fist. She bumped it with hers and snorted a laugh, still smiling.

An hour later, Jakub Kaminski called my sat phone.

"Is all well?" he asked. "Is Krystyna safe? Are you and the others safe?"

"We're good, Jakub. We still have another four hours before we hit the Senegal River."

"Could I ask you if the Senegal town of Podor is a viable option for you?"

"Hold on. Let me check the GPS map."

Podor, by appearances, was a substantial town on the river without a Mauritanian village across from it. It also wouldn't require a dramatic change in our direction. All good.

"That would work, Jakub. Tell me what the plan is."

"There is an old fort there. Stop at the riverbank opposite the fort. A boat will meet you and carry everyone across. There's a decent dirt runway at the airport. Two planes will be waiting. One for the other travelers and one for you and Krystyna."

A solid plan, and I accepted it with relief. All morning I'd mulled over our river crossing spot, with nothing definitive coming to mind. He asked to speak with Krystyna. As she spoke Polish, all I could make out was tone and tenor. She was upbeat, positive. She spoke French with the Senegalese, asking a question, and repeated the answer for her father. I later found out Jakub had enquired about what village they were from. All good.

The next several hours passed uneventful, excitement building. With no gunfire to contend with, the infant remained happy, and the two young girls whispered and giggled. I traveled across hardpan desert the entire time, a lone vehicle headed south. We approached Podor, seven miles distant, and saw the first vehicle since the previous night. It traveled east-to-west, another Land Cruiser, hauling it down what appeared a well-used sand and gravel road. We traveled perpendicular to their route. We'd spotted each other—there were no hiding spots—and I continued forward, intent on passing behind them and crossing the road. Seven more miles. Man, I could smell the barn.

They stopped in our direct path. I asked Krystyna to duck below the dashboard, her blond hair a potential signal. I had no idea how far our escape had spread, but I wasn't taking any chances. Our Cruiser rolled to a stop a hundred yards from the other vehicle. Heat waves rippled between us, no sound other than a blow-dryer-hot breeze across the barren landscape.

"Ask Mamadou to pass me my rifle."

He did. I chambered a round and stepped from the vehicle. The back hatch opened, Mamadou groaned as he unwound and exited, and the chambering of a shotgun shell sounded at my back. He and I and everyone had had enough. If these clowns wanted a fight, it would be short and nasty.

I raised my rifle, steadied against the open door, and sighted the occupants. Four men, all turbaned clansmen with sunglasses, all staring our way. Footfalls crunched hardpan as Mamadou joined me, his shotgun aimed as well. At a hundred yards it wouldn't do any damage, but the message was crystal clear. We would fight.

The Mexican standoff lasted less than twenty seconds. They shifted into gear and continued on their route. We climbed back in, crossed the road, and I upped our speed an additional fifteen miles per hour. A few irrigated green patches appeared first, then the river. Other than the irrigated areas, it remained desert. Desert with a large river winding through it. Date trees appeared on the Senegal side, then the town of Podor. The old fort wasn't a challenge to spot, nor was a lone man standing on the Mauritania side, high on the riverbank. Jakub Kaminski, with a holstered pistol, hands on hips, ball cap and dark glasses. Below him, a small wooden fishing boat with an outboard motor waited. Krystyna erupted with excitement as her father's grim face broke into a massive smile. He ran toward us as I rolled to a stop. Krystyna flew out the door and sprinted toward her father. I thought they might knock each other down. The reunion was joyous and joined with tears and Polish exultations and spinning hugs and kisses. And happy words and tears from the back seat occupants. And maybe, just maybe, a few blinked tears from the remaining front seat occupant.

In short order, I hustled everyone from the vehicle, asked Mamadou to carry the duffel, and sent them down the riverbank. Jakub and Krystyna joined them. I remained up top, rucksack over a shoulder, Colt in hand. I scanned the flat desolate area, still tuned toward any and all enemies, and listened as people boarded the small boat at my back. The end game. Hundreds of miles through isolated desolation and firefights and newly formed bonds. And now, the strange tiny tickle of regret it had ended. I couldn't help it, part of the deal, but an emotion nudged aside and never addressed.

"Mr. Lee. It is time," Jakub said.

The outboard engine fired as I approached, Jakub standing on the bank to shove us off. Before I could toss my rucksack into the vessel and climb in, he wrapped me in a bear hug, twisted me, and repeated, "Thank you," a half-dozen times. Upon release, he removed his sunglasses and wiped away more tears. As I climbed in, he couldn't resist another few back pats. I appreciated the gestures and hid a grimace when the side wound hollered. He pushed the small boat's bow and jumped in. In less than a minute we were on Senegal soil.

A fifty-year-old flatbed truck met us on the other side and carried us to the dirt strip airport. Jakub met each Senegalese with sincerity and a touch of Polish formality. When he pointed out and explained, in French, that one aircraft would take them and land near their village, they mobbed him with hugs, their voices animated and loud.

Mamadou approached and handed me the shotgun. I asked for Krystyna's translation.

"Ask him if raiders visit his village often."

He replied it was not often, but it happened every few years. I ejected the chambered shell, opened the duffel, wrapped the weapon in several towels, and retrieved the box of shotgun shells. I handed him the shotgun and ammo, and instructed Krystyna.

"Tell him the next time they do, make them regret it."

The prop plane designated for the Senegalese fired its engines and the pilot signaled it was departure time. They surrounded Krystyna with hugs and kisses and tears aplenty. Then Awa and her baby Abdou, Mamadou, Mariama, and Rokhaya all approached me. I'm not a big fan of emotional goodbyes and excessive hoopla and would just as soon exchange quick hugs and handshakes. But they weren't having any of that.

Awa and her baby pressed against my front, her arm wrapped around me. Mariama and Rokhaya, little more than head-high to my waist, plastered at my sides, arms intertwined, squeezing skin-tight. Mamadou leaned against my back, both arms draped over my shoulders, his forehead against my neck. They spoke in their native language, addressing me and rubbing my arms and torso. Awa kicked off a village song, and the others joined. Mamadou patted time on my chest. It was sweet and melodic, and their gentle swaying captured my body within their movement. And they captured my heart with penetrating sentiment. There are life moments, far too rare, when the world collapses into a pinpoint of time and place. When the ugliness and horror and death reside elsewhere. Their song lasted perhaps sixty seconds, with everyone but the baby singing. I wouldn't have minded it going on much, much longer.

We boarded our plane as Jakub, holding hands with his daughter, explained that a charter jet, courtesy of the Polish government, waited in Dakar. From there it was nonstop to DC. He asked if I needed anything.

"Well, since you ask, a couple of things."

"Anything, Mr. Lee. Absolutely anything."

"Jeans, underwear, socks, and a button-down shirt. And a couple of T-shirts. Oh, and new sneakers. Your daughter has worn mine out."

Krystyna laughed and pointed at her feet. Jakub shook his head and said, "Provide me your sizes. They will be waiting for you when we land."

"And one last thing."

"Again, anything you need."

"I need you to use your diplomatic immunity and claim that duffel bag as yours. It has special tools that US Customs wouldn't appreciate coming into the country."

"Of course."

He smiled and shook his head again, absorbing the wonderment of having his daughter back. Sleepless nights, days in agony. She was back.

The prop-plane flight, uneventful. The charter flight the same, although Poland's government had upped the amenities. Marvelous food, wine, liquor—all of which I sampled as the daughter and father sat together across the aisle and talked in their native language.

The Dakar–DC leg was eight hours, and with the time difference we'd land around six in the afternoon. I texted the world's top spook and asked for a meeting that evening. I wanted to stick a bow on this job, then call it good. Marilyn Townsend responded with an affirmative and time and place. With that, I drained the dregs of my Grey Goose on the rocks, reclined the seatback, and slept like a log. I dreamed about a slow slog through a thick dust storm as jackals howled and dark, foul entities whipped past. Head down, squinting, I forged ahead, unclear on the destination.

Chapter 40

Jakub toted his roller suitcase and my duffel bag through customs and immigration, claiming diplomatic immunity. I'd slipped Jakub my roll of Benjamins before our arrival, knowing confiscation by US Customs was a strong probability. Given his status as a diplomat flying into DC, the customs and immigration folks checked his documents and waved him and Krystyna and my duffel full of treats through. They searched me and my rucksack.

Anna Kaminski stood in the private air terminal lounge and rushed forward at the sight of her daughter. The three Kaminskis huddled, hugged, and shed more tears. I circled past and checked a nearby large shopping bag. Clothes, sneakers, the whole works. I carried it and my rucksack into the men's room, an upscale setup appropriate for dignitaries who flew in and out of DC. Marble everything, a half-dozen sinks, and two shower stalls with towels stacked on a side table. I stripped and checked the wall-to-wall mirror. I wouldn't win any beauty contests.

The peppered gouges along my left upper cheek and into my hairline had scabbed over. The side wound remained uninfected, although it would leave a small gnarly scar. Head to toe covered in grime and dust and, in spots, dried blood, ensured a beat-up and worn down appearance. Not the first time. And high odds, not the last.

Thirty minutes later I exited the bathroom feeling halfway human again with fresh new attire. If clothes made the man, I was in fine fettle. Anna snagged me upon exiting and hugged and kissed me and thanked me until it was embarrassing. I thanked her for the clothes. Then it was time for goodbyes.

Jakub and I shook hands. He thanked me again with assurances he'd lend a hand with Case Lee Inc.'s endeavors in the future. Anna gave me a last hug and kiss. Krystyna stood at the side until her parents completed their goodbyes, then approached.

She laid her head flat against my chest, wrapped her arms around me, and squeezed. I returned the hug and buried my face in the top of her head, unclear about what to say. All the usual farewells and send-offs felt shallow. We'd been to hell and back, and I struggled with the appropriate words for our departure. Krystyna bailed me out.

She stepped back and wiped tears away with her hands. Then, with a shared-secret smile, she extended her fist toward me. I cracked a mile-wide grin and returned a fist bump. It said it all.

***

The small pub near Langley held few patrons, a solid wooden bar, a dour barkeep, and the world's number one spook, seated in its farthest corner. I set my rucksack and duffel on a nearby table and bellied up to the bar.

"Grey Goose on the rocks. Make it a double."

"Anything else?"

"Nope."

"Sixteen dollars."

I laid a twenty on the bar top, collected my drink, and approached the dark-suited gun-packing phalanx at Townsend's perimeter.

"You boys and girls have an actual function this time. Watch my luggage."

I slid through a sea of indignant stares and approached Townsend.

"You need not abuse my protection," she said as I sat across from her at the small table. "It becomes tiresome."

"Let's not kick this off with abuse proclamations. I hold the upper hand on that argument, and you damn well know it."

She didn't deign a reply and sipped her white wine. The close-cropped gray hair had taken on more white, and facial lines were more apparent.

"As no doubt you are aware," I continued, "Krystyna Kaminski landed in DC this evening."

"A joyous reunion, I'm sure."

"Yeah. Joyous. Hey, thanks for the jail time in Nouadhibou. A peculiar form of assistance from the Company, but who am I to judge? Besides, the food was outstanding. Goat hoof soup."

"I'm glad you enjoyed your stay, albeit brief."

"Next time you want me on ice for the day, I'd suggest a simple request would suffice. I'm an amenable guy."

She raised one eyebrow.

"And the vehicle we provided?"

"Fine and dandy. You can recover it somewhere in the Sahara. Shouldn't be hard to find. Look for dead bodies."

"You may stop with the surly attitude, Mr. Lee. If you wish to editorialize, write me a letter."

A brief eye lock, then we both sipped our drinks. The half-dozen other customers chatted; one laughed at a joke. The barkeep wiped down the bar top and served another beer.

"How'd your man at the slave market make out? Things got a tad lively there."

"Our asset remains in good health."

"He sure took a lot of photos."

She didn't reply.

"I suppose what irritates me most, Director, is walking into these jobs with a simple mission. And it seems like every time I end up wrapped around an espionage axle. If it's not one bullshit conspiracy, it's another."

"You struggle with perspective. Years ago, as I recall, you had the same issue."

Our field ops together, back in Delta Force days, were often spiced with direct "why?" questions. Us grunts wanted to know. The Company, represented by Townsend, seldom saw a reason for higher-level elaboration.

"Guilty as charged, and no apologies. But this job was different. Find the girl. That was it."

"Which you have performed admirably. But bear in mind, again, perspective and context. The unfortunate young lady was but a tiny piece of the puzzle. I do not have the luxury of agonizing over tiny pieces. You do. Hence our varied perspectives, today as it was years ago."

Raw field ops versus three-dimensional geopolitical chess. The former filled with human life and death, pain and suffering and, on occasion, joy. The latter reserved for politicians and policymakers. People who often couldn't find their ass with both hands.

I'd vented my spleen—a personal unloading with zero expectations of any effect other than self-satisfaction. Which was about as good as it gets when dealing with the Company. One big question remained, a question near and dear, but I held off until she'd sated my curiosity about the grand conspiracy. I was sitting with one of the few people on earth who'd know.

"I brought knowledge of the Guardians to the table. How'd that end up?"

"You are fishing, Mr. Lee. I am under no obligation to assist with that endeavor."

"I'm not saying you are. But I delivered you valued intel via Jakub Kaminski. And handed you Krystyna Kaminski's location."

She lifted her near-empty wineglass at a nearby dark suit. He stood and headed for the bar to fetch another white wine.

"Hey," I said.

He turned and stared. I lifted my near-empty glass and shook it, the ice cubes rattling.

"Me, too, amigo."

A returned a scowl and a glance at Townsend. She nodded, and he turned back toward the bar.

"I believe we just discussed abusing my people."

"And again, I believe I hold the ace in the hole on that one."

She sighed and shook her head and said, "As much as you cast a skeptical eye toward my organization, we do represent freedom in this challenged world."

I kept my yap shut. A response for such utter BS would have caused a verbal shutdown. So I nodded back.

"Such freedom encompasses many concepts, including information's free flow. Our government, as you well know, encourages the open and constructive exchange of information. We support our leaders' stated goals."

Would you hold that thought, Marilyn? I require some time to find a flag you can wrap yourself in.

"Sticking with a keep-it-simple theme, were the slave market photos sufficient leverage to shut down the Guardians?"

"I won't respond to that directly. I will say the free flow of information, restrictive nations aside, remains the order of the day."

"Is it back to love and kisses between the Company and our diplomatic corps?"

"When has it not been?"

Our drinks arrived. Under normal circumstances, I never let Company personnel near my food or drink, but I figured her guy wouldn't risk altering my cocktail with a drug when Townsend had given the drink's delivery her blessing. We both sipped, and she continued.

"Perhaps you could share with me how you tracked the girl to Mauritania."

"I know a guy."

"I'm sure you do. Was, by any chance, this gentleman a transactional expert?"

I wouldn't share intel on Red or Hoolie or blockchain technology with anyone, least of all the CIA.

"Like I said, I know a guy."

She returned a sardonic smile, having few if any expectations I'd give up such information. On to my big question—did I still have a target on my back? The question coincided with a slip into a more comfortable space, a lowering of a barrier between us. The years and mileage we'd spent together would, occasionally, foster the change.

"Have they called the dogs off me?"

"You are no longer a player on that stage. Retire to your obscure dressing room. The particular audience you reference has ceased to hold any interest in you."

"Good to know." I slugged down more vodka. "I'll get back to a more normal life."

"A normal life. Yes, I suppose."

Several quiet, reflective moments passed. Laughter drifted across the room from a far table, the barkeep rattled ice in a shaker as two martini glasses waited, and a young couple, hand-in-hand, exited through the door.

"It rolls and it tumbles."

"Mr. Dickerson?"

She knew Bo well, and my "rolls and tumbles" statement about life was a direct Bo quote.

"Who else?"

"In quiet times, which are rare for me, I miss him."

"He's prospecting for gold in southwestern mountains. With a donkey."

She smiled. "And Mr. Johnson and Mr. Hernandez?"

"The cattle business still works out for Marcus. Catch is getting married. He'd appreciate it if you arrived at his wedding."

"Let us envision the mingling of my protective entourage and your liquored-up Delta teammates. Wouldn't that make for interesting interactions?"

We both chuckled and chatted for another five minutes, remembering the past. She finished her wine, tapped her cane twice against the floor as a departure signal for her security, and stood.

"One last thing." She bent at the waist, her face close. "I'm more than pleased you rescued the girl and the Senegalese captives. Life does not afford me humanitarian endeavors. And while you may not think I have a heart, such matters *do* wound me. Deeply." She straightened back up and adjusted her jacket. With a final eye lock, she said, "Each and every one of them should look back on the experience and thank their lucky stars a man named Case Lee arrived on the scene. Well done, you. Well done."

With that, she moved toward the door, surrounded with dark suits, and disappeared into the DC night.

311

Epilogue

"What's your opinion on pumps?"

Jess and I sat opposite each other on her couch in Charlotte, legs intertwined. The patio's French doors were open, the evening weather fine. She had her laptop open, I read an Alexander Hamilton biography on my Kindle, and Gillian Welch sang about hard times through hidden speakers, the volume low.

"Well, I've repaired a few. There are several on the *Ace of Spades*."

"Shoes, bub. Shoes."

She smiled over the laptop's screen.

"I guess I don't have much of an opinion. They should be comfortable?"

"Comfort is good."

She rubbed my calf, still smiling.

"I thought online shopping was a stress reliever. Are you stressed?" I asked.

"I'm waiting for my opponent's move. My hopes don't run high on this game with such lousy tiles. I've got all vowels with three of the four *U*'s."

Online Scrabble. Jess was a killer player. This was my second night at her townhouse, and it had been all good. A relationship without awkward reintroductions, we'd picked up where we'd left off several weeks earlier.

"How's Alex doing?" she asked, referencing my book.

"Interesting guy, for sure. Born in the West Indies. Was George Washington's aide-de-camp. Wrote more than half the *Federalist Papers*."

"Not an idle individual. I admire those men, our founders."

"There's lots to admire."

She retrieved her small-stemmed glass from the coffee table and took a sip. I'd tried mine. Once.

"You're not enjoying your Averna?" she asked.

"That meal was beyond stunning. I mean it. Now I'm stretched out here with a bloated belly. Maybe the digestif thing is a bridge too far."

She'd wowed me with her cooking. An Italian meal, three courses, each outstanding. As was the Italian wine. Then she introduced me to Averna, an Italian after-dinner drink meant as a digestive aid. A bittersweet liqueur made with various herbs, roots, and flowers. It tasted like shoe polish, although I didn't mention that to her. Nor did I mention they distilled Grey Goose from two ingredients—wheat and water. Period. But it was one of those things about learning each other's tastes and preferences. Not a big deal. The Scrabble game pinged—her move.

I'd flown from DC to Charleston, charter flight, and stayed two days with Mom and CC. The small facial punctures I'd acquired in Mauritania were impossible to hide, but Mom didn't grill me about them and instead focused on the rescue. I minimized details—a challenge anytime when conversing with Mary Lola Wilson.

"They kidnapped the poor thing in one country," she'd said as we both had coffee at the kitchen table. "And then toted her halfway around the world to be sold as a slave."

"That's about it."

Her jawline worked as she shook her head. It may have been a combination of things that affected her, including our current location as a major slave market a hundred and fifty years ago. The entire concept tore Mom up.

"Fourteen?" she asked.

"Fourteen."

"Good Lord." She lifted the heavy porcelain mug, then set it back down and placed a hand on mine. "I'm so proud of you, honey. I'm well aware your jobs involve strange goings-on, so I don't have a terrible amount of interest other than you being safe. But this one…" She shook her head. "Good Lord."

"I'll admit it had a pretty big feel-good element."

"As it should. Now, this job would be a good career change opportunity for you. You can end on a high note. It's something for you to think about."

"A solid point, Mom."

"It's a solid point every time I bring it up, but I never see much get-go from you about it."

"Hope springs eternal."

"My hope is flat worn out. Now, tell me what is going on with you and Jessica."

Later that day, CC came home from school, and we walked to a dog park beside Charleston Bay. Tinker Juarez glommed onto the route and would twirl at the end of his leash with excitement. We stopped at a Caribbean Creole food truck on the way.

"Just a small snack," I said, holding CC's hand and conducting a Tinker tug-of-war with the other. "We can have it while Tinker Juarez plays."

"It smells so good," she said. "But just a small snack. Mom always says about ruining supper."

"That's right. And we don't want to ruin supper. Mom's cooking chicken fried steak."

"Mmm."

"With mashed potatoes and cream gravy and fried okra."

"Mom is the *best!*"

"Yes, she is."

I bought us a small order of sweet plantains tossed with honey. At the dog park, Tinker was torn between hanging with us and a potential CC-delivered nibble, or playing with the half-dozen dogs running around. He made several false starts, returned, and soon gave up on the food and dashed around the expansive fenced-in area, chasing and being chased. A steady breeze blew, a few whitecaps danced across the bay, and several sailboats worked upwind, sails trimmed. A fine day.

"This is *so* good," CC said, popping home a plantain slice.

"I'm glad you like them."

"Not them!" she said and pointed at the small snack bag. "They are good."

She'd lost me, but that was okay. Tinker performed a flyby and let us know he hadn't forgotten us and all was well. Then back to the grand chase.

"Everything," she said.

"Everything?"

"Everything is *so* good. You and me, Case. And Tinker Juarez. And the sailboats and the snack and *everything.*"

Of course. The moment, our immediate here and now, was sheer magic through her eyes. And now, through mine as well. I put an arm around her, pulled her against me, and kissed the top of her head.

I cruised the Ditch on board the *Ace*, northbound. Man, it felt good. The weather fine, the diesel engine's gentle blue-collar rumble soothed, with solitude and reflection-time aplenty. A three-day trip to New Bern and I'd take a puddle-jumper flight for Charlotte. The schedule gave both Jess and I several days at our homes, alone, and a settle-back-in before my visit.

I shot Global Resolutions my final report. The client who'd contacted Jakub Kaminski, knew the outcome, so I kept the report short and

Mission accomplished. Invoice and expenses attached.

Twelve hours later, they planted the money in my Swiss bank account. Done and done. I owed Jules a quick note. Well, I owed her much more than that, but a short message would keep her updated.

Back. All good.

Her reply returned within an hour.

Huzzah and felicitations. I expect a full download when next we meet.

And I'd deliver it, except for Satoshi Nakamoto's location and identity. I owed Red the continued anonymity. Jules would express displeasure at the intel void, but not for the first time.

I stopped at small burgs along the Ditch, grabbed a burger and beer, chatted with locals, and spent nights pulled into isolated sloughs. CC's perspective hung with me, and I relished the several days of solitude. It didn't hurt that anticipation of seeing Jess sat like a cherry on top. Man, life was good. I wouldn't accept another contract for another thirty or sixty days, so my schedule was wide open. Off for Montana, for sure, as fly-fishing and bird-hunting with Marcus had become an annual fall routine. Maybe take a quick trip with Jess, although hanging at her place held large appeal. We'd play it by ear.

I contacted Bo and enquired about Jezebel's health. He replied she was fit as a fiddle and, as per Bo's interpretation, burned with desire for the next prospecting trip. He asked about the mission's outcome and responded with several heartfelt compliments. We wrapped up the conversation with his matter-of-fact statement that JJ remained pissed at me. Nothing new there.

Marcus and I chatted, setting a date for my arrival. He planned on asking Catch to join us, which made it even better. He enquired about the job with, as usual, a focus on the outcome. As for gory details, he only asked if heavy resistance cropped up and, if so, did I employee sufficient weaponry for the job.

"Those don't look like they'll scar," Jess said. She'd made her Scrabble move and pointed at my upper cheek. "You dodged a bullet on that one, in oh so many ways."

"I wish I could say the same about this Averna. Would you like mine?"

One eyebrow lifted, she signaled with a finger to slide it her way. I wondered if the secret ingredients included tree bark and asphalt. She finished hers off and took a sip of mine.

"An acquired taste, I suppose," I said and eased the Kindle onto the table.

I took a socked foot in both hands and massaged. She gave a small satisfied groan, closed her laptop, and put her head back.

"He saves damsels in distress and gives foot massages. I think I'll keep you around."

During supper I'd attempted to keep the conversation focused on her Tallahassee contract. Her world interested me, and I admired how she navigated interpersonal challenges among family feuds as she dug for answers. By all accounts, she excelled at her job, and her self-effacing humor toward her efforts did little to hide that fact.

But she'd kept shifting back to the rescue. I'd high-leveled events, kept ugly actions to a minimum, and avoided the desert firefight altogether. I attributed the small facial wounds to action at the slave market, where I admitted shots were fired. Even there, I tamped down the action's magnitude. And I reiterated how much her money trail suggestion had helped. Without it, I was stuck. Big time.

"I forgot to ask you," she said, opening one eye as the foot massage "What prompted you to swoop up everyone on the chopping block? I mean, six people total. I thought you special ops guys were laser-focused on the mission. In this case, the diplomat's daughter."

"I'm not sure I gave it much thought, Jess. Honestly. I just knew I couldn't walk away from them all."

She let that rest for a while. I started on her other foot. A short while later, she popped open both eyes, pulled her foot back, tucked her legs, smiled, and rolled forward. On top of me.

"Another Case Lee puzzle piece falls into place, and I'm liking the bigger picture. A lot," she said.

We kissed, and passions rose. A mockingbird warbled outside the open door, a soft evening breeze entered the room, and the night was just getting started.

THE END

THE DC JOB

ABOUT THE AUTHOR

I've lived and worked all over the world, traipsing through places like the Amazon, Congo, and Papua New Guinea. And I make a point of capturing unique sights, sounds, and personalities that are incorporated into each of my novels.

The Suriname Job

I worked a contract in that tiny South American country when revolution broke out. Armored vehicles in the streets, gunfire—the whole nine yards. There's a standard protocol in many countries when woken by automatic gunfire. Slide out of bed, take a pillow, and nestle on the floor while contemplating whether a coup has taken place or the national soccer team just won a game. In Suriname, it was a coup.

There was work to do, and that meant traveling across Suriname while the fighting took place. Ugly stuff. But the people were great—a strange and unique mixture of Dutch, Asian Indians, Javanese, and Africans. The result of back in the day when the Dutch were a global colonial power.

Revolutions and coups attract strange players. Spies, mercenaries, "advisors." I did require the services of a helicopter, and one merc who'd arrived with his chopper was willing to perform side gigs when not flying incumbent military folks around. And yes, just as in *The Suriname Job*, I had to seek him out in Paramaribo's best bordello. Not my finest moment.

321

The New Guinea Job

What a strange place. A massive jungle-covered island with 14,000 foot mountains. As tribal a culture as you'll find. Over 800 living languages (languages, not dialects) making it the most linguistically diverse place on earth. Headhunting an active and proud tradition until very recently (I strongly suspect it still goes on).

I lived and worked deep in the bush—up a tributary of the Fly River. Amazing flora and fauna. Shadowed rain forest jungle, snakes and insects aplenty, peculiar ostrich-like creatures with fluorescent blue heads, massive crocs. Jurassic Park stuff. And leeches. Man, I hated those bloody leeches. Millions of them.

And remarkable characters. In *The New Guinea Job*, the tribesman Luke Mugumwup was a real person, and a pleasure to be around. The tribal tattoos and ritual scarification across his body lent a badass appearance, for sure. But a rock-solid individual to work with. Unless he became upset. Then all bets were off.

I toned *down* the boat driver, Babe Cox. Hard to believe. But the actual guy was a unique and nasty and unforgettable piece of work. His speech pattern consisted of continual f-bombs with the occasional adjective, noun, and verb tossed in. And you could smell the dude from thirty feet.

The Caribbean Job

Flashbacks of the time I spent working in that glorious part of the world came easy. The Bahamas, American Virgin Islands, Jamaica, San Andres, Providencia—a trip down memory lane capturing the feel of those islands for ⁻l. And the people! What marvelous folks. I figured the tale's intrigue and action against such an idyllic background would make for a unique reading experience.

And pirates. The real deal. I was forced into dealing with them while attempting work contracts. Much of the Caribbean has an active smuggler and pirate trade—well-hidden and never posted in tourist blurbs. Talk about interesting characters! There is a weird code of conduct among them, but I was never clear on the rules of the road. It made for an interesting work environment.

One of the more prevalent memories of those times involved cash. Wads of Benjamins—$100 bills. The pirate and smuggler clans, as you can well imagine, don't take credit cards or issue receipts. Cash on the barrelhead. Benjamins the preferred currency. It made for inventive bookkeeping entries.

The Amazon Job

I was fortunate to have had a long contract in Brazil, splitting my time between an office in Rio de Janeiro and base camps deep within the Amazon wilderness. The people—remarkable. The environments even more so. Rio is an amazing albeit dangerous place, with favelas or slums crammed across the hills overlooking the city. You have to remain on your toes while enjoying the amazing sights and sounds and culture of Copacabana, Ipanema, and Leblon.

The Amazon rainforest is jaw-dropping in its scope and scale. 20% of the earth's fresh water flows down the Amazon River with thousands of smaller rivers and tributaries feeding it. The Amazon rainforest is three million square miles, and during flood season is covered with ten to twenty feet of water.

The wildlife is, of course, amazing. After a long field day, I'd often take one of the small base camp skiffs and fish for tucunaré (peacock bass). I'd figured out their preferred watery environments. And learned where the piranhas were less plentiful (although it's worth noting those fierce little chompers are both easy to catch and quite tasty—karmic justice, perhaps). So I was fishing a remote lagoon a mile or so from the base camp. Lily pads, tannic water, dusk and isolation. Howler monkeys broke into a verbal ruckus among the treetops circling the lagoon. When those raucous critters took a break—dead quiet.

Then soft blowhole exhales no more than five feet away. Scared the bejeesus out of me. It was two botos. Rare Amazon river dolphins. Pinkish-white, curious and content to check out the new addition to their lagoon. We shared the space a full four or five minutes until they eased away. A magic moment, etched forever.

The Hawaii Job

I've always relished visits to the Big Island. What's not to like? Gorgeous beaches, rugged coastlines, a 14,000 foot mountain, and terrain that varies from lowland scrub to tropical vegetation to grasslands to alpine turf. And, of course, an active volcano. How could I not put Case Lee smack-dab in the middle of an active lava flow?

Then there is the vastness of North Africa and its Sahara Desert. The Sahara is about the size of the lower 48 US states. I'm talking vast and empty and scattered with isolated bands of tribes and nomadic herders. The cultural chasms are enormous as well, and something I've had to deal with in the past.

The Orcas Island Job

The San Juan Islands are spectacular. Located off the coast of Washington State and close to Canada's Vancouver Island (and the city of each island is a mixture of tree-covered hills and carved-out fields. are a delight, and while I perhaps over-emphasized the rain in this novel, it is by and large a misty rain and a far cry from a deluge. The summers are spectacular, and the sea life awe-inspiring. Orcas Island—the one I'm most familiar with—was a perfect setting for Case to mix it up with the bad guys. There is a primal feel about the place which provided an excellent backdrop for his adventures.

Victoria is such a cool Canadian city and, if you get a chance, do order a Victoria Shaft cocktail when you're there. The harbor water taxis and on-foot nature of the town made for a great fit with a Case Lee scene or three.

The Nevada Job

The big lonely of America's West has a special allure. It's not to everyone's taste, but I relish not seeing another vehicle for long stretches of stark terrain. Distant desert mountains jutting above rugged expanses with alone-time the order of the day has a strong appeal for me. Much of Nevada delivers this opportunity, big time. I've spent a fair amount of time there mucking about, fishing at a special high-desert lake, and sitting with dear friends around campfires as the bottle is passed around.

The Chaco region of Bolivia is also a unique place. From dry and brittle plains to narrow mountain spines, you really are on your own. I'll never forget climbing one such mountain ridge and discovering a completely different ecology. Lush plants and trees replaced thorny brush, and small springs provided water for wildlife. I had sat down to take a break during one of these climbs when a troop of monkeys descended from treetops and wandered over to take a drink at a small spring. It was one of those magic moments, never forgotten.

The DC Job

The US's power center – Washington DC. A perfect backdrop for conspiracies and intrigue. It's also a beautiful city, one I've never tired of. The monuments, in particular, are stunning and night-time walks among them filled with never-forget moments.

The country of Jordan plays a major role in this novel. I lived in Jordan for over a year, and loved the experience. Great folks and amazing sites – particularly the ancient ruins at Petra. What a marvelous setting for a Case Lee scene or three!

Then there's Slab City. A several hour jaunt through that place and conversations with the locals (plus a sit-down at Bombay Beach) provided ample background for several great scenes in this novel. Plus, how could I not toss Bo and Marcus into that environment?

About Me

I live in the Intermountain West, where wide-open spaces give a person perspective and room to think. I relish great books, fine trout streams, family, old friends, and good dogs.

You can visit me at https://vincemilam.com to learn about new releases and insider info. I can also be visited on Facebook at Vince Milam Author.

Printed in Great Britain
by Amazon

10196